SECRETS

BOOK ONE

D. K. DeGRAW

D.K.D. PUBLISHING
WWW. DKDPUBLISHING.COM

D.K.D Publishing
6885 West Lone Mountain Road, #267
Las Vegas, Nevada 89108
www.dkdpublishing.com

First North American Publication 2011.

Library of Congress Cataloging-in-Publication Data has been applied for.

ISBN 978-0-9838508-0-9

For my beautiful and wonderful wife, Ludmila

This book would not have been written but for
her continuous encouragement and support.

To my dear friend, Roger Eves,

who was kind enough to lend his first name, but not
his last name, to one of my characters. Also for
his timely inspiration, the details of which
shall remain our secret.

To my children,
Michael
David
Jeffrey

To my bonus children,
Evgenia and Justin
Pavel and Apryl

Last but not least
to my grand baby,
Elliott
and my future generations

A special thanks to an exceptionally
talented woman, Roberta Collins,
for her encouragement and for
proof reading my book.

CONTENTS

1. ESCAPE   1
2. DELIVERY 15
3. HIGHWAY 59 27
4. ARRIVAL 41
5. MISSION 51
6. LAS VEGAS 65
7. PREDATOR 73
8. PREY 83
9. DISCOVERY 93
10. HOUSEGUEST 103
11. CHASE 111
12. FAMILY 121
13. SWITCH 133
14. CHASE 145
15. DISCOVERY 155
16. CONFESSION 167
17. GET-A-WAY 175
18. BREAKTHROUGH 187
19. REVELATION 201
20. AWAKENING 215
21. DEBUT 229
22. HOSPITAL 239
23. CLUB 251
24. CLARKSTON 263
25. HOPE 279
26. ENCOUNTER 289
27. SNATCHED 301
28. MANHUNT 313
29. HIDEOUT 325
30. KNOWLEDGE 339
31. SUSPICION 351

EPILOGUE:
EIGHT YEARS LATER 361

I REMEMBER, I remember
The house where I was born,
The little window where the sun
Came peeping in at morn;
He never came a wink too soon
Nor brought too long a day;
But now, I often wish the night
Had borne my breath away.

I remember, I remember
The roses, red and white,
The violets, and the lily-cups
Those flowers made of light!
The lilacs where the robin built,
And where my brother set
The laburnum on his birthday,
The tree is living yet!

I remember, I remember
Where I was used to swing,
And thought the air must rush as fresh
To swallows on the wing;
My spirit flew in feathers then
That is so heavy now,
And summer pools could hardly cool
The fever on my brow.

I remember, I remember
The fir-trees dark and high;
I used to think their slender tops
Were close against the sky:
It was a childish ignorance,
But now 'tis little joy
To know I'm farther off from Heaven
Than when I was a boy.

Thomas Hood

D. K. DeGRAW

CHAPTER ONE

ESCAPE

A young woman quickly stepped from the 13th South platform onto the bottom step of the TRAX light-rail tram. She climbed three steps and the tram door whooshed shut behind her. The tram jerked forward as the young woman scanned the compartment. It was empty. The young woman sat down in a seat directly across from the door and placed her small pink suitcase on the seat next to her. She used her hands to wipe tears from her eyes. She felt a pain in her lower back and pelvis as the tram began its journey northward toward downtown Salt Lake City.

The tram continued for a few miles, then made a right turn onto Seventh South. Two blocks later, it turned left onto Main Street. The tram was now in the heart of Salt Lake City. The city was completely decked out for both Christmas and the upcoming Winter

Olympics. The combination of snow, Christmas decorations and Olympic banners gave the city center a robust appearance. The tram made three more stops as it continued up Main Street. Just as the tram was about to collide with a monumental statue of Brigham Young, the tram turned right onto South Temple. The tram continued West along the southern wall of Temple Square.

The spires of the Mormon Temple and the dome of the Mormon Tabernacle towered over the walls of the block-long Temple Square. The square itself had been transformed into a winter wonderland by hundreds of thousands of glowing Christmas lights. She marveled at this display of spectacular beauty and she temporarily forgot about her troubles.

"Next stop, Temple Square Station," a computerized voice said over the intercom.

The young woman was yanked back into reality. She slid forward in her seat and grabbed the handle of the small pink suitcase. She stood up and moved toward the door of the tram.

"Temple Square Station," the same computerized voice said as the tram glided to a stop.

When the tram door hissed open, the young woman struggled to the bottom step of the tram. She steadied herself and took a giant step onto the platform. She took a few more steps forward, then stopped and looked around her. She saw the bus station across the street and waddled to the cross walk. The young woman impatiently waited for the walk signal to turn white. Clouds of vapor blew from her mouth into the freezing night air.

When the signal changed from red to white, the

young woman walked across the street to the cadence of a chirping noise coming from the signal box. Once across the street, she walked directly toward the double glass doors of the bus station. When the young woman arrived at the glass doors, she reached out with her free hand and started to push her way through. When the doors cracked open, she hesitated and started to turn away. She looked upward with closed eyes as though she were in silent prayer. After a moment, she opened her eyes and turned back and faced the doors. Without another thought, the young woman quickly pushed her way through the doors knowing she had crossed the point of no return.

The young woman was standing in a large open room filled with rows and rows of green benches. Her eyes swept the room from right to left until her gaze settled upon a green bench straight ahead. She walked to the bench, sat down, and pulled the pink suitcase against her leg. The bench faced a ticket window that was on the far side of the room. The young woman could see the back of a woman's head through the ticket window glass. To the right of the ticket window, was a single glass door. Through the door, she could see a parked bus. A sign above the door read,

"TICKETED PASSENGERS ONLY BEYOND THIS POINT."

A round clock with big black hands hung on the wall to her right. The shorter hand pointed to a space between the six and the seven and the longer hand was between the three and the four. Below the clock, bright red letters danced horizontally across an electronic sign.

"December 24, 2001 - - Welcome to Salt Lake City, Utah - - Merry Christmas and a Happy New Year - - The current temperature is 14 degrees."

"Yeah," the young woman thought to herself, "I'll be happy and merry when I'm out of this place."

The young woman looked behind her and saw a filth-covered mound on a bench in the farthest corner of the room. Toward the other rear corner of the room was a snack bar. Behind the counter, a menu board was hanging on the wall. The word MENU was written in large letters at the top of the board, but she was too far away to make out anything else. The young woman opened the pink suitcase and took out her purse. She counted her money. One twenty-dollar bill, two tens, three fives, two ones and forty-six cents in change. The young woman's stomach growled to remind her that she had not eaten all day.

The young woman's body jumped when the double doors banged open. She intentionally looked away from the door as the sound of footsteps walked closer and closer toward her. Her heart raced as blackness began to fill the corner of her eye. She instinctively cringed away. Despite her subconscious effort to avoid it, within seconds, the blackness was standing directly in front of her.

"Excuse me, Miss," a man's voice said, "may I see your ticket."

"Wwwhat?," the young woman asked as she caught her breath and looked up.

In front of her was a police officer dressed in a typical black uniform with a black winter coat.

"I need to see your ticket please," the officer said.

"I-I don't have a ticket," she sputtered, "I just got here and haven't bought one yet."

"How old are you?," the officer asked as he first

examined the young woman's face and then her pink suitcase.

"Eighteen," she lied.

In truth, she was barely fifteen.

"Where are you going?," he asked with suspicion in his voice.

"Los Angeles," she blurted out.

At least that's where she was hoping to go. She had dreams of being a famous actress.

"On Christmas Eve? All by yourself? Where's your family?," he continued.

"My family lives in Los Angeles," she said with a false conviction, "I'm in my first year at the U and I couldn't leave earlier because of finals. I'm hoping to be there on Christmas tomorrow."

The "U" was what the locals called the University of Utah, which was only a few miles east of the bus station. The officer seemed satisfied with the explanation even though he remained suspicious. He pointed his night stick to a sign.

"NO LOITERING."

"We've had complaints so I suggest you buy your ticket ASAP," he said.

"I'm sorry," she apologized, "I didn't see the sign. I'll buy my ticket right away."

At least she could be totally honest about that.

"See that you do," the officer replied, "I'd hate to send a young woman like you into the streets on a cold night like this, especially on Christmas Eve."

The young woman's gaze followed the officer as he walked over to the filthy mound. He poked it with his night stick. At first, the mound remained motionless, but the officer persisted until the mound began to wiggle, then stretch and finally sit up. The mound turned out to be a homeless man who looked like he had not bathed or shaved in weeks.

"I need to see your ticket," the officer said.

"I don't have one," the man said truthfully, "I just came in here to get out of the cold. It's freezing outside, or haven't you noticed?"

"You can't sleep in here," the officer stated without emotion, "You have to leave."

"I have no where to go," the man said loudly, "I'm not bothering anyone. Look around. The place is almost empty. Why don't you go find some real criminals to harass or is it a slow night?"

"There's a homeless shelter three blocks from here," the officer insisted, "You can sleep there."

"I already tried that," the man said with increasing agitation, "There's no room in the Inn."

"I can't let you stay here," the officer persisted, "You have to leave *NOW*."

"I'm not leaving," the man shouted, "I don't have anywhere to go. What are you going to do? Arrest me?"

"That's exactly what I'm going to do if you don't leave immediately," the officer said as a matter of factly.

"Then *arrest* me," the man shouted, "because I'm not going to leave. I'll freeze to death out there."

The handcuffs made a clicking sound as the officer locked the man's arms behind his back.

"At least the poor man will get some food and a shower," the young woman thought a little enviously to herself, "Maybe I should start making a scene myself, but then I would be stuck in this city for who knows how long."

The young woman was laughing to herself as the

officer led the man toward the double glass door. She stopped laughing when the officer passed by and looked directly at her.

"I'll be back to check on you," he said.

By the seriousness of his look and tone, she knew he meant it. The two men pushed through the double glass doors and disappeared into the dark, cold night just as the hum of a tram passed by. The young woman took a moment to regain her composure. She picked up her pink suitcase and drug herself to the ticket window. The ticket lady still had her back to the window and the young woman could see that she was reading a book. When it became apparent that the ticket lady was unaware of her presence, the young woman tapped on the window to announce her arrival. The ticket lady quickly sat upright and spun in the young woman's direction.

"I'm sorry," the ticket lady apologized with a gentle voice, "I didn't see you. What can I do for you?"

The ticket lady carefully examined the young woman who was standing in front of her. The young woman was about five-feet, six-inches tall and was extraordinarily attractive. She had long, thick, golden blond hair and beautiful blue eyes. She was wearing a grey, wool overcoat that was far too big for her and hung almost to the ground. The coat looked like it belonged to her father, or more likely, her grandfather.

"How much is a ticket to Los Angeles?," the young woman asked politely.

"One way or round trip?," the ticket lady asked.

"One way," the young woman replied.

The ticket lady punched at her keyboard and studied the monitor in front of her.

"A one way ticket to Los Angeles is sixty-three

dollars."

The young woman looked down.

"I didn't think it would be that expensive," she said with obvious disappointment in her voice.

"I'm sorry, honey," the ticket lady said sympathetically, "Why do you need to go to Los Angeles?"

"I just need to go there," the young woman said curtly.

Just as the young woman began to turn away from the window, she had a thought and turned back toward the ticket lady.

"How far can I go for fifty-seven dollars?," the young woman asked.

"The farthest you can go that's still somewhere is probably Las Vegas," the ticket lady replied, "Let me check."

The ticket lady punched on the keyboard again and studied her monitor for a few moments.

"You're in luck," the ticket lady said, "A one-way-ticket to Las Vegas is only thirty-five dollars. But you have to make up you mind quickly because the bus is leaving in less than ten minutes."

"Las Vegas," the young woman thought to herself, "I never thought about going to Las Vegas, but Las Vegas will do just fine."

Just then, the young woman heard the sound of a bus engine start up beyond the departure door. She quickly slid a twenty, a ten and a five through the slot under the window. She counted the money that remained in her purse as the ticket lady punched at her keyboard. Twenty-two dollars and forty-six cents remained. The ticket lady slid a ticket to the young woman.

"You better hurry," the ticket lady said, "The bus is leaving."

The young woman glanced toward the snack bar and then at the ticket lady.

"I have to get something to eat," the young woman pleaded, "I haven't had anything to eat all day."

The sympathetic ticket lady could see the hunger in the young woman's face and sighed.

"I'll stall the bus driver," the ticket lady said, "but hurry fast. She doesn't like to wait. I'll take your suitcase out to the bus."

"No," the young woman interrupted emphatically, "I mean, I want to keep it with me. It has all of my stuff in it, if you don't mind."

The ticket lady hesitated and looked at the young woman strangely.

"OK," the ticket lady said, "but you need to hurry. You can leave your suitcase here with me. Don't worry. I'll keep it safe. Go."

The young woman left her suitcase with the ticket lady and quickly waddled to the snack bar. The ticket lady couldn't help but to notice the young woman's strange and labored gait. As the young woman scanned the menu for something cheap, a man in his early twenties came out of the snack bar kitchen and walked behind the cash register. He instinctively smiled when he saw how beautiful the young woman was and how strangely she was dressed.

"May I help you?," he asked with a smile.

"I see you have a jumbo drink for ninety-nine cents," she asked, "How big is that?"

The snack bar man held up a jumbo sized plastic

cup.

"This is the jumbo," he said.

"I'll have a jumbo drink and that bag of chips," the young woman said pointing to a large bag of nacho cheese Doritos.

The snack bar man poked at the cash register and it started to beep.

"That will be three dollars and seventy-two cents," he said.

The young woman handed the young man a five-dollar bill and two pennies. The man handed her back a dollar bill, a quarter and a nickle. She only had eighteen dollars and seventy-six cents left.

"What do you want to drink?," the snack bar man asked.

"What do you have?"

"The usual. Coke, Diet Coke, Root Beer, Sprite ..."

"I'll have Sprite" the young woman interrupted.

The snack bar man put some ice in a large cup, filled it with Sprite and put a lid on the cup. He placed the drink, a red straw and the bag of Doritos on the counter in front of the young woman. She immediately punched the red straw though the lid and drank almost half of the contents of the cup.

"You need to move it, sweetie!," the ticket lady shouted from across the room.

The young woman couldn't resist the temptation to drink one more gulp. She immediately felt the sugar from the drink energize her body. The young woman removed the lid, smiled at the snack bar man and asked if he would refill the cup. She even added pretty please and an extra big smile to the request.

"OK," the snack bar man said, "but only because

you said 'pretty please'."

The snack bar man refilled the cup.

"COME. NOW," the ticket lady shouted from across the room.

Two horn blasts sounded from beyond the departure door which was being held open by the ticket lady.

"I'm coming," the young woman shouted back as the snack bar man gave her back the cup.

The young woman quickly replaced the lid, turned and started toward the ticket lady. At the last second, she remembered that she left the bag of Doritos on the counter. The young woman turned back to grab the Doritos.

"Come *on*, girl," the exacerbated ticket lady shouted across the room just as two longer blasts from the bus horn sounded.

The young woman grabbed the bag of Doritos and dashed with the same, awkward, labored gait to the departure door. As she approached the ticket lady, the ticket lady said,

"I'll carry your suitcase. Get on the bus. Hurry."

As the young woman walked up the steps of the bus, the bus driver stared at her with a look that was noticeably irritated.

"It's about time," the driver mumbled to herself, "Who do you think *you* are? Cinderella?"

The bus driver probably made this comment because she could see the outward beauty of the girl, but couldn't really *see* the girl. The young woman ignored the comment even though it hurt her. The bus driver felt instantly ashamed of herself and frowned as her head motioned to the back of the bus. The young woman strolled down the aisle. She passed by maybe a half dozen people who were seated toward the front of the bus and walked to the completely empty rear of the bus. The ticket lady followed closely behind her with the pink suitcase. The young woman picked a secluded seat two rows from the very back of the bus and sat down in the seat next to the window. The ticket lady placed the suitcase on the empty aisle seat next to the young woman.

"Good luck, honey," the ticket lady said.

Before the young woman could say "thank you," the ticket lady hurried toward the front of the bus.

"Thanks for waiting, Sue," the ticket lady said as she passed by the driver and walked down the steps.

The bus door immediately hissed shut. The young woman heard the sound of the bus shifting into gear and the bus immediately lurched forward. The young woman tried to put her cup of Sprite into a cup holder that was at the end of the armrest, but the cup was too big to fit in. She took another big sip from the straw and wedged the cup between her body and the side of the bus. She opened the bag of Doritos and put a chip in her mouth. She savored the flavor for a moment and started to chew. She put the open bag of Doritos on top of the suitcase and looked out the window.

The bus snaked its way westward past the Delta Center, which is the home of the Utah Jazz, and then south through the streets of Salt Lake City. It turned West again and was soon headed up a freeway on-ramp. The young woman saw a sign that hung above the roadway.

"I-15 South, Provo, Las Vegas."

The bus made a long, sweeping turn to the left and

was soon heading South toward Las Vegas. The young woman continued to munch on her chips as she took in the sights of the mountains surrounding the Salt Lake Valley. She hoped it would be for the last time. The Wasatch mountains and its ten thousand foot peaks towered to the East, while the less majestic Oquire mountains formed a distant outline to the West. The lights of the city danced past while the steady hum of the diesel engine sang out. The young woman took another large sip from her cup, reclined her seat back as far as it would go and fell asleep.

CHAPTER TWO

DELIVERY

The young woman was awakened by a sharp, painful jab to her abdomen. She bolted upright, clenched her hand into a fist and swung at her attacker. Her fist struck empty air and she was instantly hit by an awareness that she was completely alone. She felt another, but milder jab to her abdomen. She opened her grey, woolen coat and looked at her enlarged, pregnant belly. She sneered at the baby that was growing inside her as anger welled up inside her. The young woman was eventually soothed by the continuing hum of the diesel engine and the memories of her recent escape.

She wondered how far the bus had traveled while she was asleep. She looked out of the bus window, but could only see dark shadows in a sea of endless darkness. She quickly became bored as the monotony of the endless, empty scenery fueled her feelings of consuming loneliness. The young woman felt another sharp stab of pain in her abdomen that was different from the continuous dull pain she had felt up until then. She continued to feel these sharp stabs of pain in her abdomen as the minutes passed by, one after another, until distant lights appeared on the horizon.

"It must be from the food," the young woman thought, "Maybe my body isn't use to eating so much junk food."

The young woman took a few sips from the cup and turned her attention to the open bag of Doritos. She reached into the bag and took out a handful of chips. She munched on the chips as the lights of a distant town grew brighter and brighter as the bus sped southward. The young woman's thoughts drifted from her painful past to the future she would make for herself in Las Vegas. When the bus finally caught up to the lights, the young woman could see houses and buildings spread along the side of the interstate."

"Welcome to Fillmore, Utah's First State Capital - You Have a Friend in Fillmore," a billboard read.

The sign made the young woman laugh out loud.

"I've never even heard of Fillmore," the young woman thought to herself, "How could I have a friend in Fillmore? What kind of name is Fillmore anyway?"

When the last lights of Fillmore were left behind in the darkness, a sharp pain jolted the young woman upright into her seat. This was more severe than anything she had felt before. It was like a monster muscle cramp, but she didn't know exactly what it was. As quickly as the pain appeared, it disappeared. The bus continued to speed southward and the pains continued to come and go, come and go. After a while, the young woman again saw lights in the distant horizon which grew brighter and brighter until the bus came to another town called Beaver.

"Fillmore?," the young woman thought, "Now Beaver? Where do they get these names? What's next?, Rabbit?"

The young woman began to worry when the pains became more frequent, lasted longer and became increasingly severe. She also started to feel like something was pushing down on her pelvis.

"Maybe I have to go to the bathroom," the young woman thought.

She slid out of her seat and made her way the six feet or so to the bathroom door at the back of the bus. She almost fell over when the bus rocked from side to side as it passed over a rough spot in the road. But she braced herself just in time and managed to stay upright. She opened the bathroom door, stepped inside and locked the door behind her.

The young woman sat down on the toilet as the pains continued to come and go, come and go. She sat on the toilet for about a half hour, but nothing came out. She finally gave up, stood up and unlocked the bathroom door. She stepped out of the bathroom and returned to her seat. She took the grey, wool coat and formed something like a pillow. She placed it toward the back of the seat and sat down. She reclined backward hoping to relieve the pressure on her pelvis, but the pains continued to come and go, come and go. The bus passed by a sign.

"Cedar City, next three exits."

"At least that's better than Rabbit," the young

woman thought to herself.

Water suddenly gushed from between her legs. Panic gripped her body as she realized for the first time that the baby had chosen this moment to fight its way into the world.

"This can't be happening," the young woman thought, "Not now. The baby's not due for at least another month. I was hoping I'd be long gone by then. Oh, God, I *can't* have this baby now. Please God, help me."

But she wasn't really praying to God. The belief that she once had in God as a child was now long gone. For years she had prayed and prayed, but no one answered. Not God. Not anyone. So she stopped. She learned that she was on her own and whatever happened to her was up to her.

The young woman opened the pink suitcase that was on the seat next to her and removed a heavy red sweater, a pair of panties and her last dress. A dark-blue dress. She put the pink suitcase on the floor and laid the blue dress and panties neatly on the seat beside her. She wrapped the sweater around her arms and shoulders. The pains continued to come and go, stronger and longer, stronger and longer, as the bus continued to speed southward into the blackness.

The bus seemed to slow as it began to travel down a winding, steep decline. She looked out of the window and saw the outline of canyon walls on both sides of the road. When she could no longer suffer the pain in silence, she used the sweater to muffle her moans. The sweater and the constant hum of the diesel engine allowed her to avoid detection by either the bus driver or the few passengers who were seated near the front of the bus.

When the bus descended out of the canyon, the lights of a much larger city suddenly appeared on the horizon. While it was nowhere near as large as Salt Lake City, it was much larger than any of the small towns the bus had passed by so far. The young woman saw a sign.

"St. George, next three exits."

The bus drove past a golf course, a Walmart and a small shopping mall. Shortly after that, the full view of the city could be seen. The bus continued past several motels, restaurants and office buildings. The bus began to slow as it approached a sign.

"Bluff Street Exit."

As the bus exited the freeway, the young woman saw the big double arches of a McDonald's sign. It was a couple hundred feet to the right. The bus slowed to a stop, then turned right onto Bluff Street. It traveled about a hundred feet, came to a stop and turned right onto Main Street. It traveled another two hundred feet and pulled into the McDonald's parking lot. The bus stopped at the far end of the parking lot behind the McDonald's. The interior lights of the bus came on, which momentarily blinded the young woman. She heard the crackling noise of the intercom system and the sound of the bus driver's voice.

"We've arrived at St. George, Utah," the bus driver said, "We'll be stopping for a thirty-minute break. It's now a little before midnight. Please be back on the bus no later than 12:30. Be on time because this time, the bus will wait for no one."

The young woman was momentarily outraged because she knew this comment was directed at her.

"That woman knows nothing about me," she

thought, "If she only knew."

The young woman heard a pop as the intercom shut off. She was relieved when all of the passengers got off the bus. The bus driver stood up and scanned the bus. She saw that the young woman was still on the bus.

"Are you gettin off?," The bus driver shouted.

"No," the young woman shouted back just as another contraction hit that caused her to wince.

She ducked down as she stifled a cry into the sweater.

"Is everything OK?," the bus driver shouted.

"Yes," the young woman shouted back, "I'm really tired and need to sleep. Would you mind turning off the lights when you leave?"

The bus driver paused for a moment as she looked toward the young woman with a questioning stare, but the lights went off and the bus driver got off the bus. The young woman heard a noise from the bottom of the bus that sounded like the luggage compartment being opened. She heard some more noises, then a slamming noise, then complete silence. Through the bus window, the young woman saw the passengers nearing the McDonald's entrance. She also saw the bus driver and a man carrying a large suit case walking toward the entrance about forty feet behind the others.

When everyone entered the McDonald's, including the bus driver and the man with the suitcase, the young woman felt grateful to be alone. At that moment, she felt the strongest and longest contraction so far. One that lasted for at least five seconds. For the first time, she let out a cry that was so loud, it surprised even her. It was so loud that she was fearful that her cry could be heard inside the McDonald's. She kept her eye on the

McDonald's entrance and was relieved when no one ran out. She vowed to be more discreet in the future.

The young woman stood up the best she could and picked up the panties and the blue dress that she had placed onto the seat next to her. She hung the panties and the blue dress over the seat that was immediately in front of her. She rearranged the grey coat so that it was spread over the two seats she had been occupying. She reached down, removed her panties and pulled up her dress. At that moment, another contraction hit and she immediately sat down so that her back was against the side of the bus. Her left foot was on the aisle seat pressed against the armrest and her right foot was slumped down onto the floor. After five or six seconds, the pain abated and she was left sucking for air, desperately trying to get oxygen into her body.

The young woman felt down between her legs and she could feel the top of the baby's head. It seemed like about three or four inches of the baby's head was exposed. She again felt an intense contraction and this time, she instinctively knew that she had to push, push, push, push, push until she was completely out of breath. As she pushed, her head turned red, then blue, then purple until the contraction subsided and her body relaxed. The young woman was left sucking for air as she waited for the next contraction. This continued over and over until finally, the baby's head was expelled. She reached down when the baby's shoulders were expelled and pulled the baby completely out of her body. She held the baby up and looked at it for the first time. It was a girl.

The baby was covered in some kind of white gooey substance and appeared to have blue colored skin. The baby's head drooped limply from what appeared to be a lifeless body. The head merely rocked limply as the young woman gently moved the body from side to side and back and forth.

"I guess things didn't turn out so bad after all," the young woman thought to herself.

At the instant she had that thought, a man appeared in the aisle directly in front of her. The young woman's face looked terrified and she cowered away from him.

"Peace be unto you," the man said.

The young woman wasn't sure if it was a voice or just a thought in her head, but she immediately felt a peace unlike any she had ever felt before. It was a peace that pierced her soul. She had also never seen a man like this before. The man had an aura surrounding his body that appeared to be as bright as the noon day sun. Even though the man had this aura, it was completely dark inside the bus. He was wearing a white robe that covered his arms and went to his ankles and he seemed to be floating in the air.

"Wwwho are you?," the young woman stammered, "Why are you here?"

"I'm an angel sent from God," the man said.

"I don't believe in God," the young woman blurted out, "Is this some kind of trick? Wwwhat kind of angel are you? Tell me why you're here."

"You know why I'm here," the angel said with the kindest voice.

"You want the baby?," the young woman asked.

"No," the angel said, "I came for you."

"What do you mean?," the young woman protested, "Do you mean you want me to die?"

"Yes," the angel said kindly as he reached out his hand, "Take my hand and come with me."

"But I don't want to die," the young woman protested, "I can't die."

"To God," the angel said gently, "there's no such thing as death. Now take my hand."

"But I can't just leave my baby here," the young woman continued to protest, "Who will take care of her? My baby needs me."

The young woman started to cry. A little bit at first, but soon began to sob uncontrollably. The young woman wasn't crying because she was concerned about the baby. She had no love for the baby at all. Just a few minutes before, she was happy that it was dead. The reason the young woman was crying was because she was fearful of going to that Hell where she was certain she belonged. Not knowing the young woman's heart or understanding the Will of God, the angel looked at this beautiful young woman and the baby that she was holding in her arms. The angel felt compassion. As quickly as the angel appeared, the angel vanished.

The young woman sat stunned until the contractions that expelled the afterbirth brought her back to reality. Having been awakened to the present moment, she wrapped the baby inside the grey, wool coat. She removed the red dress that she had been wearing and hurriedly used it as best she could to clean herself up and the space around her. She reached for the panties on the seat in front of her and put them on. She reached for the blue dress and put that on. Finally, she put on the red sweater. She wrapped the old panties into the red dress. The young woman picked up both bundles and walked to the front of the bus. By the force of her own Will, she dragged her aching body down the stairs and got off the bus. She was surprised that the temperature outside seemed to be a lot warmer than she expected. It was still quite cold, but significantly warmer than icy Salt Lake City. She found the cold air refreshing considering her recent ordeal.

About twenty feet directly in front of the bus, the young woman saw a block enclosure that held a dumpster. She walked over to the structure, saw that the dumpster was open and tossed the red dress inside. She began to toss in the grey coat bundle as well.

"I can't just throw a baby into the trash," the young woman thought at the last moment.

She still had a flicker of a conscious no matter how cold hearted she had become. So instead, she put the grey, wool coat bundle on the cement slab behind the dumpster next to the block wall. She limped back to the bus, pulled herself up the stairs and returned to the back of the bus. She picked up her bag of Doritos and cup of Sprite and sat in the seat in front of where she had delivered the baby. She took a few more big sips from the red straw until her thirst was quenched. She reclined the seat backward and was asleep before anyone else returned to the bus. While she was sleeping, she dreamed of becoming a show girl in Las Vegas.

SECRETS

CHAPTER THREE

HIGHWAY 59

Roger Hepner struggled to stay awake as he drove down the dark, moonless highway. He glanced at the radio that no longer worked. He wished he had the money to replace it, but a new radio wasn't in his family's strained budget. He cracked open the window to let in some cold night air. Roger slowed to thirty-five miles an hour when he reached the outskirts of Fredonia, Arizona. In the center of town, he drove by a police cruiser that was parked on the side of the road. It had a dummy in the driver's seat that always fooled the tourists. The police cruiser and its dummy were the town's only form of traffic control since there were no stop lights. Roger made a right turn onto Highway 59 just before he approached the last building in town, an old abandoned gas station. He set the cruise control to eighty miles an hour and sped westward on Highway 59 that ran along the Utah side of the Utah-Arizona border.

"At least the cruise control still works," Roger thought to himself.

His stomach growled to remind him that he hadn't eaten since noon. Roger misjudged how long he would be gone from home and failed to pack enough food for both lunch and dinner. Roger had expected to be home by no later than seven, but it was now almost midnight. His mental calculation told him that he wouldn't be home until around two in the morning. He wished he had stopped to get something to eat, but stopping at a restaurant would have required him to spend too much of his family's precious dollars. On the bright side, and to Roger, there was always a bright side, his hunger was keeping him awake. He drove past an obscure sign that marked a dirt road to Toroweep.

"Sixty-one miles and he could end it all," Roger thought amusingly to himself.

He thought about the last time he had been to Toroweep, a little known place in the Grand Canyon where there is a three thousand-foot drop from the top of the Colorado River gorge to the river below. Roger thought it had the most breath taking view in the entire Grand Canyon, and perhaps, the whole earth. A surprisingly few number of people ever travel the sixty-one miles to see this sight each year in contrast to the millions of people who visit the more easily accessible locations along the canyon. The reason might be that the sign marking the road to Toroweep is so inconspicuous that even the locals fail to notice it. Or perhaps it's because the few lucky people who have visited there want to keep it a well-guarded secret. Another reason might be that Toroweep is a place where the weak of heart dare not tread.

Roger thought about the last time he went there with his family. He was a nervous wreck by the time he left. His then five-year-old son, Billy, ran around the ledge like a banshee feeling no fear whatsoever. He, himself, could come no closer than five feet to the ledge without crawling on his hands and knees. This made it impossible for him to keep his son under control despite his wife's continuous pleas.

"Do something, Roger. The kid's going to kill himself."

He remembered running into a friendly park ranger who told him that despite the obvious danger, there had only been two known deaths at the site. One was a confirmed suicide. Roger couldn't imagine voluntarily jumping off that cliff. There would be way too much time for second thoughts before he hit bottom. On the other hand, perhaps it was understandable that someone might jump off because at that particular moment, the choice between jumping off the cliff and returning home to face his wife with no money in hand was about an even proposition. The other death involved a Scandinavian couple who had camped there. According to the husband, he and his wife went to the ledge after they woke up in the morning. The husband said he returned to the tent to get a jacket and when he returned to the ledge, his wife was gone. They later found her dismembered body on a ledge that was about a third of the way to the bottom. There were no witnesses, so whether she fell off, jumped off or was pushed off, no one knows for sure. Of course, that was another thought.

"Maybe he could lure his wife there and . . . "

But that was just a fleeting thought because Roger could never do such a thing.

Since that visit three years ago, Roger read about another death in the local newspaper. According to the article, a retired couple who spent the winters in St. George, Utah had gone to Toroweep for a family outing. The grandma was taking a photograph of her entire family, including her grandchildren, who were posed near the ledge. She stepped back to get the entire family in the frame and accidentally stepped off the ledge. She fell to her death as her family watched in horror. Roger vowed then and there that if he ever returned to Toroweep, it would be without his family.

The thoughts of Toroweep gave Roger's body a shot of adrenaline that invigorated his body. Roger was so lost in these thoughts that he barely noticed passing pipe spring and he almost failed to notice a cow standing in the middle of the highway. Roger swerved to the right and hit the brakes just in time to avoid a collision. His heart pounded because he knew that if the cow had been in the middle of his lane, instead of the middle of the highway itself, he would most likely be dead. Roger was now wide awake bolstered by a full dose of adrenaline. It seemed like everything moved in slow motion as he passed by the . . .,

"Did I just see what I thought I saw?," Roger thought to himself.

Roger's car came to a stop as the image replayed in his mind. The image was not of a cow, but of a completely naked man. The man wasn't trying to flag him down, nor was he hitchhiking. Just a naked man, shivering in the cold, kneeling down in the middle of the road. Even though many people might have quickly driven on suspecting that this could be a twisted trick to get them to stop, Roger had no such thought. The idea that he could be robbed, or even worse, killed, never crossed Roger's mind. To him, this was nothing more than some poor soul in need.

Roger pushed the accelerator and made a sweeping U-turn. The object in the road was now completely illuminated by the car's headlights. Roger stopped the car about thirty-five feet away from the man. It was indeed a man, kneeling on one knee, shivering completely naked in the cold. The man's arms were pressed tightly into his body. Other than the obvious shivering, the man-made no effort to move whatsoever. Roger quickly scanned the immediate area and saw nothing except for the man and the surrounding desolate landscape. Feeling that it was safe, Roger got out of the car.

"Do you need help?," Roger yelled out.

When there was no response, Roger closed the car door and walked halfway to the man.

"Do you need help?," Roger shouted again.

Roger could hear the man mumbling something but could not make out what he was saying. Roger walked to the man and bent down.

"Do you need some help?," Roger said gently.

"Ma my . . . . na na name . . . is . . . is Gabe," The man said though his shivers.

"Why are you here?," Roger asked, "How did you get here?"

The man only repeated, "ma my . . . . na na name . . . is . . . is Gabe."

Roger stood up and again looked around in all directions. He saw nothing but his car, the road and the surrounding desolate landscape. Roger reached down and helped Gabe up to his feet. When he looked into Gabe's eyes, he felt a peace that startled him. Gabe's countenance had a certain child like quality that seemed to render the man harmless even though he was at least six-feet, five-inches tall and extremely muscular. In fact, the man seemed to have a perfect physique. Roger seemed small in comparison to Gabe even though Roger himself was six feet tall and weighed a hundred and seventy-five pounds. Roger motioned to Gabe to follow him and started to walk to his car. When Gabe didn't follow, Roger walked back and took him by the arm.

"I'll give you a ride to the next town," Roger said as he pulled Gabe toward the car.

Roger left Gabe next to the passenger side door and went to the rear of the car. Roger opened the trunk and pulled out a blanket that he kept for emergencies. Roger was always prepared because he never knew when his junker of a car might break down. Roger returned to Gabe and wrapped the blanket around him. Roger opened the door and motioned for Gabe to get inside the car. When Gabe didn't move, Roger began to push Gabe into the car until Gabe began to cooperate. When Gabe was seated, Roger put the seat belt around him and closed the door. He walked around the front of the car to the driver's side door, opened it and got in the car.

Roger put the car in gear, pushed the accelerator and made another U-turn. He closed his window, turned on the heater and resumed his westward journey. He looked at Gabe, who in turn, was staring at him with a smile.

"So what are you doing out here all by yourself?," Roger asked, "How did you get out here?"

But the man only smiled and said, "My name is Gabe."

"This guy must be mentally challenged," Roger thought to himself, "Maybe someone abandoned him here like he was some unwanted stray animal."

Before long, Roger forgot that Gabe was even in the car as his mind again began to wander. He was driving through B.L.M. grazing land that the federal government leased to cattle and sheep ranchers. In this part of the country, there are no fences and animals have the absolute right of way. He remembered a few years ago that he nearly missed hitting a black cow on the same highway. He also remembered another incident when there was a wedding in St. George. After the wedding, several guests were driving home on a similar highway north of St. George. They ran right into a herd of sheep at full speed and everyone in the car was killed.

"You can't even see them until the last second," Roger thought, "The ranchers should be at least required to put reflective vests on these animals."

Roger chuckled to himself and he began to think about the events of the day. Roger spent a disappointing day traveling through southern Utah trying to collect money on past due accounts. It was always the same story.

"I wish I could pay you," they would say, "I feel so bad, but with the economy in Japan being so down, there just hasn't been the number of tourists we expected. Look, I'm not trying to stiff you, I'm behind on all my bills. I'm one step away from filing for bankruptcy. It's Christmas, can't you give me just a few more months? Maybe when the Olympics come, things will turn around."

Roger, being a kind hearted and trusting person, or sucker, as his wife constantly told him, would acquiesce and drive to the next place only to hear the same thing over and over. In the end, he only collected a few hundred dollars. This wouldn't be nearly enough to satisfy his wife or his creditors. Roger was a jeweler, a trade he learned from his father. In addition to the jewelry store he owned in St. George, Roger also made customized jewelry that he sold to tourist shops in the region. Most of this jewelry was either native American in design or other customized designs that he believed would appeal to the thousands of tourists who visited this picturesque region from around the world. Southern Utah and Northern Arizona have some of the most spectacular and amazing natural scenery on the planet.

Roger left early that morning on his cash quest with the natural optimism that was inherent to his personality. Roger was always on the lookout for the next great idea that would finally put him over the financial hump. His tourist jewelry line was his latest idea that he believed would expand his market and bring in desperately needed cash. No matter how many times his ideas failed, he just knew that the next idea was the one that would be a home run. He had read somewhere that when Thomas Edison was asked how it felt to fail a thousand times while trying to invent a working light bulb, Thomas Edison responded by saying he had not failed a thousand times, but had succeeded a thousand times in learning how not to build a light bulb.

What was good enough for Thomas Edison was good enough for him. Roger believed that if he just hung in there long enough, success was just around the corner. If only his wife shared the same optimism. She, on the other hand, had a different point of view. With each failure, she would tell him to get his head out of the clouds and face reality.

"MacArthur Jewelers has been in this community since forever," she would say, "You know that if you went down there and applied for a job, he would hire you on the spot. I know the pay's not the greatest, but at least we would have a steady and reliable paycheck. How long are you going to put us through this?"

"How long am *I* going to put us through this?," he would think to himself, but never say to his wife.

Roger had a good job working for a jeweler in Las Vegas when he met his wife, Mary, ten years earlier. They met when Mary's sister came to Las Vegas to shop for a wedding ring. Mary had come along to give her sister a second opinion. Roger had since learned that opinions were Mary's specialty. They started dating and were married four months later. In hindsight, perhaps too quickly. Within a year, they had one child, a girl named Jen. About a year after that, they had a son, Billy. That's when Mary started in about moving to St. George. Las Vegas is evil. It's a terrible place to raise children. I want to be closer to my family. On and on and on.

Eventually, when his divorced mother-in-law got remarried, Mary and her mother thought it would be a great idea if Roger and his budding family moved to St. George. They could all move into the mother-in-law's house when Mary's mother moved out to live with her new husband. It was going to be wonderful. They could live in the house rent free. On top of that, Mary's mother would live almost next door and could help out with the kids. Mary told Roger that he was so talented and deserved to have his own store. Mary also said that she and her mother knew almost everyone in town and that they could throw him all the business he needed to get started. Success was guaranteed according to them. Roger eventually gave in to Mary's relentless nagging and moved to St. George a little over six years ago.

But things didn't exactly work out as advertised. Mary's mother was constantly demanding rent that was never agreed to. She also continually complained about what a burden it was for her to watch the children even though she was only asked to watch the children about once a week. As for business, there were already far too many jewelers in a town of only thirty-thousand people, many of whom had roots in St. George that went back generations. As for Mary's mother, she was known for nothing more than being the town gossip. Furthermore, Mary had such an abrasive personality that she alienated herself from most of the people she knew. Instead of instant success, the business struggled. Whenever Roger brought up the subject of moving away from St. George, Mary threw such a tantrum that he eventually learned to not bring up the subject at all.

Roger and Mary had two more children after they moved to St. George, a four-year-old boy named Carter and a one-year-old girl who they simply called Baby, even though her name was Emily. Even though the additional children added to the financial and marital strain, one thing was for certain - - the children were the absolute joy of Roger's life. He loved his children with all of his heart and considered them his most precious jewels of all. They were his reason for living and his reason for pushing on no matter how much the deck seemed to be stacked against him. They were the reason he got into his car that morning in a desperate effort to collect some much needed cash.

Roger drove to Springdale, a town at the entrance of Zion National Park. Because he was only able to collect about $150 of the couple thousand that he needed, he drove on to Orderville, Hatch and Panguitch, all towns on the way to Bryce Canyon National Park. He was only able to collect another two hundred dollars in these towns. His next stop was at Ruby's Inn near the park's entrance. He collected another hundred dollars there. Still being far short of his goal, he drove to Kanab, Big Water and the marina at Lake Powell. He then crossed into Arizona and went to Page, Tuba City and Jacob Lake. In all, he only collected a little over six hundred dollars. The trip to Tuba City and Jacob Lake only turned out to be a waste of time and gas because the stores were already closed before he got there. When he knocked on the owner's doors, they pretended not to be home.

Roger was brought back into reality when he heard what sounded like a squeal of delight from Gabe. Until then, Gabe had remained completely silent. Gabe was pointing to the lights of a town in the distance.

"That's Colorado City," Roger said as Gabe continued to point, "Do you like the lights?"

"Colorado City. Lights," Gabe repeated with delight.

"So you CAN talk," Roger said.

"Talk. Colorado City. Lights," Gabe repeated as he continued to point.

Colorado City straddles the Utah-Arizona boarder about an hour east of St. George. This town was settled by a polygamous group that broke away from the

Mormon church when the Mormon church banned polygamy in the 1890's. The polygamous group chose that spot in particular because they wanted to get as far away from the eyes of the government and law as possible. Back in those days, there was only one way in or out of town. They would post lookouts who would sound the alert whenever the government decided to pay a visit. If it was Utah law enforcement, everyone in the town went to the Arizona side. If it was Arizona law enforcement, everyone in town went to the Utah side. By that method, they were able to evade law enforcement for decades.

But in the 1950's, Utah and Arizona conducted a coordinated raid on the town. They arrested all the men and the images of children being torn from their parent's arms were broadcast on television. Eventually, all of the women and children wound up on welfare and it became a public relations disaster. Even though the government has left them alone ever since then, the residents remain suspicious of any outsiders. Even at noon day, the place seems completely empty. It's like the lookouts are still watching and the residents run inside whenever someone approaches town. Another strange thing about the town in addition to the lack of visible residents is that none of the buildings have finished exteriors. These two factors give Colorado City a ghost-town-like appearance.

Roger wondered what these people would think of the naked Gabe or for that matter, if anyone would even be awake. He looked at Gabe who was now sleeping and figured that Gabe seemed harmless enough. Besides that, he rationalized, even if he did stop, it would be hours before the police would arrive and even longer before he finished answering questions. Roger was too tired for that, so he just kept driving and decided to call the police in the morning. About an hour later, Roger arrived in St. George.

Roger drove up River Road to the Bloomington Hills neighborhood where he lived. After he pulled his car into the one-car garage, Roger quietly went inside the house. He opened a closet and pulled out some blankets and an extra pillow. He went to the family room, spread a blanket over the couch and put the pillow at one end of the couch. He crept into his bedroom where Mary was soundly sleeping. Roger retrieved his pajama's from a drawer along with a pair of sweat pants and his largest T-shirt. He crept back out of the room, went to the family room and put the clothes on a coffee table next to the couch. He went back into the garage, opened the passenger-side door and woke Gabe up. Roger led Gabe into the family room and handed Gabe the sweat pants and T-shirt.

"Put these on, " Roger said quietly.

Gabe just stared at the clothes as though he had never seen clothes before. Roger took the clothes from Gabe and helped Gabe get dressed. He helped Gabe onto the couch, covered him with a blanket and said good night. Gabe smiled and said good night, more as a question than as a statement. Roger put on his own pajama's, turned off the light and crept back into his bedroom where Mary remained asleep. He slipped into the bed as carefully as possible. The last thing he wanted to do was wake Mary up. As soon as Roger's head hit the pillow, he was asleep.

CHAPTER FOUR

ARRIVAL

The young woman was gone when the police officer returned to the Salt Lake City bus station about an hour and a half later.   He smiled to himself.

"Maybe my wife is right, "he thought, "Maybe I *am* overly skeptical."

He walked to the ticket window. The ticket lady was, once again, engrossed in her book with her back facing the window. The police officer rapped on the window as loud as he could without breaking the window. This startled the ticket lady so badly that she nearly fell off her chair. She turned around and saw the police officer.

"For crying out loud, Officer Decker," she yelled laughingly, "You nearly gave me a heart attack. I'm going to report you to your superior."

"All in a night's work," he jabbed back, "By the way, did that blond girl get on the bus to L.A.?"

"She sure did," the ticket lady answered, "but just barely. Why do you ask?"

"I thought she was giving me a story about having family in L.A.," Decker said somewhat pleased, "But I guess she was telling me the truth after all."

"But she's not going to L.A.," the ticket lady responded with surprise, "She bought a ticket to Las Vegas."

"Las Vegas?," Decker repeated with surprise, "I should have known."

"Known what?," the ticket lady asked.

"I think that girl's a runaway," Decker responded.

"A runaway?," the ticket lady asked rhetorically, "But she seemed so nice and is so pretty. Do you really think she's a runaway?"

"Well, I'm not certain," Decker said, "But my gut tells me that she is. Just to be safe, I'm going to notify the authorities in Las Vegas. Hopefully, someone will keep a look out for her. It's the least I can do."

"I hope she's not a runaway," the ticket lady said, "Who knows what could happen to a pretty young thing like that out on the streets."

"I hope she's not either," Decker said, "I hate to think about what could happen to her. But it's better to be safe than sorry. Good night, Myrna. Let me know if you have any more problems with loiterers."

Decker turned and started to walk away.

"Let me know if you hear anything about the girl," Myrna shouted out, "You know how boring this job would be without the gossip."

"You'll be the first to know," Decker said.

Decker returned to his precinct office, looked up the phone number for the Las Vegas Metro Police and dialed the number. When a woman answered, he explained who he was and why he was calling. She told him to wait while she transferred him to the appropriate precinct. After a couple of minutes, a man with what sounded like a New York accent said,

"This is Detective Ferraro. What can I do ya for?"

Decker again explained who he was. He told Ferraro about his encounter with the young woman at the Salt Lake bus station and asked if he would send an officer to the Las Vegas bus terminal to pick her up. Ferraro laughed.

"I don't know how busy you are up in Salt Lake," Ferraro said, "but if we spent our time hunting down lost girls in this town, we wouldn't have anything else to do."

Decker said that he knew he was asking for something unusual, but explained this wasn't an ordinary request. He told Officer Ferraro that he was asking for a favor as a professional courtesy. Decker even hinted that he had some personal interest in the matter. Even though Decker had, in fact, no personal interest in the young woman, he was drawn to help her as though some fatherly instinct had taken over. There was a silence on the other end of the phone. Just as Decker thought the line was dead, Ferraro said,

"I don't think I can send an officer, but I can notify security at the bus terminal and maybe they can handle it."

Ferraro asked for a description of the young woman.

"About fifteen or sixteen-years old," Ferraro wrote down, "golden-blond hair, blue eyes, about five-feet, six-inches tall, long grey wool coat, small pink suitcase."

Ferraro said he would forward the information to the security office at the bus terminal and would ask them to detain the young woman if they found her. Ferraro made it clear that he couldn't make any promises. Decker responded by telling Ferraro that any assistance he could offer would be greatly appreciated. Decker gave Ferraro his phone number and asked Ferraro to let him know if they found the young woman. Ferraro told him that he would. After he hung up the telephone, Ferraro immediately dialed the telephone number of the bus terminal security office. After a few rings, a voice said,

"Security Office."

"This is Detective Ferraro with the Las Vegas Metro Police Department. Who am I talking to?"

"This is Ralph Wray," the voice said, "What can I do for you?"

"There's a police officer in Salt Lake who's looking for a run away girl. Seems like it's some relative of his. She purchased a ticket to Las Vegas and she's headed your way. He wanted to know if you would keep a look out for her when the bus arrives from Salt Lake. He wants us to detain her if we can. Maybe ask her a few questions at least."

"OK," Wray said, "So what do you want me to do?"

"I want you to detain her," Ferraro said, "Make up some excuse. Then call me when you have her. I can be there within ten minutes and I will take it from there."

"Is that legal?," Wray asked.

"Just do what I tell you to do," Ferraro said harshly.

"I guess I can do that if you say so," Wray said hesitantly.

Ferraro gave Wray his telephone number and the description of the girl.

"What's her name?," Wray asked.

"I didn't get that information," Ferraro responded, "Look, just call me as soon as you have her. How hard can that be?"

Ferraro abruptly hung up.

Wray was perturbed by Ferraro's arrogance.

"These Metro people act like they can order us lowly security guards around," he thought to himself.

Even though Wray wasn't fully committed to the task, he decided he would at least give it a half-hearted effort because, if nothing else, it added a little excitement to an otherwise mundane job. Wray left the security office, walked to the dispatch office and went inside. He walked up to the dispatcher, who seemed to be shuffling through some paperwork on his desk.

"Can you tell me when the bus from Salt Lake is scheduled to arrive?," Wray asked politely.

The dispatcher continued to shuffle the papers and held up a hand as if to gesture,

"Wait until I'm finished."

"Just another humiliation," Wray thought, "I'll bet they wouldn't keep Detective Ferraro waiting."

After a while, the man looked up at Wray.

"Now what did you want?," the dispatcher said.

"I asked if you could tell me when the bus from Salt Lake is scheduled to arrive," Wray said less politely.

"Wait here and I'll find out," the dispatcher said.

The man walked past Wray and out of the office. About fifteen minutes later, the man returned with a cup of coffee in hand.

"It's scheduled to arrive at two-thirty in the

morning and is on schedule," the dispatcher said, "It will display 'Los Angeles' on the destination sign"

"Thanks," Wray said aloud and, "for nothing," to himself.

"I guess I interrupted his coffee break," he seethed.

In not so good a mood, Wray waited for the bus to arrive. At about 2:15, Wray walked out of his office and out the front door of the bus terminal. He waited on the sidewalk for the bus destined for Los Angeles to arrive. The air outside was cold, but not freezing. He watched several buses pass by, but none of them was the bus he was looking for. The cold air seemed to refresh Wray's mood just a tad and the tension began to relax from his body.

A tourist bus passed by, immediately followed by another bus that displayed the "Los Angeles" sign above the windshield that he was looking for. He watched closely as the bus passed in front of him and made a left turn into the station. When the bus disappeared from sight, Wray went back into the terminal, passed a line of waiting passengers and out of the terminal through a door on the back side of the terminal. He saw the bus flicker by as it passed the parked row of buses. The bus pulled into the last stall to his right. Wray heard a hissing sound as the bus came to a stop.

Almost immediately, Wray saw a dark-haired woman wearing a red sweater dash around the front of the bus. The person didn't match the description he had been given so he continued to walk somewhat casually toward the bus as more people got off. He arrived at the bus just as the driver stepped off. The driver almost ran into him as she turned in his direction.

"Excuse me," Wray apologized, "I'm looking for a

girl who I was told was on this bus. Golden blond hair, blue eyes, grey wool coat"

"Yeah," the bus driver said, "There was a girl on the bus who fit that description. But she already got off."

"Where?," Wray asked.

"Here," the bus driver said, "Where else."

"When?," Wray asked.

"Just now," the bus driver responded, "She was the first person off the bus."

"But I didn't see anyone who fit that description," Wray argued.

"That's right," the bus driver explained, "She's not wearing a grey wool coat anymore. She's wearing a red sweater. She's also wearing a dark dress. I think it was black or dark blue. Something like that."

"Did you see where she went?," Wray asked.

The driver pointed to the Plaza Hotel and said, "That way. I saw her go into that building. She seemed like she was in a hurry."

Wray ran to the casino entrance, opened the door and entered in. He was immediately met with row upon row of slot machines. The girl was nowhere to be seen.

"I'll never find her in that jungle," he thought to himself, "She could be anywhere."

After searching for several minutes around the casino with no luck, Wray returned to the bus where the driver was talking to the dispatcher.

"Did you find her?," the bus driver asked.

"No," Wray said.

"She got on the bus with a suitcase," the bus driver said, "but she didn't have it with her when she got off. I think she left it on the bus."

"A small pink suitcase?," Wray asked.

"That would be the one," the bus driver said, "She was sitting near the back."

Wray got on the bus and walked to the back of the bus. He found the abandoned suitcase under a seat next to a window. There was also a large empty soda cup and an empty bag of Doritos. Wray grabbed the handle of the suitcase and pulled it toward him. As he did so, the suitcase came open. It had not been latched shut. The suitcase was empty. As an afterthought, Wray threw the empty cup and empty Doritos bag into the suitcase and latched the suitcase shut. As he did so, he noticed some faint writing between the latches. Wray got off the bus and took the suitcase to the security office. He examined the writing on the suitcase and could see faded words that had been written in magic marker,

"ANNA HANSEN."

Wray picked up the telephone and dialed Ferraro's number.

SECRETS

CHAPTER FIVE

MISSION

Officer Decker hung up the telephone after talking to Ferraro. Ferraro told him that the young woman got off the bus in Las Vegas, but had escaped before she could be apprehended and questioned. Ferraro said that the pink suitcase was recovered and that the name "Anna Hansen" was written on it. Decker sat back in his chair and couldn't help feeling like he had failed the young woman in some way.

Decker, whose first name was Richard, grew up in Provo, Utah. Even though Provo's only about 45 miles south of Salt Lake City, it seems much farther away than that because it's separated from Salt Lake City by a mountain pass called the Point of the Mountain. In fact, while growing up in the tranquility that Provo offered, Richard felt almost completely isolated from the rest of the world and its problems.

He graduated from Provo High School where he had been a basketball star earning All-State honors. Richard accepted a scholarship offer to play basketball at Brigham Young University, the local university just across the street from Provo High. Richard's dream was to play in the NBA. But before Richard had the chance to play in even one varsity game, he tore ligaments in his knee during practice. That was in the days when freshmen couldn't play on the varsity team. Just like that, his basketball career and his NBA dream was over. From that day on, Richard would be just another anonymous student among the thousands who attended BYU.

After the end of his disappointing freshman year, Richard, being a member of the predominant Mormon religion, went on a church mission to Brazil. Richard spent the first six months of his mission at the church's Mission Home in Salt Lake City where he received language and religious training. His time at the Mission Home was mostly spent with other American missionaries who were being sent by the church to either Brazil or Portugal.

From the beginning of his arrival at the Mission Home, he and the other missionaries in his group were expected to speak only in Portuguese, or Portuglish, as the missionaries called it. Since they knew few words of Portuguese, they had a game of making up a hybrid Portuguese/English word to communicate. The most creative word won the day. For example, the Portuguese word for a fork, as in spoon and fork, is garfo. The missionaries made up the word garfork, which they used as a verb that meant to fork something over. By the end of the six months, Richard and the other missionaries had the illusion that they were fluent in Portuguese since they had little trouble communicating with each other.

This illusion was shattered as soon as he arrived at the airport in São Paulo, Brazil. When he went through customs, the Brazilians could have been speaking Japanese for all he knew. He didn't understand a word they said and as far as he could tell, they didn't understand a word he said either. They certainly didn't understand what garfork meant nor the humor of the word. The reality of his inferior language skills was further confirmed when after going through customs, there was no one on the other side waiting for him and his companion as they were expecting. Mormon missionaries are always required to travel together in pairs. They refer to each other as their "companion." They do this for one reason - - to keep themselves out of trouble, both of their own making and the making of others.

After waiting in vain for someone to pick them up at the São Paulo airport for over an hour, the pair eventually decided to call the mission office using the local payphone system. With a great deal of patience on both their part and the part of the native Brazilians who tried to help them, they managed to complete a telephone call to the mission office. Richard and his companion were informed that the mission office had no idea that they were expected to arrive in Brazil and were told to wait where they were. Someone would be dispatched to pick them up.

About an hour later, another pair of missionaries, each sporting the appropriate hair cut and trade mark white shirt and tie, arrived at the airport. The missionaries loaded themselves into what appeared to be a twenty-year-old version of a Ford Galaxy 500, except that the vehicle seemed to be almost brand new. Richard and his companion got in the back seat and the other two missionaries got in the front seat. Richard later learned that outdated Ford models continued to be manufactured in Brazil. They drove through mile after mile of what Richard considered to be urban blight. Potholed roads, sidewalks in complete disrepair and old worn-down buildings made of homemade brick that were no more than two or three stories tall. The rivers they passed by seemed to be extremely polluted with everything from sewage to industrial waste to garbage. Eventually, the vehicle pulled up to an old house surrounded by a three-foot-high adobe wall.

"Where are we?," Richard asked.

"This is the mission office," the missionary in the driver's seat answered.

"But at the Mission Home in Salt Lake," Richard protested, "they told us that the mission office was in the good part of town."

Richard will never forget when the two missionaries in the front seat turned around in unison and said,

"This is the good part of town."

Richard had no idea what he was in for from there. When Richard entered the mission office, he saw a missionary sitting in a chair with his pant legs pulled up. He was scratching what appeared to be dozens of large mosquito bites that covered his legs.

"They must have some nasty mosquitos here in Brazil," Richard said.

"These aren't mosquito bites," the missionary scratching the bites said, "These are pulga bites."

"Pulga bites?," Richard asked, "What's a pulga?"

"I forgot the English word," the missionary said, "Let me think . . . . Oh yeah, fleas."

"FLEAS," Richard said with disgust, "I thought only DOGS have fleas."

"Fleas are everywhere here," the missionary responded.

"How long have you been here?," Richard asked.

"In Brazil?," the missionary asked.

"No," Richard said laughing, "sitting in that chair."

The other missionary joined in the laughter.

"Yes, in Brazil," Richard said

"You got me on that one," the missionary said, "A little over a year and a half. I'm going home tomorrow. Did you just get here?"

"Yes," Richard said with the look of disgust still on his face.

"Don't worry," the missionary said, "You'll get used to it. I did. Everyone does."

"I hope not" Richard said to himself unable to shake the look of disgust from his face.

"Exactly how long does it take to get used to that?," Richard asked still looking in disgust at the flea bites.

"Trust me," the missionary answered, "In a few weeks, all of this will seem normal. Within a few months, this will seem like home."

At that moment, a door opened and a voice called out. The missionary got up, said "good luck" and walked though the open door which quickly closed behind him. Richard sat in a chair that was as far away from the chair where the missionary had been sitting as possible. Immediately thereafter, and for at least two or three weeks after that, every time Richard felt what he thought was even the hint of something crawling on his skin, he would immediately slap at himself and check to see if he had squashed anything.

As was the custom of the Mormon missionaries, Richard spent about six months in a given location, or "area" as it is known to the missionaries. He would then be sent to another area. His first area was a city on the far west end of São Paulo called Osasco. Osasco was in what turned out to be the worst part of the city. Richard lived in a shack with three other missionaries. Two of them were Brazilians and the other one was from Argentina. None of them spoke English. The transition was hard.

Upon waking up on his first morning in Osasco, Richard asked where the shower was. He was told it was down the stairs to the right. Richard went down the stairs as instructed and opened the door to the right. He saw a toilet in the middle of a room the size of a small closet, but he saw no shower. He returned to the shack thinking that he had misunderstood what he had been told.

"Where did you say the shower is?," he asked the other missionaries.

He was again told that it was down the stairs to the right.

"I went there and the only thing I saw was a toilet," Richard said.

He was told to do it again, stand in front of the toilet and look up. He followed the instructions and when he looked up, he saw a pipe hanging down from the middle of the ceiling. He followed the pipe from where it hung down from the ceiling to the wall. From there, the pipe ran down the wall to where he saw a garden hose like faucet. That was the shower. The trick, he learned, was to shower while straddling the toilet which had no seat. More important, he had to do this without dropping the bar of soap into the toilet. During the summer, that wasn't too difficult.   But during the winter months, it wasn't so easy.

The temperature during the winter months in São Paulo, which is during the summer months in the United States, approaches freezing and is often below freezing. In Brazil, at least in the places where Richard lived, there was no such thing as central heating and there was also no such thing as a hot water heater. Both the shower closet and the water that came out of the pipe were freezing cold. The only tolerable way to shower was to turn on the shower long enough to get wet. The water was then turned off while Richard scrubbed himself as quickly as possible with the soap. Doing that three times in a row without the soap squirting out of his hands was only accomplished when Richard was a seasoned veteran. The water was then turned back on long enough for Richard to rinse off. The whole process took less than thirty seconds.   Richard's father, who had continually complained about Richard's long showers back home, would have died of shock to see it.

Another challenge was that the shack was infested with cockroaches.   When they returned home in the evening, the roaches would scatter as soon as the lights were turned on. One time, Richard tried to use a broom to knock a cockroach off of the ceiling. That was the night Richard learned for the first time that cockroaches could fly. He ran from the shack totally freaked out as a large roach flew around the shack. The missionaries also shared the shack with lizards. Richard was told this was a good thing because the lizards ate the bugs and cockroaches. At night, when the lights went out, the roaches came out of their hiding places and could be heard scurrying around. He also heard sounds like little feet running on top of the ceiling. It turned out that the little feet belonged to rats.

Richard hardly slept at all for about the first week and he was constantly slapping at himself and waking up to every sound. But soon, he was so tired at the end of the day that he just fell asleep. Within weeks, Richard's body was covered with the same red sores that he had seen on the missionary in the mission office when he first arrived in Brazil. They itched like crazy. The Brazilians, who seemed immune to the flea bites, kept telling Richard that he had the chicken pox. Richard knew this wasn't possible because he had the chicken pox when he was a child.

After a couple months of torture, an American missionary was transferred into the shack in place of one of the Brazilians. This American missionary confirmed that Richard's ailment was in fact, flea bites. The American missionary also taught him how to catch the fleas. Each night when they returned home to the shack, they began hunting the nasty creatures together. Fleas are extremely difficult to catch because they have a hopping ability that allows them to disappear in a nanosecond. Richard learned that it takes a lot of practice to master the art of hunting fleas. Richard was taught to get a piece of transparent tape in one hand and to pass his other hand, completely stretched out, palm down, closely over the parquet wood floor. When he did this, a flea would hop up and hit his hand. He then had to quickly spot the flea and press the sticky side of the tape onto the flea before it hopped away. Once the flea was stuck on the tape, Richard was told to fold the tape over the flea. The flea would then be entombed in the tape. He then hung the tape with the entombed flea on the wall.

Within a week, there were about one hundred and fifty fleas hung on the wall. Richard also learned that he had to check his clothes when he took them off each day to make sure he didn't bring new fleas into the shack. The fleas would usually be around the seams of his clothing and he would find about two or three each week. After that, the flea problem disappeared. Richard's aversion to dogs; however, has never abated even to this day because of his original belief that only dogs have fleas. To Richard, it doesn't matter whether his belief is true or not, he just doesn't want any more trouble with fleas and isn't willing to take any unnecessary chances.

Richard also learned how to wash clothes the old-fashioned way. With a scrubbing board. But one of his most memorable moments was when the owner of the shack asked Richard if he was flushing soiled toilet paper down the toilet. When Richard confirmed that he was, the owner gave Richard an ass chewing and was told to never do it again. The owner said the toilet paper was clogging the sewage pipes. When Richard asked what he was supposed to do with the soiled toilet paper, he was told to put it in the waste basket next to the toilet. Before that, he had always wondered why there was so much toilet paper in the waste baskets next to the toilets in Brazil. Question answered.

The funny thing is, within a couple of months after Richard's arrival in this new country, all of this seemed normal and didn't faze him in the slightest. He happened to be in the mission office when one of the missionaries he had been friends with in the Mission Home arrived in Brazil. Wanting to share his hard-earned wisdom with his newly arrived friend, Richard told him about the flea hunting expeditions and the soiled toilet paper disposal method. His friend became so enraged that he nearly punched Richard in the face. This reaction hurt Richard's feelings and left him puzzled. His friend was also sent to Osasco and later apologized to Richard a month later. When Richard asked why his friend became so enraged, his friend said that he thought Richard was playing an initiation prank on him. He thought Richard was just trying to scare him and to make him look like a fool when he put soiled toilet paper in the wastebasket.

"I guess some people just have to learn the hard way," Richard thought to himself at the time.

Even though Osasco was one of the worst parts of São Paulo in the physical sense, it was one of the best parts of São Paulo as far as the people went. Being a lanky six-foot, five-inch tall white guy, Richard literally stood out amongst the Brazilians, who for the most part, came up to about the middle of Richard's chest. Brazilians, for the most part, are also dark skinned since they are mostly a mix of African, European and Native American ancestry. It was particularly funny when he rode the public transportation buses because he would have to bend his head down to even fit in. Richard distinctly remembered the first time he rode the train from downtown São Paulo to Osasco. As the train was pulling into the São Paulo train station, Richard noticed that all the windows were missing. Before the train even came to a stop, everyone, including his companion, began diving through the windows into the train car.

"What the heck?," Richard thought at the time.

He learned that was the only way to get a seat. Since he didn't dive in, he had to stand. In fact, Richard learned that there is often no room inside the train for all the passengers, so some people even have to ride on top of the train. The next time he took the train, Richard joined in and dove into the train with reckless abandon.

Wherever he went, the Brazilian's would call out, "Que horas são?" meaning "What time is it?"

They did this because they wanted to hear Richard speak Portuguese with his gringo accent. But being a gringo amongst the poor also made him quite a celebrity and he had a lot of success working with the people. There was always a group of kids who followed him around like he was the pied piper of Scotland. Those were happy years for him and made him forget about the basketball career he had lost. Despite the hardships, Richard saw the lives of many people change for the better and there were always tears when he left an area.

After Osasco, Richard went to Campinas, which was further west into the interior. After Campinas, he went to Dourados, which was near the border of Paraguay. While in Dourados, Richard presided over a church congregation. One of the highlights of his time in the interior of Brazil was seeing fireflies for the first time in his life. He had never seen fireflies before and walking amongst them at night seemed almost magical to him. Another highlight was looking at the stars at night. Being in almost complete darkness, the number of stars seemed multiplied by a thousand and seemed to be so close that Richard could reach up and grab them. The remainder of his mission was spent in the center of São Paulo itself.

When Richard returned to Provo after his mission, he continued his studies at BYU, or the "Y," as it is known locally. After his junior year, he got married, which is common among the students at the Y. He and his new bride moved into Wymount Terrace, the University's married student housing complex. The single students call the place "Why Me Terrace," perhaps in reference to the many babies who also live there. Shortly thereafter, Richard got a job working at the BYU police department office, which has its own police force. It was then that he first decided to become a cop.

After Richard graduated from the Y, Richard went to the police academy and was hired by BYU. After a couple of years and a couple of children later, Richard moved on to the Provo Police Department. He eventually wound up working for the Salt Lake Police force. That's where he had worked for the past twenty something years.

Richard was now fifty-two years old and had five children ranging in age from twelve to twenty-three. His plan was to retire in a few years and move to St. George, Utah, a city near the Arizona border at the south end of the state. St. George was becoming a preferred retirement destination, particularly within the Mormon community, because of its great weather, beautiful scenery and small town pace of life. By then, his youngest child would be well established in college and he and his wife could live out their golden years in relative peace and comfort.

SECRETS

D. K. DeGRAW

CHAPTER SIX

LAS VEGAS

    The bus drove over the crest of a hill and the Las Vegas Valley magically came into full view.   The bus descended into the Las Vegas Valley as it sped toward the city center. Anna Hansen was awakened from her deep sleep when the intercom system popped on.

    "We will be arriving in Las Vegas in twenty minutes," the bus driver announced.

    Anna yawned and stretched her arms as her body returned to life. She ate the remainder of her Doritos chips and drank the last of her Sprite. Anna looked out the window and could see lights spread throughout the Valley. She also saw the distinctive lights of the casinos that formed "The Strip." Within minutes, the bus passed by the Las Vegas Speedway where NASCAR races are held each year.   Minutes later, the bus entered the outskirts of Las Vegas. Building after building began to wiz by. The bus veered to the right as it approached downtown Las Vegas.

The bus exited Interstate 15 by making a wide sweeping left turn on an elevated ramp that spanned the Interstate. Now heading east on Highway 95, the bus took the first exit to the right and came to a stop light. When the light turned green, the bus continued south on Casino Center Boulevard. A few blocks later, the bus passed by Fremont Street, the Plaza Hotel and then the Golden Nugget Casino. Two blocks later, the bus began to slow. Anna saw three big blue squares, one below the other, hanging from the side of a building. A white letter B was on the top blue square. The square below that had a letter U. The bottom square had a letter S.

Anna noticed a uniformed guard standing in front of the bus terminal's entrance. He seemed to be watching the bus with particular interest. She continued to watch the guard until the bus made a right turn into the bus terminal. When she lost sight of the guard, Anna's heart began to race and she could feel drops of sweat beading on her forehead.

"Maybe they already found the baby," Anna thought to herself,
"My God, what will they do to me if they catch me?"

Anna began to panic. But in an instant, Anna's finely honed survival instincts kicked in. She quickly opened the suitcase and pulled out a black scarf. She tied her long golden blond hair into a knot above her head and wrapped the scarf so that it completely covered her head. She tied the ends of the scarf into a knot under her chin and looked back into the suitcase. The suitcase was nearly empty except for a few items of clothing and a large brown envelope. Anna stuffed the items of clothing into the bodice of her dress and put the envelope inside her sweater. By this time, the bus had made another right turn and was heading north along the back side of the bus terminal.

Anna arose and began walking toward the front of the bus as it traveled the length of the building. She left the suitcase behind. The bus passed by buses that were already parked diagonally along the building. Anna arrived at the front of the bus just as it made a diagonal turn into the last stall. The bus came to a hissing stop as the engine continued to idle. Anna looked out the window for signs of the security guard.

"Open the door," Anna thought to herself as her heart raced.

Finally, the door swung open and Anna stepped out of the bus as quickly as she could without seeming to draw attention to herself.

"Didn't you forget your suitcase," the bus driver yelled out.

Anna ignored the bus driver and she immediately turned to the left and dashed around the front of the bus. When she was on the opposite side of the bus, she paused for a few seconds to look for an escape route. She immediately noticed a side entrance into the Plaza Hotel and Casino that was less than thirty feet away.

"How lucky," she thought to herself.

She knew this path would conceal her from the guard if he was, in fact, looking for her. Without hesitation, she raced toward the entrance, opened the door, and entered into a jungle of slot machines. Anna began to dodge between the rows and rows of slot machines. She grabbed the brown envelope that was under her red sweater, and quickly took the sweater off. She was less conspicuous in only her dark blue dress. Anna glanced over her shoulder toward the entrance. There was no sign that she was being followed. Within seconds, Anna could no longer see the entrance door. She hoped this meant that she was also no longer visible to any potential pursuer. She continued past rows and rows of slot machines and gaming tables that went on for nearly an entire city block. Anna finally spotted a row of large glass doors. By the size and number of the doors, she concluded that this must be the hotel's main entrance.

A door automatically opened when she approached it. Anna walked through and found herself on a street brightly lit by the neon lights of the surrounding buildings. This initially alarmed her because she was afraid she could be easily spotted now that she was in the light. She thought about going back into the casino, but knew she had to press forward if she wanted to escape. The western end of Fremont Street was directly across the street from where she stood. The bus had passed this exact spot just minutes before.

Anna looked ahead and saw that Fremont Street, even in the middle of the night, had a number of pedestrians strolling down the sidewalk. She looked to her right and saw the three blue squares that spelled BUS just a few blocks down the road. Anna looked for the security guard, but he was no where to be seen. She decided that she would chance crossing the road. She kept a few pedestrians between her and the bus terminal as a precaution, trying to fit in as best she could with the other pedestrians. Anna passed by the Golden Gate Casino and began walking eastward on Fremont Street.

This part of Fremont Street, which is now known as the Fremont Street Experience, is not actually a street in the traditional sense. It's a pedestrian walkway covered by a canopy that's called the biggest television screen in the world. She walked past a big neon cowboy who was smoking a cigar on the right side of the walkway. On the other side of the walkway, directly across from the neon cowboy, was a neon cowgirl who seemed to be welcoming him. Just as Anna walked past the historic Binion's Horseshoe Casino, everything went dark and the pedestrian traffic came to a halt. The lights of the canopy above her came to life as a show played to the beat of blaring music. Anna didn't stop to watch.

Anna continued walking down the walkway, dodging pedestrians along the way. She walked past one casino after another until there were no more casinos. She walked past a long row of souvenir shops until the canopy finally ended at Las Vegas Boulevard. A block after Anna crossed Las Vegas Boulevard, Fremont Street became a real street with a roadway and sidewalks on each side of the road. Anna continued to walk eastward on Fremont Street's south-side sidewalk. She walked block after block until she came to an all-night diner. A street sign on the corner said,

"Maryland Parkway."

By now, the souvenir shops had been replaced by old, one story, U-shaped drive-in motels with swimming pools in the middle of the U. Anna looked eastward down Fremont Street and could see that the motels continued for several more miles. She looked down Fremont Street to the west where she had just come. She could see the Plaza Hotel in the far distance, but saw no sign that she was being followed. Realizing that her getaway now seemed certain, Anna suddenly felt weak. The adrenalin that had been flowing through her body was being replaced with nervous exhaustion. She sat down on the side walk with her back against the wall of the diner. She put the brown envelope and her red sweater on her knees, rested her head on the sweater and fell asleep. Anna was abruptly awakened by a male voice.

"Excuse me, Miss," the voice said, "Can I buy you something to eat?"

SECRETS

CHAPTER SEVEN

PREDATOR

A man dressed like a cowboy stepped into his garage. He slapped a button on the wall and the mechanical motor of the garage door opener sprang to life. Cold night air rushed into the garage as the garage door rumbled upward. It was nearly midnight and the cowboy was going hunting. He swaggered toward his pink, mint condition, 1969 Cadillac DeVille convertible. The steel taps on the heels of his Tex Robin full quill ostrich cowboy boots clicked on the concrete floor. Despite his unsavory occupation, the cowboy was proud of who and what he was. He was a wealthy man far removed from his impoverished upbringing in east Texas. In his mind, he simply did what he needed to do and he made no apologies for it.

The cowboy opened the door of his pink Cadillac

and slid in behind the steering wheel. He put a key in the ignition, started the car and pushed a button on the console. He heard a whirring sound behind him as the Cadillac's white top began to close. When the top came to a stop, he fastened the latches that locked the top to the front windshield. The cowboy shifted the car into reverse and backed out of his spacious three car garage. He made a reverse U turn in his spacious driveway. He pushed a button on the garage door opener on the visor. When the garage door began to close, he shifted the car into forward and drove down a quarter mile long road.

When the cowboy arrived at the gate that guarded his property, he pressed on the brake and the Cadillac came to a stop. He pushed another button on the garage door opener. The cowboy waited as the gate slowly opened. When he was satisfied that there was enough room for the Cadillac to pass through the gate, he pressed the accelerator pedal. The car instantly lurched forward and passed through the gate as it was continuing to open. Once the car was completely through the gate, the gate reversed its motion and began to close. The cowboy pushed the brake pedal and the car came to a stop at the edge of Patrick Lane. The cowboy watched the gate in the rearview mirror until the gate completely closed.

The cowboy turned right onto Patrick Lane and continued eastward until Patrick Lane ended at McCarran Airport. He made a right turn onto Eastern Avenue and drove northward toward old downtown Las Vegas. Old downtown Las Vegas is a rectangular area a few blocks wide and fifteen blocks long. It begins at Main and Fremont Street on the West side and continues east to Fremont and 15th Street. Decades ago, before the southern end of Las Vegas Boulevard became "the Strip," this part of Fremont Street was known as the strip. Except for a few high class places on the west end of Fremont Street that are adjacent to the Fremont Street Experience, Fremont Street is a run-down part of town that has seen its better days. The farther east, the more run down it becomes. The eastern end of Fremont Street is now a place where drunks, drifters, misfits and runaways congregate. In other words, the cowboy's kind of people.

The cowboy continued north on Eastern Avenue until he reached Fremont Street. When he turned left onto Fremont Street, the hunt for his prey began. To say that the cowboy is a pimp isn't exactly correct. He was part of an international prostitution ring that made hundreds of millions of dollars every year. He ran the Las Vegas operation and his cut was in excess of a hundred thousand dollars every month. In exchange for all this money, he was expected to do two things. First, oversee the ring's assets, meaning the prostitutes in Las Vegas and second, recruit new prostitutes. The cowboy was already a wealthy man, so the money he received was no longer his primary motivation. His primary motivation now was the expectation that if he didn't pull his weight, he would be replaced with someone more effective. Of course, "replaced" meant killed unless he payed a king's ransom. That's what kept the cowboy motivated.

Even though it was easy to find prostitutes walking the streets of Las Vegas, these weren't the kind of prostitute the cowboy was looking for. The prostitutes who walked the streets were mostly drug-addicted, over-the-hill women with several teeth missing. Prostitutes like that were a dime a dozen and not appealing to the

Ring's big money clients. The cowboy was looking for young, attractive women who were in their prime. A teenage, runaway girl fit the bill perfectly. Another big reason why the Ring recruited runaway girls was that no one was usually looking for them. Even if someone was, who would know to look for them in Las Vegas? Because of that, it's easy to make these girls disappear once they're recruited. That's why the cowboy felt comfortable hunting for these girls himself. On top of that, it gave him an adrenalin rush of excitement that made him feel alive. It also made him feel powerful compared to the powerlessness he felt as a small cog in the huge prostitution ring.

The cowboy left the other methods to his subordinates. One of the easiest of these other methods was to find a suitable girl walking down a dark, lonely street and simply abduct her. Even though that happened on occasion, this kind of abduction was relatively rare since it left too much to chance. Much more effective and less risky methods had been developed. One of the more effective methods was to have his subordinates, young, attractive men, hang out at places popular with young women, even girls as young as junior high school age. It could be the mall, a fast food joint, or a club. Virtually anywhere young women hang out. The subordinate, who was well trained in what he was doing, would strike up a conversation with a potential target. His goal was to eventually become the target's boyfriend. Of course, he would never actually go to the target's house or meet her parents. He would always arrange to meet the target somewhere else. If the target was too young to drive, he would pick her up somewhere within walking distance from her house. He also had a prearranged excuse for why they had to keep their relationship secret, such as he had just broken up with a girl who was extremely jealous. He told the target that if this prior girlfriend saw them together, she might severely injure the target, perhaps even kill her. This concocted story seemed to make the whole affair even more thrilling to the target.

If the target took the bait and a relationship developed, the subordinate would ask the target to sneak out of her house in the middle of the night so they could meet at a predetermined place. When the target arrived, she would willingly get into the car of who she thought was her boyfriend. But instead of her "boyfriend," the car was full of his associates. Before the target knew what was happening, the doors would lock, a hood would be over her head, and her neck would be duct taped tightly to the head rest. A gun would then be pressed against the target's ear and she would be told not to make a sound. The car would drive away and that would be last time the target ever saw her neighborhood or family again.

If somehow the "boyfriend" had been seen with the target and became a suspect, he always had an air tight alibi because he never abducted the target himself. They would also use a stolen car just in case the car was traced to the abduction. The police would later find the stolen car burned to the ground leaving behind no trace of evidence. There were several variations on this same theme that all worked equally well, including having a girl befriend the target.

Once the target was abducted, her initiation into prostitution would begin. First, the target would be gang-raped repeatedly and told that she was worthless and disgusting. The target would be told that nobody, including her own family, would ever be able to stand the sight of her. She was also told that if she escaped, that the target and every member of her family would be killed. The target was also given drugs until she was addicted and dependent on the drugs. This continued until the target's spirit was completely broken and she believed she had no choice but to submit to this tragic life of forced prostitution. In addition, the target was consumed with guilt and shame that she had allowed herself to be duped by this supposed "boyfriend." Once broken, the target would then be shipped to another city within the ring's operation. The target was now worth up to a million dollars in potential earnings. The target would never be brought back to the city where she was abducted, and would never remain in any city for more than a few months.

Even though recruiting girls from within the United States was the easiest and cheapest way to recruit girls, the ring also recruited impoverished girls from countries in South and Central America, Eastern Europe and Southeast Asia. The ring would place advertisements in these foreign countries advertising jobs in the United States. The jobs could be anything from working as a nanny, to being a fashion model, to working a summer job as a waitress. The job didn't matter as long as the girls believed it was a real job. To these impoverished girls, it seemed like a passport from poverty. The Ring would arrange to interview the "applicants" in their native countries. If the girl was found suitable, the Ring would arrange a Visa for the girl to come to the United States. Once in the United States, the girl would disappear and go through the same initiation process as a girl who was abducted from within the United States.

However, recruiting foreign girls was falling out of favor for several reasons. First, the Ring had to arrange for a "legitimate" job for the girl in the United States in order to apply for a Visa. Second, the travel expenses and fees for the Visa compared to simply abducting a girl who was already in the United States were substantial. Third, the paper trail that could potentially expose the Ring was greater than that of a local abduction. And lastly, even though this method had once been extremely effective, over time, the word had spread and foreign girls were becoming much more cautious about accepting jobs from strangers. They had learned the maxim "If it sounds too good to be true, it probably is." With the advent of the internet, these foreign girls were doing a lot more research about whom and what they were getting themselves involved with. For these reasons, it was becoming increasingly difficult to recruit girls from foreign counties and it was no longer worth the expense considering how easy and inexpensive it was to simply abduct a girl who was already in the United States.

The Ring also discovered an additional benefit if they abducted American girls. The ring learned that it's far easier to deliver an American girl to a foreign client than a foreign girl. That's because American citizens can simply get on a plane and travel to a multitude of countries without a Visa. The foreign girls, on the other hand, typically have to go through a rigorous screening process to get a Visa. With that discovery, the Ring began advertising its products world wide. The ring found this to be extremely profitable and relatively hassle free. The ring would simply sell a girl to the highest bidder. One girl could go for as much as a half of a million dollars, and sometimes even more. The Ring would take the money and ship the girl to the country of the purchaser's choice. And that was that. The girl would never return to the United States again. The Ring made a substantial profit with none of the hassles of running the prostitutes themselves.

While all of this was good for the Ring, it was bad for the cowboy. Because of the decreasing supply of foreign girls and the increasing demand for American girls, the cowboy's quota for the number of American girls he was expected to recruit each month was nearing the point of impossibility. He was beginning to wonder if it was time for him to get out of the business altogether. The cowboy had a substantial fortune deposited in offshore bank accounts, so money was not the issue. His problem was how much money the ring would allow him to keep for himself. He knew that if he simply tried to run, the Ring would hunt him down until it was satisfied that he was dead. The cowboy had become a prisoner in the world he had chosen for himself. He was now wondering whether the money was worth the sacrifices he had made. As he was thinking this thought, he saw a girl sitting on the sidewalk. It looked like she was asleep.

SECRETS

CHAPTER EIGHT

PREY

"Excuse me, Miss," the man repeated several times until Anna awakened, "Can I buy you something to eat?"

"What?," Anna said as she looked up.

A man was standing over her.

"I asked if I could buy you something to eat," the man repeated.

Anna studied the man. He seemed to be in his mid-thirties and was dressed like the neon cowboy she had passed earlier. He even smelled of cigar smoke.

"What do you mean?," Anna asked.

"I mean you look like you need something to eat," the man said, "The diner is right here so it wouldn't be much trouble."

"OK," Anna said because she was starving, "But it's

just something to eat. Do you understand?"

"That's all I had in mind," the man said with a friendly smile as he extended his hand to help her up.

She took his hand and he pulled her to her feet and they walked the short distance to the entrance of the diner. The cowboy held open the door as Anna walked through. The cowboy walked in behind her. When a hostess seated them, they sat on opposite sides of a booth. The hostess handed each of them a menu and left.

"My name's Dwayne," the man said, "What's your name?"

"Cindy," she lied.

"Where're ya from?," he asked.

"Colorado," she lied again.

"When did ya get into town?," he asked.

"Why ya ask so many questions?" she said trying to mimic his country accent.

There was an awkward silence for a few moments that was broken up when a waitress arrived to take their order. Anna ordered a breakfast special with eggs, hash browns, a stack of pancakes and a large glass of orange juice. Dwayne ordered the same thing and the waitress left.

"I'm sorry," Dwayne said, "Just tryin' to be friendly."

"I'm not looking for a friend," Anna said, "It's just a meal. Remember?"

"Look," Dwayne said, "I'm just tryin' to help. I think you can at least be friendly."

"What makes you think I need help?," Anna asked.

"What?," Dwayne laughed, "Do ya think you're the first girl who's run away to Vegas? I see 'um all the time.

Same story. No money. Am I right?"

Anna looked down and didn't answer.

"So what's your real name and where're ya really from?," Dwayne asked.

"I'd rather not say," Anna said honestly.

"Why not?," Dwayne asked, "Are ya in trouble with the law? Did you do something real bad?"

Anna continued to look down without answering. Dwayne grinned like he had just hit the jackpot.

"Look," Dwayne said, "You can either let me help ya or not. Makes no difference to me. But if ya want my help, you should at least be sociable."

"I'm sorry," Anna finally said, "You're right. I can at least talk to you."

Anna asked questions about Dwayne until the waitress delivered their food. As they, or rather she ate, Dwayne continued to talk. She found out he was originally from east Texas. A place called Lufkin. Dwayne said he moved to Los Angeles in his mid-twenties hoping to become the next John Wayne. After drifting from job to job in L.A. for several years, he moved to Vegas a few years ago where Dwayne said he hit it big. He said he ran a very successful and profitable business enterprise, but didn't exactly say what it was when she pressed him.

When Anna finished her meal, Dwayne offered her his, which he hadn't even touched. Since Anna didn't know when she would have her next meal, she took him up on his offer. As Anna continued to eat, Dwayne bragged about the cars he owned, the names of which she had never heard of. Dwayne said he had a big house that was almost next to Wayne Newton's, who she also had never heard of. He said his house sat on a huge piece of property that had horses and stables.

"Do you like horses?," Dwayne asked.

"I don't know," Anna answered, "I've never been around horses before."

"Maybe you should come to my house and you can see them,"
Dwayne said, "I think you would like that."

"Maybe some day," Anna said, "but not now."

Dwayne asked her if she had a place to stay. When Anna didn't answer, he asked her if she wanted to stay with him. Dwayne said there was plenty of room at his house and that it wouldn't be any trouble at all. When Anna said she didn't feel comfortable staying with a stranger, Dwayne said she should at least let him get her a room at a nearby motel. Anna thought about it for a few moments. Since Dwayne seemed harmless enough so far, she finally agreed.

"But it's just a room," Anna said, "Right?"

"Right," Dwayne answered with his fingers crossed, "Nothing more. I promise."

After Dwayne paid the bill, they got up and walked out of the diner. Dwayne told Anna that he knew a good place to stay just a block down the street. Dwayne said he knew the manager and could get a good rate. They walked to a place called the Starlight Motel.

"Wait here while I get the room," Dwayne said.

Anna waited outside the motel office as she looked through the window. She saw Dwayne talking to a man behind the counter. A few minutes later, Dwayne returned and handed her a key. The number "222" was inscribed on the key.

"I asked for a quiet room at the back so you wouldn't be disturbed," Dwayne said, "The motel will be mostly empty for the next couple of days until the New Year's Eve crowd arrives. You can have the room until the twenty-seventh. Let me show you where the room is."

"That's OK," Anna said, "I can find it myself. You have done more than enough. Thank you for all of your help."

"Maybe you can return the favor some day," Dwayne said as he winked at her.

A cold chill went down Anna's spine. She wondered if she had made a mistake by accepting help from this man. But she was grateful to have a place to lay low for the next couple of days. More importantly, she avoided sleeping on the street or spending the last of her money. Anna found room two-twenty-two, which was the farthest room from the motel office on the second floor. Anna unlocked the door, stepped inside the room and immediately closed the window curtain. The next thing she did was turn on the heater. She waited until she felt warm air blowing from the unit. It was a clean, but modest room with a double bed, a night stand and a dresser. The room also had a small round table next to the window with a chair. She opened one of the dresser drawers. She took out the clothes she had stuffed in her bodice and put them on the small table. She folded her red sweater and the other items of clothing, put them in the open drawer and closed it. She opened another drawer, put in the brown envelope and closed it.

Anna scanned the room and saw a telephone, a clock and a lamp on top of a night stand. The clock said it was now 4:33 a.m. Anna walked into the bathroom. It had a bathtub shower combination, a toilet and a small sink. Anna put the stopper in the bathtub and turned on the water. She adjusted the water so that it was as hot as she could tolerate. She took off her clothes and dropped them on the floor. She stepped into the bathtub, sat down and leaned back. At first, the bathtub wall was uncomfortably cold on her back. She leaned forward and splashed some hot water along the back side of the tub. She leaned back, and this time, the wall of the tub was warm enough.

Anna closed her eyes as the hot water first covered her legs then continued up her body. She turned off the water when the water was just a couple of inches from the top of the tub. She savored every moment as the hot water massaged her aching muscles. She also savored the complete quietness of the bathroom. For once, it felt good to be alone. When the water began to cool, she washed every inch of her body. Anna then washed her long, golden blond hair with the complementary shampoo that came with the room. Her body resisted her attempt to stand up, but her mind eventually won the battle. Anna arose from the water and stepped out of the tub. She dried herself off with a towel and wrapped the towel around her head. She then washed her blue dress and underwear in the bath. Anna hung the clothes over the shower curtain rod to dry. She went into the bedroom and climbed onto the bed. She covered her naked body with a sheet and a blanket. Within seconds, she was asleep.

Hours later, Anna sensed the smell of cigar smoke filling her nostrils. Anna stretched out her arms and slowly woke up. She was completely startled when a male voice said,

"You're finally awake."

Anna looked toward the sound of the voice and saw

Dwayne sitting in the chair next to the window. He was completely naked.

"What are you doing here," Anna screamed, "Get out of my room."

"No one can hear ya," Dwayne said with a calm voice, "I told ya, the place is almost empty. Besides, what do ya mean YOUR room. I'm the one who paid for it."

"How did you get in?," Anna asked angrily.

"I told ya," Dwayne said, "the manager's a friend of mine."

"Why are you here?," Anna continued, "What do you want?"

"Ya know what I want," Dwayne said with a wry smile, "I want what men want. You're not stupid. I'm calling in my favor."

Anna saw that the clock displayed 1:36. Because there was a bright light behind the curtain, she knew it was in the afternoon.

"You're not getting that from me," Anna said sternly, "You promised me it would only be a room."

"Well," Dwayne said, "men say what they need to say to get what they want. You should know that by now."

"Get out of my room now, you son of a bitch," Anna screamed.

"Look, whatever your name is," Dwayne said as he stood up and approached the bed, "We can do this the easy way or the hard way. We both know you can't call the police. So the way I see it, you don't have much of a choice."

Dwayne walked to the bed and yanked off the blanket and sheet. Anna's nakedness was completely exposed.

"So which way's it gonna be?," Dwayne said as he climbed on the bed, "The hard way or the easy way.".

"This can't be happening AGAIN," Anna thought to herself, "I thought I had escaped."

"This can't be happening," Anna repeated in her mind over and over again as she began to cry softly.

Dwayne yanked the towel off Anna's head and grabbed her by the hair. He then pulled her toward him. Anna's instincts kicked in once again and her body and mind completely shut down. Anna's body went completely limp.

When Dwayne was finished, he climbed off of the bed and walked to the desk where he had piled his clothes. Dwayne put his clothes on and took his wallet out of his back pocket. He removed two twenties and a business card and put them on the desk.

"There's a lot more money where this came from if you're interested," he said.

"I'm not interested," Anna cried, "Get out."

"I've heard that before," Dwayne laughed, "We'll see about that in a few weeks when you're starving with no money and no where to go. My number's on the card."

"I won't be calling you," Anna cried, "That's a promise."

"We'll see about that," Dwayne said.

Dwayne walked out of the room and slammed the door shut behind him. Anna got out of the bed sobbing and walked to the table and picked up the business card.

"Baby Doll Escort Service. Dwayne B. Goode, Proprietor," she read.

Anna ripped the card into tiny pieces and threw the

pieces angrily against the curtains. She propped a chair up against the door handle and walked into the bathroom. She turned on the water and took another bath like the one from earlier that morning. She sobbed, this time loudly, as the hot water climbed up her body.

CHAPTER NINE

DISCOVERY

Lieutenant Atkin's telephone rang just before five in the morning. He was on call, but was hoping this Christmas would be uneventful.

"Hello?" Atkin answered with an emphasis on the first syllable.

"You need to go to the McDonald's on Main Street and Bluff," a familiar voice said.

"Was there a shooting?," Atkin asked.

"No," came the reply, "They found an abandoned baby."

"Is it dead?," Atkin asked.

"I don't know," said the voice, "but you need to get down there right away."

"What is it?," Atkin's wife asked.

She had also been awakened by the telephone call.

"They found an abandoned baby," Atkin said yawning.

"I was hoping we could be together as a family this Christmas," his wife said with a pout.

"I know," Atkin said, "It's a tough job, but someone has to do it. Besides, you were happy when I got the promotion."

"I know," she said, "But I didn't know that you were going to be yanked out of bed at all hours of the night."

"I guess that's why I get paid the big bucks," Atkin said with a laugh.

"That'll be the day," his wife laughed back.

"I'll try my best to be home before the kids wake up," Atkin said, "But if I'm not home by nine, go ahead without me."

"Just promise me that you'll get home as soon as you can," his wife said, "We'll wait for you."

About a half hour later, Atkin arrived at the McDonald's. Several police officers had already arrived at the scene.

"What's up?," Atkin asked the first officer he encountered.

"A McDonald's employee found a baby by the dumpster," the officer said, pointing to a nearby dumpster.

"Is the baby dead?," Atkin asked.

"It was alive when it left here in an ambulance," the officer said, "It was rushed to Dixie Medical. I don't know if it died in route."

"Who found the baby?," Atkin asked.

"A college kid," the officer answered, "He's inside."

Atkin went into the McDonald's. He saw a young man sitting at a table with an officer. The boy looked really shaken, like he could start crying at any moment.

"Is this the boy?," Atkin asked when he approached the table.

"Yes," the officer said.

Atkin sat down at the table next to the boy.

"I know you're quite upset," Atkin said to the boy.

The boy didn't respond.

"Can you tell me what happened?," Atkin asked the boy.

"Am I in trouble?," the boy asked in response.

"Not at all," Atkin assured the boy, "You probably saved the baby's life. Now why don't you just relax and tell me what happened."

"OK," the boy said.

The boy took a few deep breaths and his body relaxed just a little.

"I went outside to throw out some trash," the boy explained, "I heard some noises that sounded like crying. At first, I didn't know what it was. But the closer I got to the dumpster, the sound became louder and louder. I could hear that the crying sound was coming from behind the dumpster. When I looked behind the dumpster, I saw a grey coat. Something was moving inside of it. I opened the coat and found the baby. That's all I know."

"Did you see anyone around the dumpster?," Atkin asked.

"No," the boy said, "There was no one around. Just the baby."

"What did you do after you found the baby?," Atkin asked.

"I was scared to death," the boy said, "I didn't know what to do. I ran inside and told my manager. My manager went to the dumpster and brought the baby inside. She's the one who called the police."

"What time did you find the baby?," Atkin asked.

"I don't know," the boy said, "Maybe about an hour ago."

"I know this must be hard for you, " Atkin said, "But anything you can remember might be helpful. Did you notice anything else that was unusual?"

"Not that I can think of," the boy answered confidently.

"Well, thanks for your help," Atkin told the boy as he handed the boy a business card, "if you remember anything else, anything at all, don't hesitate to call me. Anything you might remember could be helpful."

"Do you really think I saved the baby's life?" the boy asked.

"If the baby lives," Atkin responded "it certainly owes its life to you.

Atkin spoke to the manager who confirmed the boy's story. Atkin asked the manager if any pregnant women came into the McDonald's during the night.

"No," the manager answered. "But the bus from Salt Lake City stopped by around midnight."

"Were you working when the bus came in?," Atkin asked.

"Yes," the manager answered, "I work from ten at night to six in the morning."

"Did you see any pregnant women get off the bus?," Atkin asked.

"I can't see the bus from here," the manager answered, "but no pregnant women came into the restaurant while the bus was here."

After interviewing the manager, Atkin went outside to inspect the scene. Atkin asked an officer standing by the dumpster if anything of interest had been found. The officer told him the baby was found wrapped in a grey wool overcoat. He said the wool overcoat probably saved the baby's life. He said a red dress and a pair of panties were found in the dumpster. The officer told Atkin that the dress and the panties probably belonged to the mother. Atkin looked around and saw that a group of reporters had already arrived on the scene.

"Are the articles of clothing still here?," Atkin asked the officer.

"Yes," the officer answered.

"Where are they?" Atkin asked.

"The items have been bagged and are in one of the squad cars."

"Get me the wool coat," Atkin said.

"Why do you want the coat?"

"Just get me the coat," Atkin said impatiently, "It's too early in the morning to start explaining everything to you. Trust me. I have my reasons."

The officer left and returned with the clear plastic bag that contained the grey wool coat. He also brought Atkin a pair of latex gloves. Atkin snapped on the gloves and walked over to the reporters.

"Is anyone here looking for an interview?" Atkin asked with mock sarcasm.

Several microphones were shoved near Atkin's face and the camera lights turned on. Atkin pulled the grey wool coat out of the bag and held it up. Atkin started to speak into the microphones.

— — — — — —

Richard Decker's family was already awake when he returned home from his shift. His wife and family, except for his oldest son who was serving a Mormon mission in Mexico, was waiting for him to arrive so they could open their Christmas presents together. This included his oldest child, a daughter. She was pregnant with his first grandchild. She and her husband had come from Colorado to spend the Christmas holiday with the family. He also had a son, who was a senior in high school, and two daughters, who were fifteen and twelve. After opening presents and eating breakfast with the family, Richard and his wife settled into their lazy boy chairs in the family room. Richard's wife picked up her crochet hooks and continued working on a blanket that she was making for the expected grandchild.

"How was your shift?," she asked Richard.

"Like usual," he said, "but there were a couple of interesting things that happened at the bus station."

"Like what?," she asked.

Richard told her about the homeless man and the young woman.

"She could be just about anyone," his wife said, "Hansen's a common name. She might not even be from around here at all."

"I know," Richard said, "But I couldn't help thinking about my own daughters. I would hope that someone would look after them if I couldn't."

"You're just an old softie," his wife said, "That's one of the reasons why I love you so much. But you can't save everyone."

"You're right as always," Richard said.

"That's another reason why I love you," his wife said, "You know I'm always right."

"That's why my first rule is 'always listen to my wife'," Richard laughed.

"But it's supposed to be 'always listen to your wife the first time'," his wife laughed back.

Richard turned on the television and tuned into the local news. Richard watched as Atkin gave his interview. He saw Atkin holding up a grey wool coat just like the one the young woman had been wearing the night before. Atkin said that a new born baby had been left abandoned inside the coat. A number appeared on the screen and Atkin said that anyone who might have any information about the abandoned baby should contact the telephone number on the screen. The camera then cut to a television reporter.

"Again," the reporter said, "the headline story is a newborn baby was found wrapped in a grey wool overcoat next to a McDonald's dumpster in St. George. Back to you in Salt Lake."

"Which McDonald's location was the baby found at?," the anchor asked the reporter.

"It's the McDonald's on Main and Bluff Street," the reporter answered.

Richard Decker went into his bedroom and called the number that was on the television screen.

"St. George Police Department," a woman answered.

Richard explained who he was and said,

"I think I have some information about the baby that was found abandoned in St. George this morning."

"I will connect you to Lieutenant Atkin," the woman replied, "He's handling the investigation."

After a few rings, a man answered.

"Atkin," the man said.

Richard again explained who he was and told Atkin the story about the young woman who got on the bus in

Salt Lake.

"Are you sure it's the same girl?," Atkin asked.

Richard told Atkin that he was certain that the grey wool coat he saw on the television was the same coat he saw the young woman wearing the night before. Richard gave Atkin Ferraro's telephone number and explained that he and Ferraro were already in communication about the matter. Atkin thanked Richard for calling and said he would follow up with Ferraro.

As soon as Richard hung up with Atkin, he dialed Ferraro's telephone number. But a different voice answered the phone this time.

"Sergeant Roos," the voice said.

"I'm trying to reach Detective Ferraro," Richard said.

"His shift ended over an hour ago and he has already left the building," Roos said, "Is there something I can do for you?"

"My name is Officer Richard Decker. I'm with the Salt Lake P.D. I spoke with Detective Ferraro a few hours ago about something we were working on together. I need to speak to him as soon as possible. It's urgent. Is there another number I can reach him at?"

"I can't give out personal information over the phone," Roos said, "But I can call him myself and let him know that you called. I'm sorry, but that's the best I can do."

Richard gave Roos his home telephone number and emphasized that the matter was urgent. Richard stressed that he needed to speak with Ferraro as quickly as possible. Roos said he understood and that he would call Ferraro immediately. When Roos hung up, he immediately dialed Ferraro's number as promised. After several rings, an answering machine kicked in and Roos left Ferraro a message.

After speaking with Roos, Richard walked absent mindedly back into the family room.   His wife immediately noticed that Richard was in some other world.

"Is something wrong?," his wife asked.

Richard sat down in his lazy boy chair.

"You know that young woman I told you about?," he said.

"Yes," she replied, "Did something happen to her?"

"She was wearing a grey wool coat just like the one they found that baby in St. George wrapped in," he said somberly.

"That's terrible," his wife said, "Do you think she's the one who abandoned the baby?"

"I'm certain of it," Richard responded.

"What kind of person would just abandon a baby like that?," his wife asked rhetorically.

"I don't know," Richard responded, "But it can't be good."

CHAPTER TEN

HOUSEGUEST

Roger bolted upright in his bed. Piercing screams resonated in his ears. He jumped out of bed and ran to the bedroom door. As he reached out to twist the door knob, the door crashed open and slammed into his body. Knocked off balance, he fell to the floor. His wife, Mary, pushed past him and ran to the closet. Roger returned to his feet as Mary frantically rifled through the closet.

"What's going on?," Roger asked earnestly, "What are you looking for?"

"Where's the gun?," Mary screamed.

"The gun?," Roger asked confused, "Why do you need the gun?"

Mary continued to search through the closet without responding.

"What's happening?" Roger repeated, now frantic

himself.

"Someone broke into the house," Mary screamed.

"Who? Where?," Roger said with alarm as he moved toward Mary.

"I don't know," Mary screamed, "A black man. He's in the family room."

Roger instantly remembered the events of the night before and relaxed. He grabbed Mary by the shoulders and held her as she resisted his attempt to restrain her.

"Calm down," Roger said firmly, "Let me explain."

When Mary continued to resist, he repeated even more firmly,

"You need to calm down."

When Roger felt Mary's body relax, he let go.

"We need to sit down," Roger said

As they sat on the bed, Roger took Mary by the hands and told her about the strange events that happened the night before.

"So who is this Gabe?," Mary asked.

"I don't know," Roger said, "The only thing I know is he keeps saying his name is Gabe."

"Where's he from?," Mary asked.

"I don't know," Roger answered, "I only know that he was standing completely naked in the middle of the road when I found him."

"And you thought it would be a good idea to bring him home?," Mary asked incredulously.

When Roger started to answer, Mary cut him off.

"I didn't expect you to answer the question," Mary said, "For all you know, we could all be dead by now."

"We're not dead," Roger said exasperated, "You always assume the worst. Everything will be fine. You'll see. You're judging him and you haven't even met him."

"Oh, and you have," Mary laughed in his face, "This is just like you. This isn't a stray puppy we're talking about. This man could be a dangerous criminal."

In Mary's mind, all black men were dangerous criminals. Having lived in St. George for most of her life, the only black people she knew were on television, in the movies or singing gangster rap. There was not even a single black person in the schools she attended while growing up.

"You have no idea what could've happened," Mary said as she started to cry.

"I'm telling you," Roger implored, "there's something about this guy that tells me he's completely harmless. I promise you. This guy's not a psycho killer. He's as innocent as a baby. You should at least meet him before you judge him."

"Well," Mary said, "you need to call the police like you planned. Maybe they know something about him that you don't."

"OK," Roger said, "I'll call the police right now."

Roger picked up the telephone and dialed 9-1-1.

Mary's screams also woke up the children who immediately ran into the family room to see what Santa had brought them. They were immediately stopped in their tracks when they saw a black man sitting on the couch. They had never been this close to a black man before and a black man had certainly never been inside their home. This unexpected houseguest left the children in an emotional state that was somewhere between frightened and curious. Not knowing what to do, the children stood completely motionless, jaws agape, staring at Gabe.

A short while later, their father walked in and

explained that this black man, whose name is Gabe, was a special Christmas visitor left by Santa. He told the kids that Santa would pick him up on his way back to the North Pole. This explanation immediately disarmed the children who then ran to Gabe. They crowded next to him on the couch and bombarded him with questions about Santa and the North Pole. Does Rudolph's nose really glow? How tall is an elf? How many elves live at the North Pole? Does Santa have any children? When Gabe only repeated what the kids said to him, Roger told the children that they were asking Gabe to reveal top secret information. Roger warned them that if they didn't stop pestering Gabe with questions, they would be put on Santa's permanent naughty list and would never receive another Christmas present ever again. This immediately stopped the interrogation just as their mother entered the room.

Mary gave Roger a concerned glance when she saw her children sitting so close to this still unknown man. Roger looked at her and mouthed,

"Relax. Everything's fine."

Roger then asked in a loud voice,

"Who wants to open presents?"

"I do. I do," the children shouted back in unison.

The children sat around the Christmas tree and they all took turns opening presents. When all the presents were opened, their daughter, Jen, asked,

"Where's Gabe's presents?"

"Yeah," their son, Billy, added, "Didn't Santa leave any presents for Gabe?"

Roger told the children that Santa didn't leave any presents for Gabe because Gabe's presents were at the North Pole where he lives.

"Well," Jen said, "I think Gabe should have at least one present."

Jen handed one of her presents to Gabe. Gabe took the present and smiled.

"Me too," Billy said as he gave Gabe one of his presents.

Their son, Carter, joined in and gave Gabe one of his presents. Even Baby, mimicking her siblings, joined in by taking the pacifier out of her mouth and handing it to Gabe. Gabe took the pacifier and put it in his mouth. He started sucking on the pacifier just like he had seen Baby do. Everyone rolled with laughter, even Mary. For just a moment, Gabe began to shine as if he were an angel.

At that very moment, the door bell rang and Roger was now regretting that he called the police. By now, Gabe was playing with the kids just like he was one of them and the kids, likewise, had taken a liking to Gabe. Roger ruefully opened the door and invited the police officer into the house. He introduced himself as Sergeant Johnson. While Gabe and the kids played in the family room, Roger and Mary sat with the police officer in the living room as Roger told about how he had found Gabe.

"So," Roger said when he was finished telling the story, "do you have any idea who this man is?"

"We haven't received any reports of a missing man matching his description," Johnson said, "but this is starting to be a very strange day."

"Why's that?," Roger asked.

"Something else happened early this morning."

"What was that?," Roger asked.

"Last night," Johnson said, "or rather, early this morning, a baby was found abandoned next to a dumpster at the McDonald's near Main Street and Bluff."

"How old was it?," Roger asked.

"Brand spanking new," Johnson said, "It was wrapped in an old wool coat and left by the dumpster behind the building. The wool coat probably saved the baby's life."

"The baby's alive?," Roger asked.

"It was the last time I heard," Johnson said, "An employee who works at McDonald's heard the baby crying when he went to take the trash out. The manager called 911 and it was immediately taken to the hospital."

"What kind of person would abandon a baby like that?," Mary asked.

"I don't know," Johnson said, "But we think it was someone who came in on the midnight bus. There was a report of a young woman who was wearing a coat like the one the baby was wrapped in. We think she rode on to Las Vegas."

"Well," Mary said, "I think she must be a horrible person to just abandon a baby like that."

"I don't know if she is or not," Roger said, "But I hope they find her."

"I heard a security guard at the Las Vegas bus terminal was on the look out for her," Johnson said, "but she slipped past him."

"Are they still looking for her?," Mary asked.

"I don't know," Johnson said, "that's not our call. That's up to the Vegas Metro Police. Well, I need to get going. We're short staffed since it's Christmas and I have another call to make."

"What are you going to do with Gabe?," Roger asked.

"I don't know," Johnson said, "I'll probably take him

over to Purgatory."

"You're going to put him in jail?," Roger asked.

"I don't know what else to do with him," Johnson said.

"Is there any reason why he can't stay here?," Roger asked.

"You want him to stay with you?," Johnson asked.

"I'm not sure that's a good idea," Mary said.

"We can't just let him go to jail," Roger said, "I wouldn't feel good about that. I don't think he's a criminal."

"I guess it's up to you, ma'am," Johnson said.

Mary looked at Roger who was looking at her imploringly.

"How long would he need to stay here?," Mary asked after an awkward pause.

"I guess until we find out who he is or until you change your mind," Johnson said, "If you change your mind, all you need to do is call and I'll pick him up."

"I guess he can stay here for now," Mary said hesitantly, "But you better come back if I call you," Mary said sternly.

"That's a promise," Johnson said.

"I guess it's settled then," Roger said, "He'll stay with us for now."

"Call me if you have any problems," Johnson said as he handed Mary a business card.

The name Sergeant Jeffrey Johnson was engraved on the card along with the address and telephone number of the St. George Police Department . With that, Johnson was out the door leaving Roger and Mary alone in the doorway.

CHAPTER ELEVEN

CHASE

As the hours passed away, Richard Decker rushed to the telephone every time it rang hoping it would be Ferraro returning his call. But each time, it was some kid asking to speak to one of his teenaged children. Richard couldn't help feeling annoyed.

"Keep it short," Richard said before handing the telephone over, "I'm expecting an important phone call."

Each time, his kids would roll their eyes as if to say,

"Sure dad, we'll never speak to any of our friends again just for you."

Richard's children went about their conversation as usual, completely ignoring his admonition. As time rolled by, Richard's agitation increased. He began to think that Ferraro must have called, but had gotten a busy signal.

At about five in the afternoon, Richard couldn't stand it any longer and he called the Las Vegas Metro Police. When Roos answered the telephone, Richard asked if Roos had given Ferraro his message. Roos explained that he had gotten an answering machine and had not heard back from Ferraro. Roos told Richard that Ferraro would be working later that evening. Roos assured Richard that Ferraro would certainly call him by the end of the day. Richard ate dinner with his family and returned to his lazy boy chair to watch TV. Almost as soon as he was reclined in the chair, Richard was fast asleep. At precisely ten in the evening, Ferraro reported for duty. He found the message in his box to call Decker. The message said that the matter was urgent. There was also a message from a Lieutenant Atkin from St. George, Utah. Ferraro dialed Richard's telephone number and a woman answered. She told him that her husband was asleep and that she didn't want to wake him. Ferraro told her who he was, that he was returning her husband's phone call and that her husband said the matter was urgent.

"Oh yes," the woman perked up, "He's been waiting for your call all day. Let me get him."

A few minutes later, Ferraro heard Richard's voice.

"I have some new information about the girl," Richard said, "I've been trying to reach you all day."

Ferraro explained that he had not been home between shifts and that he had spent Christmas day at his girlfriend's house. He apologized for not calling sooner and told Richard that he called as soon as he got the message. Richard told Ferraro about the abandoned baby.

"Are you certain it's the same girl?," Ferraro asked.

"I'm certain," Richard said, "I saw the coat on the

news. It's the exact same coat. It has to be her."

Ferraro told Richard that he would investigate further, but reminded him that the girl had almost a full day's head start. Ferraro also explained that the girl may have left Las Vegas by now. Richard said he understood and asked Ferraro to let him know if he discovered anything new. Ferraro told Richard he would do his best and hung up.   Ferraro called Lieutenant Atkin who confirmed what Decker had told him about the baby and the grey wool coat.

— — — — — —

Ferraro walked to the bus terminal, which was a short distance away from his precinct station, with a renewed emphasis on the investigation. Ferraro saw a janitor mopping the floor when he entered the bus terminal. When Ferraro asked him where the security office was, the janitor pointed to a door across from the ticket counter. Ferraro knocked on the door.

"Come in," a voice behind the door said.

Ferraro opened the door and stepped in. A blond haired man in his early twenties was sitting in a chair in front of several small black and white television monitors. The monitors displayed several locations in and around the bus terminal. Underneath a table, he saw a small pink suitcase.

"I'm looking for a guy named Wray," Ferraro announced.

"You found him," Wray said as he stood up.

Ferraro explained who he was and Wray said he remembered the telephone call.

"Is that the suitcase?," Ferraro asked pointing to the suitcase.

"Yes," Wray replied, "Do you want it?"

"No," Ferraro said, "That suitcase is now evidence and I don't want anyone to touch it until the CSI detective shows up. I don't want it contaminated any more than it already is."

Ferraro asked Wray if the video from the surveillance cameras was recorded. Wray answered affirmatively and explained that the video cassettes were kept for thirty days before they were reused. Ferraro asked if Wray could give him the video cassette from when the young woman got off the bus.

"It's over there on the shelf," Wray said pointing to a shelf.

Wray walked to the shelf and examined the cassettes on the top shelf. He found the one marked "December 25, 2001, Rear Entrance North" and pulled it off the shelf.

"This is it," Wray said, offering the cassette to Ferraro.

When Ferraro asked if he could watch the video, Wray put the cassette into a video cassette player and pressed the play button. As the video began to play, Ferraro could see that the video was shot from a camera that was hung above the rear entrance of the bus terminal. The camera was pointed northward toward the Plaza Hotel. The video initially showed a line of buses parked diagonally along the building. On the bottom right corner of the screen, there was a stamp that showed the date and time. The date remained the same, but the seconds and minutes ticked by as they watched the video.

"What time did the bus arrive?," Ferraro asked.

"It was around two-thirty in the morning," Wray

said, "I'll fast forward the video."

The video fast-forwarded for several minutes. When the time stamp approached two-thirty, Wray pushed the play button on the remote control. The video returned to normal speed and they continued to watch for several minutes. Finally, a bus pulled into the stall farthest from the camera and stopped. Within seconds, they saw a figure dart around the front of the bus. It was an image of a dark-haired woman who was wearing a sweater and a dark dress. The image quickly disappeared behind the bus. They continued to watch as another figure strolled toward the bus.

"It doesn't seem like you were in much of a hurry," Ferraro said dryly.

Wray didn't respond. They continued to watch as the image of the woman reemerged from behind the bus. The woman disappeared into the hotel entrance as Wray began to engage in a conversation with the bus driver. Seconds later, they saw Wray run around the front of the bus. Wray disappeared for a moment and then reappeared as he followed the woman into the hotel entrance.

"We're not going to get much information from that," Ferraro said, "It's too dark and too far way. I don't even think she looked toward the camera."

When Wray didn't respond, Ferraro looked at Wray who was looking down at the floor.

"The woman didn't match the description so I didn't . . .," Wray said hesitantly.

"That's OK," Ferraro interrupted, "The casinos have top notch surveillance systems. I'm sure I can get something useful from them."

"What's so important about this girl anyway?,"

Wray asked.

"When I first called you," Ferraro began, "nothing. But she's now suspected of abandoning a newborn baby up in St. George."

"That's awful," Wray said, "I'm sorry I . . . ."

"It's not your fault," Ferraro said interrupting him again.

Ferraro put a hand on Wray's shoulder.

"I need to find out where that bus is now," Ferraro said.

Wray walked Ferraro to the dispatch office and said, "Maybe they can give you that information."

Ferraro thanked Wray for his help and walked into the dispatch office. Ferraro learned that the bus had gone to Los Angeles and then to San Diego. The bus was now making a return trip the same way it had come.

"So it will be returning to Las Vegas?," Ferraro asked.

"Yes," responded the dispatcher.

"The exact same bus?," Ferraro quickly followed.

"Yes," the dispatcher confirmed, "Unless there was a breakdown. It's scheduled to arrive here in about two hours."

"Same driver?," Ferraro asked hopefully.

"No," responded the dispatcher, "They change drivers in San Diego."

"I need to keep that bus for at least a day," Ferraro said, "Can you make arrangements to switch out the bus?"

"I'll see what I can do," the dispatcher said.

"No," said Ferraro emphatically, "I need to know if you can do it, otherwise, I'm going to get a warrant. And if I have to get a warrant, I'm going to keep it for a month. Do you understand what I'm saying?"

"OK," said the dispatcher, "I'll make sure you get the bus."

"Don't double cross me or I will get a warrant for every bus that stopped at this terminal during the entire day," Ferraro said emphatically, "Kapeesh?"

"I get it," the dispatcher said equally emphatically, "I'll make sure you have your bus."

Ferraro left the dispatch office and walked out the back entrance of the bus terminal. He retraced the steps that Wray and the young woman had taken and walked through the door of the hotel entrance. Ferraro found the hotel's security office and explained who he was. He said he was looking for a woman who came into the casino in the early hours of Christmas morning. Ferraro asked if he could look at the surveillance tape of the entrance nearest the bus terminal.

"What time was it?," Ferraro was asked.

"About two-thirty in the morning," he replied.

Ferraro was handed a cassette and was directed to another room that had a VCR and television. This time, a clear color image of the young woman could be seen entering through the entrance door. She was dressed in a dark blue dress and a red sweater. She was wearing a black scarf that disguised her hair. Her face could clearly be seen. Within seconds, the girl disappeared from the screen. Ferraro returned to the security office, explained that he found the woman he was looking for, but that she had quickly disappeared from the camera's view. Ferraro asked if there was another camera that captured a view from where the last camera left off. A man went with him into the viewing room and watched as the video was briefly replayed.

"I will get it for you," the man said.

The man returned with another cassette. Ferraro once again found the young woman. This time, he saw the young woman remove a large brown envelope from under her sweater and then the sweater itself. The young woman glanced back toward the entrance over and over again as she wove her way through the rows and rows of slot machines. Within a minute, the young woman disappeared again. Ferraro repeated the process of getting additional cassettes until he finally saw her exit the hotel. Ferraro watched the young woman disappear from view when she crossed the street toward the Fremont Street Experience pedestrian walkway.

After getting a copy of the hotel's surveillance videos, Ferraro returned to the bus terminal. When he entered the security office, a CSI detective was sitting in a chair shooting the breeze with Wray.

"What's happening here?," the CSI detective asked.

Ferraro told him the details about the young woman, then pointed to the suitcase.

"I need that suitcase taken into evidence and analyzed," Ferraro explained, "A bus should be arriving here any time now. I need the bus analyzed as well. I see you've met Mr. Wray. He can show you where he found the suitcase. I want you to check out the bus and find out if anything was left behind. You know, blood, body fluid, the usual things."

For the first time in his life, Wray felt like a real cop.

"Sure," Wray said hoping to play a bigger role in the investigation, "Is there anything else I can do?"

Wray's countenance drooped when Ferraro said,

"No, that's it. I'm going back to the precinct."

Ferraro looked at the CSI detective and added,
"Let me know what you find as soon as you find it.
I want a rush put on this."

Ferraro handed the video tapes from the casino to
the CSI detective.

"Make me some still photographs of the woman,"
Ferraro said, "The best picture is going to be where she
first enters the hotel."

D. K. DeGRAW

CHAPTER TWELVE

FAMILY

"I can't believe you did that to me," Mary said angrily when Roger closed the front door.

"Did what?," Roger asked.

"Put me on the spot like that without even discussing it with me first," she huffed.

"I don't think I had any other choice," Roger said, "I wasn't going to let Gabe go to jail. You've seen him. He's practically like a child. Who knows what would happen to him in jail. I can't believe you're making an issue out of this."

"OK," Mary said, "But he stays with you at all times. That means he goes to work with you."

"Agreed," Roger said.

With that, the matter was settled for now. Roger watched Sergeant Johnson get into his squad car and drive away. Mary went into the kitchen to prepare breakfast. When the squad car disappeared down the street, Roger went into the family room and found the kids playing with their new Christmas toys. Mary could hear the sound of laughter, which only added to her displeasure. She set a bowl, a spoon and a glass on the table for each of the three older children and Gabe. She also put a small bowl, a tiny spoon and a sippy cup on the kitchen table near the high chair. When breakfast was ready to eat, Mary put a stack of cinnamon toast on a plate in the center of the kitchen table along with a pot of oatmeal.

"Breakfast is ready," Mary yelled.

Mary took a gallon of milk out of the fridge, picked up the sugar bowl and put these items on the table just as Jen, Billy and Carter ran into the kitchen. The children took their usual places at the table.

"Can we start?," they started shouting, "We're hungry."

"Not yet," Mary said "You need to wait for Gabe and Baby."

The children began pounding their spoons on the table as they chanted,

"We want to eat. We want to eat. "

Roger walked into the kitchen holding Baby in one arm and pulling Gabe with his free hand.

"Settle down kids," Roger said with a stern voice.

The children instantly stopped the pounding and chanting. Roger put Baby into the high chair, secured the restraining strap around Baby's waist and clipped the plastic tray onto the arms of the high chair. Roger dragged Gabe over to the table and seated him at the table next to Billy. Roger saw that there were only enough settings for the children and Gabe.

"Where's my place?," Roger exclaimed, "Don't I get to eat?"

"No," Mary said, "We have some things to talk about first."

Mary poured some milk into the sippy cup, snapped on the lid and put it on the tray in front of Baby. She then put some oatmeal, milk and sugar into the tiny bowl and placed the bowl and the tiny spoon on the tray as well. She then looked at Roger.

"Follow me, Mister," Mary said.

She walked down the hallway and into the bedroom with Roger in tow behind her. When the bedroom door closed, the children passed the pot of oatmeal around the table as each one, in turn, scooped some oatmeal into their bowls. The pot of oatmeal was followed by the milk jug, sugar bowl and plate of cinnamon toast. Eventually, everything was log jammed next to Gabe, who acted as though he didn't know what to do. The children stared at him with an encouraging look. Finally, Gabe reached for the spoon in the pot and scooped some oatmeal into his bowl. He poured some milk into the bowl along with a teaspoon of sugar just like he had seen the children do.

The children all laughed and smiled as they start eating their breakfast meal. Gabe also laughed as he watched the children. After a few moments of observing the children, Gabe took his spoon and began eating the oatmeal. After eating a few spoonfuls of oatmeal, he reached for a cinnamon toast, put it to his mouth and took a big bite. He instantly tasted the sweetness of the cinnamon and sugar on his tongue. Gabe smiled and for just a flicker of a moment, he seemed to glow as though he were transformed into an angel. This startled the older children. They instantly stopped eating as they looked at each other, then starred at Gabe. They silently wondered what had just happened.

At that moment, Baby reached into her bowl, grabbed a handful of oatmeal and smeared it all over her face and head. Baby squealed with delight. Upon seeing this, Gabe reached into his bowl, grabbed a handful of oatmeal and smeared it all over his face and head just like Baby had done. Everyone at the table squealed with laughter. Baby, encouraged by the laughter, took her bowl of oatmeal and dumped it over her head. When everyone laughed even harder, Baby began slapping the top of her head. The older children suddenly became silent because they didn't know whether they should approve of this or not. But Gabe, following Baby's example, took his bowl of oatmeal and dumped it over his head. Mimicking Baby, Gabe began slapping the top of his head. Baby laughed and laughed and Gabe joined in. The other children continued to sit in awkward silence for a while, but they soon joined Baby and Gabe in laughter as each one, in turn, dumped their bowl of oatmeal over their heads and began slapping the tops of their heads. They laughed and laughed as Baby began slapping her hands on the tray of the highchair. Milk and oatmeal splashed everywhere. This added to Baby's amusement. Soon Gabe was slapping his hands on the table in front of him and the children soon followed. With that, the kitchen was filled with joyous laughter, noise and mischief.

Upon hearing the noise in the kitchen, Mary stopped her conversation with Roger in mid-sentence.

"I think the kids are having too much fun out there," she said, "and that means nothing but trouble."

Mary got off the bed and walked out of the bedroom. Roger followed behind her. Mary saw what was happening in the kitchen and the mess that had been made.

"What is going on out here?," Mary shouted angrily.

The older children became instantly silent, but Baby and Gabe continued on, oblivious to Mary's presence. Mary glared at Gabe until he, too, became silent, followed by Baby.

"I said, what is going on out here," Mary glared. "I want some answers NOW!"

"We were just having fun," Jen said and began to explain.

But Mary cut her off abruptly.

"This is completely unacceptable," Mary yelled, "You have turned this kitchen into a pigsty. I'm ashamed to be your mother. I want this kitchen cleaned immediately."

Billy snickered to himself because he had recently watched a Bill Cosby video where Cosby had joked about mothers being pigsty experts.

"Do you think this is funny, young man," Mary yelled.

"No," Billy said trying his best to stifle another snicker.

After a pause, Mary looked at Roger and said, "This is all your fault."

Mary burst into tears and ran back into the bedroom. Roger remained in the kitchen with the children.

"I'll help you clean this up," Roger said, "Why don't you tell me what happened."

Roger and the children cleaned the kitchen as the

children told the story. Gabe joined in with the cleaning as he observed and mimicked the others. Soon, they were all laughing together until every thing was spic and span.

"Why's mom always so grumpy?," Billy asked his dad.

"Your mom has a lot of things to worry about," Roger answered, "I think having Gabe here is one more thing for her to worry about."

"But why?," Billy continued, "Gabe's so nice and so funny. I'm happy he's here. Why isn't mom?"

"I think your mom just needs some time to adjust to this new situation," Roger answered.

"Do you think mom will ever adjust?," Jen asked.

"I hope so," Roger said with a melancholic voice.

The days passed by without any further incidents at the kitchen table. Roger carefully supervised Gabe until he was confident that Gabe had mastered the art of table manners. Gabe's vocabulary increased day by day and he was soon talking in complete sentences. Gabe also liked to sit at the kitchen table and observe Mary as she prepared meals. This made Mary feel uncomfortable.

"Why do you sit there and watch me like that?," Mary finally said with a surly voice.

"I want to learn how to do that," Gabe responded kindly.

"Do what?," Mary asked.

"What you are doing," Gabe answered.

"You mean cook?," Mary said with surprise.

"Yes," Gabe said. "I want to learn how to cook."

That was the first time anyone in her house had ever expressed any interest in helping Mary with the cooking.

"Come over here and I'll teach you how to cook," Mary said warmly.

Mary showed Gabe the recipe she was working on and explained how to add each ingredient. She also demonstrated how to use the measuring cups and spoons. Mary explained how the oven and stove worked and soon, the first meal they prepared together was ready to eat. Mary proudly told the family how Gabe had helped her. She also told them how nice it was to have some extra help for a change. Gabe continued to help Mary in the kitchen along with other household chores. In particular, Gabe loved to vacuum. He seemed completely mesmerized by the vacuum cleaner and would sit and study it for hours. Gabe turned it on and off, over and over again, trying to figure out the source of the suction. Gabe would always cheerfully do whatever he was asked to do without complaint or hesitation. Gabe would simply say,

"Yes, I would like to do that."

Gabe would even ask from time to time if there was anything he could do to help. Before long, Mary noticed that the whole atmosphere around the house seemed to be more cheerful, peaceful and pleasant.

Near the end of the children's Christmas school vacation, the family made its traditional trip to Brian Head. Brian Head is a small ski resort an hour and a half drive north of St. George. Jen and Billy were beginning to hound their parents about letting them snow board, but Roger and Mary thought they were still too young. They told the kids they would stick to the tubing hill this year, but maybe next year. Jen and Billy took the news with a groan.

"Why do you always treat us like we're babies?,"

they asked.

The evening before the trip to Brian Head, the family loaded all of their snow gear into the back of the minivan. They wanted to be ready to leave first thing in the morning. When the minivan was loaded, they realized that there was no winter clothing for Gabe. Roger took Gabe to Hurst Sporting Goods, which rented snow outfits and equipment.

The store was partly owned by Bruce Hurst, a local boy who had been a pitcher in the major leagues. In fact, he had pitched for the Boston Red Sox in the 1986 World Series. Hurst had been anointed the series most valuable player just minutes before the ground ball between the first baseman's legs fiasco snatched the trophy away from him and propelled the Mets to the World Series title. Even though Bruce Hurst no longer lived in St. George, he still owned several business interests in town and was involved in local charity work. One of the most visible was the baseball stadium at the local community college. Bruce Hurst had donated the money to renovate the stadium and it was now named in his honor.

The family woke up early the next morning and loaded into the minivan. They drove north up I-15 past Cedar City and exited I-15 at Parowan. The family drove through the tiny town and headed up Parowan Canyon. They continued up the twisting road until they reached a chain up area. Roger pulled over to the side of the road and put chains on the front tires. They continued up the canyon road as it became increasingly steep and windy. They passed by several vehicles that had ignored the chain up warning sign and were now stranded at the side of the road. These cars were attempting the difficult task of turning around on the narrow, slippery road. A few miles further up the road, Roger made a couple of sharp, hairpin turns and the Brian Head Town sign came into view. At a base elevation of almost ten thousand feet above sea level, Brian Head is one of the highest elevation ski resorts in the world.

A few more miles up the road, ski lifts came into view. After a few more miles, Roger made a right turn into the Navajo Lodge parking lot. Because of their early arrival, the lot was mostly empty. Within an hour, the lot would be packed with cars. Roger pulled into a parking space close to the lodge and the tubing hill. Roger went into the lodge to purchase passes while the rest of the family remained at the minivan and put on their snow gear. Still waiting for Roger to return, the children began throwing snow balls at each other. At first, Gabe didn't know what to think of this. The idea of intentionally throwing an object at someone seemed to bewilder him. But he soon joined in the fun when he realized that the soft, fluffy snow was harmless. That was until someone accidently hit Baby in the face. Even though Baby was unhurt, she began to wail at the top of her lungs. Fortunately, Roger returned with the tubing hill passes and quickly defused the situation.

"Who's ready to go tubing?," Roger yelled.

"I am, I am," the older children yelled back as they raced toward Roger to get a pass. Roger attached a pass to Jen's jacket and then to Billy's.

"Can we go?," Jen asked, "We don't want to be treated like babies."

"Yes," Roger answered. "You and Billy can go."

"What about Gabe?," Billy asked.

"You can take Gabe with you," Roger responded.

After Roger attached a pass to Gabe's jacket, Jen and Billy ran to the tubing hill pulling Gabe along with them. When they reached the stacks of tubes, Jen and Billy each selected a tube for themselves. They searched for the biggest tube they could find for Gabe. They gave the tube to Gabe and pulled their selected tubes to where an attendant was waiting.

"Do what I do," Jen said to Gabe.

Jen handed the attendant a rope that was attached to the tube. Jen sat down on the tube and the attendant hooked the rope onto the tow cable. Jen and her tube were jerked forward toward the top of the hill. Billy urged Gabe forward to take his turn. Billy helped Gabe sit on the tube and the attendant attached the rope to the tow cable. Even though Gabe had the largest tube in the stack, the size of the tube looked comically small in comparison to Gabe. It was like seeing a person wearing a hat far too small for their head, but upside down. Gabe gave a startled yell as he and his tube followed Jen up the hill. Billy was soon following Jen and Gabe up the hill.

At the top of the hill, another attendant unhooked the tubes from the tow cable and the threesome pulled their tubes to the nearby sliding lanes. Jen and Billy situated their tubes in adjacent sliding lanes and helped Gabe do the same. They showed Gabe how to sit on the tube. When they were all in position, they showed Gabe how to scoot himself forward using his feet and hands. In unison, they began to slide down the hill faster and faster. Gabe yelled all the way down while Jen and Billy laughed along side him. The rest of the family joined them for the next trip up the hill and they spent the rest of the day laughing and having a wonderful time together.   It was the first time Gabe had seen all members of the family happy at the same time. For just a moment, he glowed like an angel.

CHAPTER THIRTEEN

SWITCH

Anna Hansen got dressed and walked to the window. She cracked open the curtain and looked out the window. She saw no sign of Dwayne, or anyone else for that matter. She walked to the back of the room and retrieved the plastic laundry bag that was dangling from a hanger. She walked over to the dresser and pulled open the top drawer. She removed the clothes from the drawer and stuffed it into the laundry bag. She opened the other drawer, took out the brown envelope and put it in the laundry bag as well. Anna tied the bag shut and returned to the window. She again cracked open the curtain and looked out of the window. Seeing no one, and believing it was safe to leave the room, she removed the chair. She opened the door and cautiously stepped out.

Anna paused to make one last sweeping scan of the motel parking lot. Still seeing no one, she walked quickly to the stairs. She descended the stairs and made her way to the motel office. Through the office window, she could see a dark-skinned man doing something behind a counter. He looked like he was from India or Pakistan. Anna opened the door and walked in.

"You son of a bitch," Anna yelled with her eyes blazing like fire.

Anna threw the key at the man as hard as she could. The man ducked out of the way at the last second. The key narrowly missed hitting the man's head and bounced off the wall behind him.

"Why are you yelling at me?," the man protested with an accent that confirmed that he, indeed, was from India or Pakistan.

"You know why," Anna said with rage in her voice.

"I didn't do anything," the man continued to protest, "Why are you so angry?"

"What about your friend, Dwayne B. Goode," Anna seethed, "What about HIM? How much did he pay you?"

"That piece of garbage is no friend of mine," the man said defensively, "I work the day shift. You must be talking about the fellow who works the night shift."

Anna continued to silently glare at the man.

"Look," the man said, "I've heard about a man named Dwayne B. Goode, but I can assure you, he's no friend of mine. He's a very evil man. I don't know what he did to you, but trust me, from the stories I've been told, the fact that you're here now means it could have been much worse for you. You should feel very lucky."

"Well," Anna snarled, "I don't feel lucky."

"From what I've heard," the man continued, "this

Dwayne B. Goode hangs around here at night looking for runaways who have no money and no where to go. He turns them into drug addicts and prostitutes. I hear he lures them to his house, injects them with heroin and once they're addicted, turns them into prostitutes. Did he try to get you to go to his house?"

Anna looked down at the floor and didn't answer.

"At least you were smart enough not to go with him," the man said, "See, you're one of the lucky ones. I strongly suggest you get out of here before this Goode returns. I need you to be honest with me. Are you a run away?"

Anna stood silently for a while, but decided to trust the man.

"Yes," she said still looking at the floor.

"Right now," the man continued, "you don't have any good options. But I can help you. I know of a woman who will help a pretty girl like you. It's not a very good option, but I promise you it's a lot better than being a drug addict and prostitute. Do you want me to call her for you? There's no obligation."

"Yeah," Anna said sarcastically, "I've heard that before. As recently as yesterday as a matter of fact."

"I promise you," the man said, "This woman won't hurt you. You have my word on that. If you're not interested in what she has to offer, you can walk away."

Anna considered this for a moment.

"OK," Anna finally said, "But I promise you. If you're lying to me, some how, some way, I will hunt you down. When I find you, I'm going to chop off your balls. That's if YOU'RE lucky."

"Hey," the man protested, "there's no reason to make threats. You will not be hurt. I promise you."

The man picked up the telephone and dialed a number.

"I have a run away girl at the Starlight Motel who needs help," the man said, "She's a real beauty and I thought you might be interested."

After a pause, he studied Anna.

"About five-six, golden, blond hair, blue eyes, nice body, a real looker," the man said.

After another pause, the man asked,

"How old are you?"

"Eighteen," Anna answered.

"You don't want to know," the man said, "But I think with some makeup, she could be made to look at least twenty-one."

After another pause, the man hung up. He told Anna that someone would be there to pick her up in about fifteen minutes.

"So what's in it for you?," Anna asked the man.

"What makes you think there's something in it for me?," the man said with pretended surprise.

"Because men don't do anything unless there's something in it for them," Anna said, "So don't act so surprised."

"Truth be told," the man said, "I do get a small finder's fee if I refer someone who turns out to be a keeper."

"How small? ," Anna asked.

"I'd rather not say," the man answered.

"At least he's honest," Anna thought to herself, "that's more than I can say about most men."

"Where are you from?," the man asked.

"I'd rather not say," Anna responded, "Where are you from?"

"Pakistan," the man answered.

"Why did you come to America?," Anna asked.

"To get a better life," the man answered.

"That's why I came to Las Vegas," Anna said.

After that, the man returned to his work and didn't ask any more questions.

A little while later, a Black Cadillac limousine arrived at the motel. A man got out of the back seat and walked into the office. He was wearing a black suit and a dark blue shirt with an open collar. He was wearing black sunglasses with black lenses that hid his eyes. He had black hair, a dark tan and was very tall. He had the muscular build of a defensive lineman. The man had three parallel white scars about an inch apart on his face. The scars ran from the middle of his forehead, behind the left lense of his sunglasses and almost to his left ear. The man had another scar that ran from the bridge of his nose, across his left cheek toward his neck. The scars stood out against his dark tan and gave the man an extraordinarily menacing appearance.

"Are you sure I'm going to be safe?" Anna said to the Pakistani man, "Remember, your balls are depending on it."

"I promise you will be safe," the man assured her, "especially when you're with him."

The scar faced man walked through the door and looked directly at Anna.

"You must be the girl," he said.

Anna nodded.

"Come with me," the scar faced man said.

Anna followed the scar faced man to the limousine and he motioned for Anna to get in. When Anna was situated in the rear seat, the scar faced man got in the limousine and sat in the seat opposite her closest to the driver. The scar faced man rapped on the window behind him with the back of his right hand. The limousine immediately lurched forward. It pulled out of the Starlight Motel parking lot and turned right onto Fremont Street.

Anna asked the scar faced man where they were going, but the scar faced man remained silent as though he hadn't heard her question. A few miles later, the limousine turned right onto Boulder Highway. It continued south for a couple of miles until it turned left into a parking lot. Anna saw a sign near the street in front of a windowless building.

"Pussy Kat Club," the sign read.

The limousine drove behind the windowless building. Expensive cars were parked along a block wall behind the building. The limousine stopped next to what appeared to be the building's rear entrance. The driver got out of the limousine and opened the door. The scar faced man motioned for Anna to get out. When Anna exited the limousine, the scar faced man followed behind her. He walked up to the door and knocked a unique rhythm on the door with his knuckles. The door opened.

The scar faced man motioned for Anna to walk in, which Anna reluctantly did. Anna walked past an equally large and menacing man who held the door open. This man was dressed exactly like the scar faced man, sunglasses and all.

"It must be their uniform," Anna thought to herself.

When the scar faced man followed Anna into the building, the door slammed shut behind them.

"Follow me," the scar faced man said.

The scar faced man continued down a short hall

way. Anna followed closely behind. The scar faced man continued walking down a maze of hallways until he reached a door. The scar faced man knocked on the door and waited until a woman's voice could be heard behind the door. Anna didn't understand what was said, but it seemed to be said in a foreign language. The scar faced man opened the door and motioned for Anna to walk in. The woman said something to the scar faced man. The fact that it was said in a foreign language was now unmistakable. The scar faced man left the room and closed the door behind him. The only word Anna could make out was a word that sounded like "Sergay." She assumed this was the scar faced man's name. Anna glanced around and saw that she was alone in the room with the woman.

"Pleaze zit down," the woman said as she studied Anna up, down and up again, "My name iz Kat."

Kat had black hair and equally black eyes. She looked to be around fifty years old, but was still very attractive despite her age. Kat wore a deep vee necked top that exposed the cleavage of her ample, but firm, breasts.

"What kind of place is this?," Anna asked.

"In aMERica, zhey call zhis a strip club," Kat answered.

Kat's foreign accent gave her an extra boost of sexiness that she really didn't need given her physical appearance.

"What do you do here?," Anna asked.

"I'm za owner," Kat answered.

"No," Anna said confused, "I mean, what's a strip club?"

Kat laughed out loud.

"You must be young," Kat said.

Anna's cheeks turned red with embarrassment.

"Well," Kat continued, "to put it zimply, girls takes off zheir clothes vhile drunk men gives zhem money. Za drunker za man iz, za better for za girl. Vhen za man iz drunk, he loses track of how much money heez throwing away and spending on za booze."

Kat gave another laugh.

"Now I vant you to take off your clothes," Kat said matter of factly.

"What do you mean?," Anna asked confused.

"I mean," Kat said, "I vantz you to take off your clothes right now. Zhat should be a zimple request. I vant to zee vhat you have."

"I don't want to take off my clothes like that," Anna said in astonishment, "I want to be a showgirl."

"Oh," Kat said with a laugh, "You vantz to be a showgirl. I zinks you're a little too young to be a show girl. Are you twenty-one?"

"No," Anna answered slowly.

"Do you have any special training?," Kat asked.

"What do you mean by special training?," Anna asked.

"Do you zinks you can just shows up in Las Vegas and be a show girl?," Kat asked not expecting an answer, "A show girl must have years and years of danze training. Zhese show girls have training at za best studios and schools. Do you have any training like zhat? Ballet? Modern danze? Any zhing like zhat?"

This time, Kat waited for a response.

"Well, no," Anna said slowly.

"Zhat's vhat I thought," Kat said, "Are you ready to gets zeriouz now or do you vants to live in a fantasy vorld?."

After a moment, Anna said,

"So what do you want from me?"

"I vant you to take off your clothes," Kat repeated.

Anna stood up slowly and unbuttoned her dark blue dress. She removed her arms from the dress and the dress fell to the floor.

"Now za bra," Kat said.

Anna reached around her back and unhooked her bra. She removed the straps from her shoulder and it too fell to the floor on top of the dress. Anna stood there ashamed with her arms folded across her breasts.

Kat again laughed.

"You poor and innozent girl," she said, "Put your arms by your side so I cans zee you and turns around slowly."

"I might be poor," Anna thought to herself, "but I'm not as innocent as you think."

Anna did as she was told and turned around as Kat inspected her. Kat saw that Anna had a wonderful figure from top to bottom. She had firm, round, breasts that were not too large to be unnatural, but large enough to delight any man. Anna also had a beautiful face and a long graceful neck. Kat instantly knew that Anna would be a star attraction at her Club.

"You can puts on you're clothes and zit down," Kat said when she was finished with her inspection.

Anna put on her clothes and sat down as instructed.

"Zo tell me," Kat said, "Are you just a normal run avay or are you in some zeriouz troubles? You need to be completely honest vith me if you vants me to help you."

"I might be in some trouble," Anna answered.

"A little or a lots?," Kat continued, "Are za poleez looking for you?"

"The police might be looking for me," Anna answered, but not giving any details.

Kat looked at Anna for a moment, then laid out the terms of her offer. Kat said Anna could become a dancer at her club. In return, Anna would get 25 percent of her tips along with room and board. Kat told Anna that she maintained a house where Anna would live with the other dancers. She said that there were strict rules. The dancers were not allowed to have boyfriends, no men in the house, no drug use anywhere and no alcohol outside the club. Kat said she would keep all of Anna's share of the money, except for a small monthly allowance. Anna would be given the remainder of her money when her three year contract was completed. Kat told Anna that she would be taken to the house and would be expected to master the arts of the trade within a few weeks.

Kat said there was another matter that needed to be addressed. Anna was told that normally someone like her would be provided a false identification, which cost about a thousand dollars to obtain. But in Anna's case, given her legal problems, she would need an entirely new identity. Kat explained that this would be much more difficult and costly. Twenty-five-thousand dollars difficult. Kat explained that she would advance this cost, but that Anna would need to repay her from Anna's share of her earnings. Kat emphasized that a contract like that was not legally enforceable, so any violations of the contract would be enforced by Serge. Kat explained that Serge was the scar faced man she had met earlier. Kat explained minor violations would be dealt with swiftly and appropriately. If there was a major violation, Anna might simply "vanish into thin air."

After explaining the terms of the contract to Anna, Kat said,

"You vill not get a better offer any vhere else. Do vee have an agreement?"

"I don't know," Anna said, "I need to think about it."

"Zhink about it all you vant," Kat said, "I understand you already met a man named Dwayne B. Goode. I vill a have Serge take you back to za Starlight vhile you zhink."

Kat stood up, walked to the door and opened it. Anna remained seated.

"I think I will accept your offer," Anna said.

Kat walked over to Anna and put her hands on her shoulders.

"I zhink you made a very vise decision," Kat said, "Now let's pick out a new name for you."

Kat returned to her desk and opened a drawer. She pulled out a binder and opened it. Kat sat back in her chair as she shuffled through the binder. After a few minutes, she looked at Anna.

"Amber Gould," Kat said, "I zhink zhat name would be perfect for you. Vat you zhink?"

"I like that name," Anna said.

"Vee vill need to change your eye and hair color," Kat said, "Maybe brown eyes and amber brown hair like your name. Vith za right makeup, maybe vee can change you into a whole new perzon."

CHAPTER FOURTEEN

CHASE

Ferraro returned to work at ten o'clock on the evening of December 26. He hoped that the same people who worked the Christmas Eve night shift would be at work that night as well. He found two envelopes on his desk when he arrived. The first envelope contained several eight-and-a-half by eleven inch photographs of Anna. Her face could clearly be seen and it was indeed, a very beautiful face. The second envelope contained two reports prepared by the CSI detective. The first report showed that traces of two types of blood were found on and around several of the seats where the suitcase had been found, A positive and AB negative. There was also traces of ambiotic fluid found around the same area of the bus. This evidence clearly indicated that a woman on the bus had recently given birth to a baby.   The other report was an analysis of the fingerprints that were found on the suitcase. This report showed that Wray's fingerprints were found along with several fingerprints that could not be identified. There was also one major surprise. The fingerprints of a man named Gerald Hansen were lifted off the suitcase. Hansen's fingerprints were in the criminal investigation data base because he had a police record.

The police record showed that Gerald Hansen's first conviction was in Montana for the statutory rape of a minor. Hansen had served five years in the Montana State Prison for that conviction. He was released about fifteen years ago. Since then, Hansen had also been arrested several times for minor crimes ranging from disorderly conduct to soliciting prostitution. The record showed that Hansen had served short stints in various local jails throughout the Western United States. He had most recently served six months in the Salt Lake County Jail and had been released less than a week ago. The record listed a current address for Hansen in Salt Lake City.

Ferraro picked up one of Anna's photographs and left his office. Ferraro walked to Fremont Street across from the Plaza Hotel. Ferraro began walking east and stopped at all the hotels, casinos and stores along the way. He showed Anna's picture to the staff and asked if anyone had seen her early on Christmas morning. Knowing that she could be using an alias, he also asked each hotel if anyone checked in during the early hours of the morning under any name.   All responses were negative.

Ferraro continued eastward on Fremont Street until he came to the diner at the corner of Maryland Parkway.

Ferraro showed Anna's picture to the hostess.

"Yeah," the hostess said, "I remember that girl. She came in with an older man. About mid thirties. Gloria waited on them."

"When was that?," Ferraro asked.

"A couple of nights ago," she answered, "I remember it was in the middle of the night."

"Is Gloria working tonight?," Ferraro asked.

"Yeah, she's right over there," said the hostess, pointing to an older, heavyset woman, "Why don't you sit down and I'll get her for you."

Ferraro sat at the nearest empty table and waited for Gloria. After a few minutes, Gloria walked up to his table.

"I hear you want to talk to me," Gloria said.

Ferraro introduced himself and held out Anna's picture.

"Do you remember waiting on this girl the other night?," Ferraro asked.

"I sure do," Gloria said, "A really pretty girl. She was with a man."

"Do you know the name of the man she was with?," Ferraro asked.

"I think his name is Duane or Wayne, something like that," Gloria answered, "I see him around here from time to time. He's always with a different girl, mostly young girls. It's always at night and he always pays cash. A good tipper, too."

"Have you seen him today?," Ferraro asked.

"No," Gloria shook her head, "I haven't seen him since the night he came in with that girl."

"Can you describe what he looks like?," Ferraro asked.

"Thirty something," Gloria said, "Brown hair, dresses like a cowboy and I'm pretty sure he smokes."

"Do you remember if they left together or separately?," Ferraro asked.

"Together for sure," Gloria answered, "I heard them talking about getting a motel room. But she didn't seem like that type, if you know what I mean"

"Do you know which motel they would have gone to?," Ferraro asked.

"No," Gloria answered, "I didn't listen that closely because I didn't want to snoop into their business."

Gloria used the fingers of her hands to indicate quotation marks when she said the word "business."

"Thanks for the information," Ferraro said as he handed Gloria a ten-dollar bill, "I'll tell you what. There's another twenty in it for you if you call me the next time this Duane, Wayne or whatever his name is shows up here again. Here's my card. Call me anytime, day or night."

Ferraro got up, made the same offer to the hostess and walked out. Ferraro scanned the blocks of motels that stretched down Fremont Street.

"I have a long night ahead of me," Ferraro thought to himself.

Ferraro continued his search and eventually entered into the office of the Starlight Motel. He showed the motel clerk behind the counter the picture of Anna.

"Have you seen this girl?," Ferraro asked the clerk.

"Never," the clerk answered honestly because in fact, he had never actually seen the girl.

"Are you sure?," Ferraro said paying close attention to any sign of deceit.

"Positive," the clerk said.

Ferraro sensed that the clerk was telling the truth. Ferraro asked to see the log books and found that someone had checked into a room at about four in the morning on Christmas day. Room 222. It had the name John Smith. Ferraro pointed to that entry.

"Who was this John Smith?," Ferraro asked.

"Some man," the clerk said, "I really don't remember."

"Was he dressed like a cowboy?," Ferraro pressed.

"Look," the clerk insisted, "I really don't remember."

Ferraro now sensed that the clerk was lying.

"Look, buddy," Ferraro said as he leaned toward the clerk's face, "Obstructing justice and harboring a fugitive is a crime that can send you to prison. Your memory better improve right now or I will be hanging around this place like white on rice. Get it?"

"OK," the clerk said, "he was dressed like a cowboy but that's all I know. He paid cash and I didn't ask any question. He said his name was John Smith, so that's what I wrote."

"What's his real name?," Ferraro asked unsatisfied.

"I swear to God I don't know," the clerk pleaded, "I've told you everything I know."

"Is this cowboy still checked in?" Ferraro asked.

"No," the clerk answered, "the room was vacated when I came back to work the next night. He must have checked out the next day."

"You weren't working when he checked out?," questioned Ferraro.

"No," the clerk said emphatically, "Another guy works during the days."

"Who's that?," Ferraro asked.

"Rahim," the clerk said.

"Is that a first or last name?," Ferraro asked.

"I don't know," the clerk responded, "I only know him by Rahim."

"I want to see Room 222," Ferraro said still unsatisfied, "Is anyone checked in the room now."

"No," the clerk answered, "No one is expected to check in until tomorrow. The room has been cleaned, so please don't make a mess."

The clerk handed Ferraro a key marked "222." Ferraro continued to glare at the clerk for a few seconds, then turned around and walked out of the office. Ferraro entered Room 222 and saw that it was clean and empty. He searched the room and then the bathroom. Ferraro opened every drawer and found nothing out of the ordinary. Ferraro even looked under the sheets, the mattress and the furniture. Ferraro found no sign that Anna or anyone else had been there. Ferraro determined that it was pointless to take any of the bedding as evidence because it was obvious that the bedding had been changed since the room was last occupied. As Ferraro was about to walk out of the room, he saw a tiny scrap of paper under the air-conditioning unit. Ferraro picked up the scrap and examined it. It looked like a scrap from a business card. The only thing that was written on the scrap of paper were the letters "e B."

Ferraro returned the key to the office and showed the scrap to the clerk.

"Does this help your memory?," Ferraro asked.

The clerk looked at the scrap.

"Nope," the clerk said, "Never seen anything like that."

"Are you sure about that?," Ferraro asked staring

the clerk directly in the eyes.

"Positive," the clerk said making sure that he stared right back at Ferraro.

"By the way," Ferraro said, "I'm afraid I made a mess of the room. You might want to have the maid remake the bed."

Ferraro turned around and walked out of the office. When the clerk was certain that Ferraro was gone for good, he picked up the telephone and dialed a number. A voice on the other end answered the telephone.

"Hey Dwayne," the clerk said, "A Cop was here asking about you. He had a picture of a girl."

"What did the girl look like?," Dwayne asked.

"Real pretty," the clerk answered, "Golden blond hair. She was wearing a dark blue dress."

Ferraro stopped by the remaining motels along Fremont Street, but came up empty. It seemed certain that the Starlight Motel had to be the place where Anna had gone. He made a note to return to question this guy named Rahim. Ferraro returned to his precinct office and started to think. He put the names "Duane" and "Wayne" that the waitress had given him with the "e B." that was on the scrap of paper.

"Duane B. or Wayne B. Something," he thought to himself.

Following a hunch, he went to the sex unit division.

"Has anyone here ever heard of someone who goes by the name of Duane B. or Wayne B. something?," Ferraro asked.

They told him there was a suspected sex trafficker named Dwayne B. Goode, spelled D-W-A-Y-N-E.

"What do you know about him?" Ferraro asked.

They told him Goode was the lowest scum bag on

earth.   He was suspected of being involved in a nationwide sex trafficking ring that may even be international. They told Ferraro that Goode had been arrested several times, but nothing ever stuck. They told Ferraro that Goode was very smart. He always had alibis and was too distant from any crime to be implicated. Ferraro was told that the sex division was chomping at the bit to nail this guy. Ferraro asked to see Goode's file. When Ferraro opened the file, he saw a booking photograph of a thirty-something, brown haired, man dressed in a cowboy shirt. Ferraro asked if he could get a copy of the file including the photograph. Half an hour later, Ferraro left with a copy of Goode's file and photograph in hand.

Ferraro returned to his office and called Decker. When Richard Decker answered the phone, Ferraro said,

"This is Detective Ferraro. I have a name for you."

SECRETS

CHAPTER FIFTEEN

DISCOVERY

When Richard Decker typed the name Gerald Hansen into a computer, a screen popped up that confirmed the information Ferraro had given him. Hansen was forty-one years old and was recently released from the Salt Lake County Jail. His current address was on Lucy Avenue, which was only a few miles south of downtown Salt Lake City. Lucy Avenue was in one of the oldest parts of Salt Lake and was rapidly becoming one of the poorest parts of the city. Lucy Avenue was also less than a block north of Franklin Covey Field, the home of the city's Triple-A Baseball franchise.

Richard knew this area well because he had attended many events at the ball field, both in his childhood and as an adult. In addition to baseball games, the ball field also hosted concerts and the best Fourth of

July fireworks show in the Salt Lake Valley. He attended the fireworks show there every year with his family for as long as he could remember. His family had to arrive earlier and earlier over the years in order to get a good seat as the population of the city grew. It was almost to the point where it was so crowded that it wasn't worth going any more. He remembered thinking that the past Fourth of July would probably be the last year he and his family would attend the fireworks show. Because the ball field had no parking of its own, Richard had parked on Lucy Avenue several times when he attended events there. He couldn't help but wonder if Anna Hansen had also attended the Fourth of July show and whether they had walked along the same sidewalk together. Maybe Richard had even parked in front of her house.

Richard ordered a hard copy of Gerald Hansen's file. Richard drove to Lucy Avenue when Ferraro's photograph of Anna Hansen arrived. He parked in front of a house that matched the number of the house in the file. The house was on the south side of the street and had wide wooden siding that was painted a light shade of green. He noticed that the house had been recently painted. This was in stark contrast to the worn and peeling paint he could see on the other houses along the street. A short sidewalk led to a small porch that was centered in front of the house. He saw a very small, detached one car garage to the right of the house. The garage had also been recently painted in the same shade of light green.

Richard got out of his car and walked up the short sidewalk. Just as he began to ascend the porch stairs, he saw the movement of a window curtain in the corner of his eye. He looked directly at the window and saw the curtain swaying. He climbed the four steps and walked to the front door. He pushed the doorbell button and heard a chime ringing inside the house. When no one answered the door, he rang the doorbell again and followed up with a hard knock on the door. When the door remained unanswered, Richard banged on the door with his fist.

"I'm with the Salt Lake Police and I know someone's in there," Richard shouted, "Open the door right now, or I'll come back with a search warrant and break the door down."

A few seconds later, Richard heard the floor creak inside the house followed by the sound of a deadbolt unlocking. The door cracked open and he saw the partial face of a woman. The woman had gaunt hollow eyes and looked nothing like the girl in the photo. A gold colored chain stretched tightly from the edge of the door to the door frame. Richard introduced himself to the woman and asked if Gerald Hansen lived there. The woman hesitated. She looked back into the house and then at Richard.

"He's not here," the woman said.

"I'm here about a girl," Richard said, "I believe her name is Anna Hansen."

Richard held out the photograph of Anna and he could see a glimmer of recognition on the woman's face.

"Is she in trouble?," the woman asked.

"Are you her mother?," Richard asked.

"Uh, no," the woman responded, "She's Jerry's daughter. He already had her when we met."

Richard could hear some banging noises inside the house.

"Are you Gerald Hansen's wife?," Richard asked.

"No," the woman responded, "We just live together. We met a couple of years ago."

"How did the two of you meet?," Richard asked.

"In a bar," the woman answered.

"When was the last time you saw Anna?," Richard continued.

"I don't know," the woman said as more banging was heard inside the house, "Sometime before Christmas."

"Have you reported her missing?," Richard pressed.

"I wanted to," the woman said defensively, "But Jerry wouldn't let me. He said she needed to learn a lesson. Jerry said she would be back soon begging us to let her come back home."

A loud bang and the sound of dishes crashing could be heard inside the house.

"Who's inside the house?," Richard asked.

The woman looked back into the house and remained silent.

"He's drunk," the woman said, "You need to come back later."

The woman started to close the door, but Richard put his foot in the opening, preventing the door from closing.

"If he's in there," Richard said with authority, "I need to talk to him."

"You better leave," the woman insisted, "He can get violent when he drinks."

"If he doesn't come to the door right now," Richard said sternly, "I will wait right here until a search warrant arrives. I'm not leaving until I talk to him."

The woman thought for a few seconds.

"Wait here," the woman said.

The woman's face disappeared leaving the door ajar. A few seconds later, Richard heard shouting and arguing inside the house.

"Tell him to go the hell away," a man's voice said with a drunken slur.

"He said he's not leaving until he talks to you," the woman said, "Just go talk to the man so he will leave."

Richard heard the man curse for a while, but after a few minutes, a man's face appeared in the crack.

"Did you find the slut?," the man asked in his drunken stupor.

"No," Richard said, "but I need to ask you some questions."

"Well, I ain't got nothing to say to you," the man said, the smell of alcohol strong on his breath, "I ain't saying nothin without an attorney. I have a right to an attorney. You can't make me talk. I know my rights, you god damned pig"

Before Richard could respond, the man spit at Richard.

"Get off my property," the man yelled, "You ain't got no right to be here."

The man tried to close the door, but Richard's foot still prevented the door from closing. The man stumbled for a moment and when he figured out what was blocking the door, the man yelled,

"Get your god damned foot out of my door or I will sue you. I know my rights you god damned pig"

The man spit on Richard one more time. Richard removed his foot and the door slammed shut. Richard Decker waited for a moment, then turned around and started to walk away from the door. Richard knew there was nothing more he could do for now. But before he reached the end of the porch, Richard heard yelling from inside the house. He walked back toward the door just as the woman yelled,

"I swear to god. If you hit me again, you son of a bitch, I'm going to get the shot gun and shoot your head off."

Richard heard several smacking sounds.

"I'm really going to kill you this time," the man shouted, "You ungrateful bitch."

The smacking sounds continued along with the woman's screams as Richard unholstered his revolver and kicked the door open. Without hesitation, Richard ran into the house, his revolver in a two-handed grip, his arms extended forward. Richard knew that a warrant wasn't needed because he, as a police officer, was allowed to enter the house in order to protect the woman from an immediate and present threat to her life. Richard thought how fortunate it was that this drunken man gave him an excuse to enter the house. At the same time, he knew he was entering into a potentially lethal situation to both himself and the woman.

Richard began to sweep an empty living room as he continued toward the yelling that came from an opening that led to the kitchen. He entered the kitchen, which he also found to be empty. The shouting was now louder and was coming from a hallway just around a corner to the left. Richard slowly walked to a corner where a hallway began. He quickly glanced down the hallway where the shouting was coming from. At the end of the hallway, Richard saw the back of the man who was pounding on a door.

"You better open the door, you ungrateful bitch," the man shouted.

He could hear a woman crying behind the door.

"If you step one foot in this bathroom," the woman yelled, "I swear I'll get the shotgun and blow your head off."

Richard quietly stepped forward and aimed his revolver at the center of the man's torso.

"This is the Police," Richard shouted, "Put your hands above your head and slowly back away from the door."

"What the hell?," the man said as he started to turn around.

"Stop," Richard shouted, "I said put your hands above your head and slowly back away from the door. Do it now, or I will shoot you right where you stand."

The man looked over his shoulder and saw the revolver aimed directly at him.

"Do what you were told right now," Richard shouted, "I'm not going to tell you again."

The man slowly put his hands above his head and took a few steps backward from the door.

"Kneel down on the floor with your arms above your head," Richard said.

The man started to lower his hands.

"I said," Richard yelled, "keep your hands above your head."

The man knelt down as he was told, but continued to shout obscenities that were directed at both the woman and Richard.

"This isn't over bitch," the man yelled toward the door.

"I'm going to sue you, you god damn pig," the man screamed at Richard.

Richard removed the handcuffs from his belt and

walked toward the man.

"Now lie down on your stomach," Richard ordered.

The man began to comply.

"Keep you hands where I can see them," Richard shouted.

Richard approached the man and put one knee in the center of the man's back. As Richard knelt on the man's back, the man continued to shout obscenities.

"Shut up," Richard said to the man sternly.

Richard grabbed one of the man's arms and locked a cuff around a wrist. When the man continued shouting profanities, Richard shoved the man's face into the floor and put additional pressure from his knee into the man's back. The man yelped in pain as Richard grabbed the man's other wrist and locked a cuff around that wrist. The man's arms were now safely secured behind his back

"Now shut up or I'm going to make it lot worse," Richard commanded.

The man stopped shouting and Richard checked the man for weapons. Finding none, Richard rose and grabbed the man's feet. When the man started to kick, Richard kicked the man in the crotch as hard has he could.

"You want to give me trouble?," Richard asked, "You can have all the trouble you want."

The man jolted with pain and began to groan as Richard once again grabbed the man's feet and drug him belly down into the kitchen.

"Don't even think about moving," Richard said to the groaning man.

Richard aimed his revolver at the center of the bathroom door.

"Ma'am," Richard yelled, "this is Officer Decker. I

just spoke with you out on the porch. I want you to open the door slowly and come out with your hands above your head."

By now, the crying had stopped and the bathroom was silent. After a few moments of continued silence, Richard yelled,

"It's safe to come out. Drop your weapon, open the door slowly and come out with your hands above your head."

"I don't have a weapon," the woman shouted, "I'm coming out. Please don't shoot me."

The door opened slowly and the woman stepped out with her hands above her head. Richard could see blood trickling down the woman's face. The blood was coming from around both of her eyes and her mouth.

"I want you to walk into the kitchen slowly," Richard said, calmly, "Are you going to give me any trouble?"

"No," the woman said meekly.

"OK," Richard said, "I want you to step around that man there and walk toward me until I tell you to stop."

Richard backed away when the woman entered the kitchen. He watched as the woman skirted around the man as though she was expecting him to reach out and grab her at any moment. But the man just lay there groaning. The woman walked slowly toward Richard, hands up, until she was just a few feet way.

"Stop," Richard commanded, "I need to check you for weapons. Face the wall and put your hands against the wall."

Richard searched the woman and found no weapons. He pointed to a chair in the living room and told the woman to sit there. When the woman sat in the chair,

Richard told her not to move from that chair until he told her to.

"Do you understand?," Richard asked.

"Yes," the woman said and nodded.

"Is this Gerald Hansen?," Richard asked.

"Yes," the woman answered.

Richard holstered his pistol and walked over to Hansen. Richard read Hansen his Miranda rights and pulled Hansen to his feet. When Richard pushed Hansen toward the living room, Hansen moved forward cooperatively and they both exited the house. Richard secured Hansen in the back seat of his police cruiser and radioed for backup. Richard went back into the house and sat in a chair across from the woman.

"So what can you tell me about Anna Hansen?," Richard asked.

"I can tell you her real name's not Anna Hansen."

SECRETS

CHAPTER SIXTEEN

CONFESSION

"So if her name's not Anna Hansen," Richard asked with surprise, "what is it?"

"I don't know," the woman answered, "The girl thinks her name is Anna Hansen, but I know it's not."

"How do you know that?," Richard asked.

"Because Jerry told me," the woman answered.

"When did he tell you that?," Richard continued.

The woman looked down at the table and remained silent.

"You need to tell me everything you know," Richard said gently.

"Jerry told me he would kill me if I told anyone," the woman said still looking at the table.

"You need to trust me," Richard said with a reassuring voice, "If you help me, I will make sure he never hurts you again."

The woman looked at Richard with anger in her face.

"You know you can't guarantee that," the woman said, "You have no idea of what that man's capable of."

"You're right," Richard apologized, "I can't make any guarantee. I can only do my best. But is this how you want to live for the rest of your life? You need to help me if you want me to help you and Anna."

The woman sat for a moment.

"OK," the woman softly said, "I'll tell you what I know. Where do you want me to start?"

"Start by telling me your name," Richard said.

"Nina Larson," the woman answered.

"OK, Ms. Larson," Richard said "Let's start from the beginning. Tell me how you met Gerald Hansen."

"You can call me Nina," the woman began, "I first met Jerry, that's what his friends call him, at a bar a couple of years ago."

"Where was that?," Richard asked.

"Some place in North Salt Lake, along the old highway," Nina answered, "Jerry was decent looking. At first, he was very charming and nice. He bought me a drink and we seemed to hit it off right away. Jerry was new to town. He told me he had nowhere to stay and was living in his Van. He said that didn't bother him much, but that he had a fifteen-year-old daughter. It was winter time and I remember it was really cold outside. Jerry said his daughter was having a hard time and that he was worried for her. We chatted for a while and Jerry asked me if I wanted to meet his daughter. When I told him that maybe I would like to meet her some day, Jerry said he meant right then. I was surprised that his daughter was at the bar. Jerry told me she was in the van out in the parking lot. He took me out to the parking lot. His daughter was waiting for him in the van. She was a really pretty thing, but had the saddest eyes I'd ever seen. I couldn't help feeling sorry for her, so I asked Jerry if he wanted to stay with me until he got on his feet. They moved in with me that night."

"When was that exactly?," Richard asked.

"It was around the first part of December two years ago," Nina answered.

"That would be December 1999, correct?," Richard asked.

"That's right," Nina said, "At first, everything was wonderful. Jerry helped out around the house. He kept the house clean while I was at work and fixed things here and there. He even painted the house and helped out with the expenses. I started to think we might get married some day. But after awhile, things started to change."

"When did things start to change?," Richard asked.

"About four or five months after he moved in," Nina answered, "I remember it was around the first part of spring, so maybe around the end of March or first of April."

"What changed?," Richard asked.

"At first it was little things," Nina answered "Jerry started coming home drunk now and then. He would get violent when I confronted him about it. He would slap me at first. Then he started whipping me with his belt. Before I knew it, he began beating me up something terrible. That was when I told him to leave. Jerry refused to leave. He said he wouldn't leave until he was good and ready and that no woman was going to tell him what to do. One time, I picked up the telephone and started to call the cops. Jerry ripped the cord right out of the wall and told me that if I ever tried that again, he would kill me. He was so angry that he was spitting the words and his eyes were nearly popping out of their sockets. I had never seen anything like it. I was terrified. Then other things started to happen."

"Like what?," Richard prodded.

"Jerry would leave with Anna during the evening and they wouldn't return until the next morning," Nina said, "When I asked him where they had been, he beat me and told me that I would mind my own business if I knew what was good for me. There were also many times when woke up in the night and heard noises coming from Anna's room. When the noises stopped, Jerry would sneak back into our room and get back in bed. I pretended to be asleep most of the time, but one time I asked him if he went to check on the noises. Jerry said 'What noises?' I said 'The noises coming from Anna's room.' Jerry said I wasn't supposed to hear any noises and began slapping me on the sides of my head over and over again. He said it wouldn't be good for my hearing if I heard any more noises. I suspected that he was doing something bad with Anna, maybe even selling her to men, but I was too afraid to find out the truth. So I just left it alone. Then one day . . ."

Nina paused in a trance as though she were looking at something in the far distance.

"You need to tell me what happened?," Richard prompted her.

"Richard came home drunk," Nina continued, "He told Anna to go to her room. Jerry had his pants off even before he followed her into her room. He slammed the door behind him, but I could hear Anna pleading with him to leave her alone. She was saying she was too sore from the night before. I heard him beat her. I could hear that animal satisfy himself. I just sat here at the kitchen table with my head in my hands. I did nothing.

When he came out of Anna's room, I asked him how he could do that to his own daughter. He looked at me with an awful smile. Jerry told me that Anna wasn't his daughter. When I asked him what he meant, he asked me if I was both stupid and deaf. He repeated that Anna wasn't his daughter. I asked him whose daughter was she if she wasn't his. Jerry answered by saying how was he supposed to know. His exact words were, 'I took the slut right off the street. How should I know who she belongs to, but she ain't mine.' When asked more questions about Anna, he gave me the worst beating I ever got. He said that's what I got for asking too many questions. I think that's the night Anna got pregnant."

"You knew Anna was pregnant?," Richard asked.

"Yeah," Nina answered, "I don't think Jerry would have let her keep the baby, but he went to jail before he found out. By the time he got out, it was too late to get an abortion."

"What happened next?," Richard asked.

"Jerry was livid when he got out of jail and found out that Anna was pregnant," Nina said, "He called some of his friends who he'd met in jail and they came over. They gang raped her for hours on end and the next day, they did it again. That's when I decided I wasn't going to just do nothing anymore. I couldn't take it. I think I was going crazy."

"When was that?," Richard asked

"A few days before Christmas," Nina answered, "I think Jerry was hoping it would cause Anna to lose the baby. That's when I knew if Anna stayed here, she would end up dead. I knew I had to do something. I didn't care about myself anymore. I also knew Jerry would probably kill me too, but if was going to die, I didn't want to face God knowing that I just stood by and did nothing to help that girl. I waited until Jerry left the house. I remember it was the day before Christmas. I helped Anna take a bath and clean up. I told her that she needed to get out of here now while she had the chance.

At first, Anna didn't want to go. She asked me where she was supposed to go. I gave her all the money I had, which wasn't very much. I helped her load everything she had, which wasn't very much either, into her little pink 'princess suitcase.' That's what she called it. I took her to the tram station at the end of the street. I told her to get off at the Temple Square stop and that the bus station was across the street.

I told Anna to buy a ticket to Los Angeles if she could. I told her that Los Angeles is a big place and it would be easy for her to get lost there. I told her that Jerry would never be able to find her if she made it there. I told her she was pretty enough to be a movie star and that maybe I would see her in the movies one day. I said that to give her some hope. She told me she always dreamed of being an actress. I told her to get on the bus and get away from here as far and as fast as she could.

I remember we were so nervous standing at the tram station. We kept looking back towards the house expecting Jerry to show up at any moment. When we saw the head light of the tram coming toward us, we hugged each other. We were both crying. I whispered in her ear to do exactly what I had told her to do. When the tram arrived, she gave me a kiss on the cheek. The last thing Anna asked me was what Jerry was going to do to me when he found out that she was gone. I told her to not worry about that. As long as she was safe, I would be fine. I told her to get to the bus station, get on a bus and never look back. I also told her to never contact me because it would be too dangerous for her. The last time I saw her she was on that tram as it sped away."

"What did Jerry do when he found out Anna was gone?," Richard asked.

"I told him that I left the house to get groceries and when I came home, Anna was gone," Nina said, "He gave me a beating, but I don't think he knows that I helped her. He has left the house every night since then and doesn't return until morning. I think he's looking for her. I think he thinks she's still in Salt Lake. Do you know if she made it out of Salt Lake?"

"Yes," Richard said, "She made it out of Salt Lake." "Thank God for that," Nina said as her face began to return to the present.

"That's good," Nina repeated.

"Is there anything else you can tell me?," Richard asked.

"No," Nina said, "That's all I can remember."

Richard stood up and began to leave.

"Wait," Nina said, "There's one more thing. I also put a large brown envelope into her suitcase."

CHAPTER SEVENTEEN

GET-A-WAY

Dwayne B. Goode knew he had stepped into a big pile of shit the instant he hung up the telephone. He had no idea who this girl was, but the fact that the police were making an effort to search for her meant big trouble for him. Perhaps his luck had finally run out. A feeling inside of him said it was time to get out of town and lay low for a while. His original plan was to return to the Starlight Motel and snatch the girl whether she was ready to go with him or not. This didn't seem like a good idea anymore. Instead, Dwayne decided to make a quick get-a-way. He had made preparations for this eventuality some time ago. Dwayne knew that it wasn't a matter of if his past would catch up to him, but when.

In addition to the millions of dollars he had stashed in offshore bank accounts, Dwayne also had a safe house prepared in St. George, Utah. This safe house was stocked with everything Dwayne needed to stay out of sight for several months. It was also stocked with a supply of untraceable cell phones so that he could keep in touch with both his bosses and subordinates. Dwayne knew he could continue running his Las Vegas operation from St. George for at least two months, maybe even longer. Dwayne wasn't ready to take any drastic actions just yet. For all he knew, this whole thing might blow over and he would be back in Las Vegas just like nothing had happened. For now, he only needed to buy some time so he could assess the gravity of the situation.

Dwayne always made sure there wasn't a shred of evidence at his house that could connect him to any of his criminal activities. All of the legitimate information about his personal and business affairs was stored on computer servers located outside the United States. These servers were safely off limits to all law enforcement agencies that he needed to worry about. He accessed this information remotely over the internet using secret passwords. His computers were programmed to automatically delete any information about these internet sites the instant he logged off the site. This meant that if any law enforcement agency seized his computers, they wouldn't be able to access any illicit information.

The only person in the world who knew where and how to access this information was Goode himself. If any of his computers' hard drives were searched, there would only be benign letters and documents that demonstrated that he was a highly successful businessman. Dwayne was purposely involved with prominent charitable organizations in the city in order to enhance his reputation and personal contacts. His computer hard drives only contained information that would confirm he was a stellar member of the business community.

The only thing Dwayne had to fear was the girl. She had seen his face and could potentially expose him as the man he really was. Even so, the only thing the girl could pin on him was the rape. If it came to that, it would be her word against his. Who would a jury believe? A criminal running from the law or him, a man known in the community as a prominent philanthropist and business man? But Dwayne had no intention of taking any chances with the law. He had no desire to risk spending any time in jail, whether it be for one day or a hundred years. It was clear to Dwayne that the best course of action was to go to his safe house and wait things out.

Dwayne took a small suitcase out of his large bedroom closet. This suitcase had been prepared well in advance for such an occasion. He placed the suitcase on the bed and opened it up. He saw that everything was in order. The suitcase was filled with cash and a false driver's license and passport. The name on the false documents was Duane Goodey. This false name was close enough to his real name that he felt like he could never be tripped up if he ever accidentally spoke his real name. Dwayne put the false driver's license in his wallet and closed the suitcase. Dwayne wheeled the suitcase out of the bedroom and down the hallway. He entered into the great room where he saw his housekeeper, Juanita.

"I'm taking a trip," Dwayne announced, "I'm not sure when I'll be back."

"Where to?," Juanita asked with her Spanish

D. K. DeGRAW

accent.

"I don't know," Dwayne answered. "I guess wherever the wind takes me."

"That's very impulsive, Mr. Goode," Juanita said, "Why did you decide to take a trip all of a sudden?"

"I've been feeling burned out and decided I need to get away for a while," Dwayne explained. "I don't know how long I'll be gone. I'll keep in touch and let you know"

"Is there a number where I can call you while you are away?," Juanita asked.

"No," Dwayne said, "I want to be left alone so I can relax. I'll call you if I need anything."

"What if there is an emergency?" Juanita asked.

"I give you permission to handle the emergency the best way you can," Dwayne answered.

"OK," Juanita said puzzled, "But don't blame me if I don't do it right."

"You don't need to worry about that." Dwayne said, "You've been handling things around this house for a long time. You'll do just fine without me."

"Do you need help with any luggage?," Juanita asked.

"No," Dwayne said, "I've already taken care of that myself. Thanks for asking."

"Goodbye, Mr. Goode," Juanita said as Dwayne was walking toward the garage door, "I hope you have a nice and relaxing trip."

"Thanks Juanita," Dwayne shouted back.

Dwayne stepped into the garage and walked to a car that was covered by a canvass car cover. He removed the cover and revealed an ordinary mid-sized sedan. Dwayne always kept this sedan covered so that none of his staff ever saw it. That way, they would never be able to describe it to anyone. He figured that the staff probably assumed it was an exotic car, like the ones he always drove. This car was registered under the same fictitious name as Dwayne's fictitious driver's license. Dwayne opened the trunk and threw in the suitcase. He closed the trunk and walked to the driver's side door. Dwayne opened the door and slid into the car. He reached for a garage door opener that was clipped to the sun visor and pushed a button. When the garage door opened, Dwayne shifted the car into forward and drove away.

With the information Ferraro had gathered, he obtained a warrant to search Goode's house and property on Patrick Lane. Goode's house was near Pecos and Sunset in the far south end of Las Vegas. Most of the houses in this part of town were very large and situated on equally large parcels of land. Usually five acres or more. Almost all of the property owners in this area kept horses and sometimes other kinds of livestock. That was one of the primary reasons why the owners purchased these properties in the first place.

— — — — — — —

Ferraro and his team of a dozen officers arrived at the front gate of Goode's property. Ferraro got out of the car and walked to a brick pillar. He pushed a button on an intercom panel and heard the sound of a telephone ringing. Eventually, a woman with a Spanish accent answered.

"Who is there?," the woman asked.

"This is Detective Ferraro with the Metro Police," Ferraro said "I have a warrant to search this property. I need you to open the gate immediately."

"I'm sorry," the woman said with a hesitant voice, "but the owner is not here. Maybe you can come back later."

"Who am I speaking with?," Ferraro asked with a stern voice.

"My name is Juanita Lopez," the woman said even more hesitantly. "I am just the maid. I don't know if I can let you in without . . ."

"Look Ms. Lopez," Ferraro interrupted. "I have a warrant to search this property and you don't have a choice. Either you open the gate right now or we will break it down."

"OK," Juanita said after a pause, "But I hope Mr. Goode doesn't fire me for this."

"Trust me," Ferraro said. "You're doing the right thing."

The gate began to slowly open and Ferraro got back into his car. Ferraro and his team drove up the road that led to Goode's mansion. Ferraro parked the car in front of the mansion and got out. He walked to the front door of the Mansion with three officers behind him. The rest of the team got out of their vehicles and began to make a perimeter around the house. Ferraro rang the door bell. Shortly thereafter, the door opened revealing a middle-aged Hispanic woman dressed in a maid's uniform. Ferraro showed the woman the warrant and explained that they had the right to search the property. Ferraro and the three officers stepped forward and the maid stepped aside. The three officers began to spread throughout the house while Ferraro remained behind and questioned the maid

"You must be Ms. Lopez," Ferraro said.

"You can call me Juanita," the woman said, "What's happening here?"

"Nothing you need to be worried about," Ferraro attempted to reassure her, "What do you know about Mr. Goode?"

"I'm his maid," Juanita said, "He pays me on time. That's all I know."

"How long have you been his maid?," Ferraro asked.

"About ten years," Juanita answered.

"Have you ever noticed anything unusual or suspicious happening around here?," Ferraro asked.

"Like what?," Juanita asked.

"Like drug use or an unusual number of young women coming in and out of here," Ferraro answered. "Anything like that?"

"I don't know," Juanita answered, " Mr. Goode has parties with many guests several times a month. Famous people and politicians come to these parties. I guess that's unusual. He also has people and friends stay at the house when they come from out of town. Sometimes they drink a lot. I think some of these people use drugs, but I don't know much about drugs. I don't know if you think that is unusual?"

"Have you ever seen Mr. Goode use drugs?," Ferraro asked.

"No, never," Juanita answered.

"Does Mr. Goode frequently have women stay overnight with him, I mean in a sexual way?," Ferraro asked.

"Oh yes," Juanita answered. "He has his way with women, but not more than I think is unusual for a rich, single man."

"Do any of these women seem like they are not with Mr. Goode voluntarily?," Ferraro asked.

"You mean forced to be with him?," Juanita asked.

"Yes," Ferraro said.

"Oh, no," Juanita said emphatically, "These women seem to very much want to be with Mr. Goode. Since he is not particularly attractive, I think it is because he is rich. But he has no trouble finding women, that's for sure."

"You said that Mr. Goode isn't here right now," Ferraro said, "Do you know where he is?"

"No," Juanita said.

"Do you know when he left?," Ferraro asked.

"I would say about four or five hours ago," Juanita answered. In fact, it was less than two hours ago, but Juanita felt she could lie at least that much for her boss.

"Did he take anything with him?," Ferraro continued.

"I saw him take a small suitcase," Juanita answered.

"Just one?," Ferraro asked.

"That is all I saw," Juanita answered.

When Ferraro asked what the suitcases looked like, Juanita described it to him.

"Did you ask him where he was going?," Ferraro asked.

"Yes," Juanita answered.

"What did he tell you?," Ferraro asked.

"He said on a trip to relax," answered Juanita. "Wherever the wind took him were his exact words."

"Do you have a way to contact him?," Ferraro asked.

"No," Juanita answered, "He said he didn't want to be disturbed and that he would call me if he needed anything. That is all I know about his trip."

"You have no telephone number for him?," Ferraro asked suspiciously.

"That is correct," Juanita answered

Since he seemed to be getting nowhere with Juanita, Ferraro ended his interrogation and went to look around the house.

"What's the status?," Ferraro asked when he ran into an officer.

"As far as we can tell," the officer said, "this place has fifteen bedrooms and twenty bathrooms. It also has a very spacious living, dining and recreation rooms. It has a kitchen that any chef would die for, a gym and a theater. There is an Olympic sized swimming pool outside behind the house and two guest houses that appear to be about fifteen hundred square feet. There is a massive garage on the property filled with exotic cars including Ferraries, Porches, Mercedes-Benzes, Cadillacs, Aston-Martins and even a Lamborghini. If that's not enough, there's also a large stable filled with horses. I've never seen anything like this place. It's incredible. It's going to take us weeks to process the entire property, but so far, we've come up with nothing."

"What about people?," Ferraro asked.

"In addition to the maid you were talking to," the officer said, "we found a horse trainer, a couple of gardeners and a handy man. They claim they only speak Spanish."

"Are they all legal?," Ferraro asked.

"It seems so," the officer answered.

"Where are these people now?," Ferraro asked

"Officer Mendoza is interrogating them in the recreation room," the officer answered.

Ferraro could faintly hear Mendoza voice speaking in Spanish. Ferraro walked toward the sound. He found Mendoza in a huge recreation room with four Hispanic men. These men obviously made their living working outside. There was also a distinctive odor of horse manure inside the room.

"What have you learned?," Ferraro asked Mendoza.

"These guys don't seem to know shit," Mendoza answered, "well, except for the guy who smells like shit. But that's not the kind of shit we're looking for."

Ferraro chuckled in agreement as another officer walked into the room. The officer told Ferraro that he found a car cover inside the garage. The officer said this must be the cover for the car that Goode left in because the spot in the garage where he found the slip cover was now vacant. Mendoza asked the group being interrogated whether anyone knew what the car looked like. They all said that they had never seen the car because it was always covered up. They said they assumed it must be a very expensive car like the ones Goode always drove. Once the interrogation was over, it was clear that the four men knew even less about Goode than the maid did. Goode was gone and there were no leads.

SECRETS

CHAPTER EIGHTEEN

BREAKTHROUGH

Richard Decker continued interviewing Nina Larson as a team of police officers entered the house. The officers immediately went to work searching the house.

"What was in the large brown envelope that you gave to Anna?," Richard asked.

"Photographs," Nina answered.

"What kind of photographs?," Richard asked.

"Photographs of a little girl," Nina responded, "I'm not certain, but I think they were photographs of Anna before Jerry abducted her."

"Why do you think that?," Richard asked.

"The little girl in the photographs was about five or six years old," Nina said, "She had flaxen hair and it seemed like she was being stalked. The little girl in the photographs looked like she could have been Anna when she was that age.."

"Where did you get the photographs?," Richard asked.

"When Jerry went to jail," Nina answered, "I wanted to find out more about him. Who he really was and where he came from. I searched all of his things and couldn't find anything helpful. Then one day, I stumbled upon a hard-shelled, Samsonite brief case that was hidden in the basement. It was locked. I took it to a locksmith to see if he could open it."

"Could he open it?," Richard asked.

"The locksmith gave me a key that could open it," Nina answered, "When I opened the brief case, it had thousands of dollars in hundred dollar bills. I also found several large brown envelopes like the one I gave to Anna. Each one of these envelopes had photographs of a different little girl inside."

"There were photographs of more than one girl?," Richard asked to clarify.

"Yes," Nina said as she nodded, "Each of the envelopes had photographs of a different girl. All of the girls in the photographs seemed to be between three and six years old. I went through each envelope and only one of the envelopes had photographs of a girl who I thought might be Anna."

"How many envelopes were there in total?," Richard asked.

"About ten to fifteen," Nina answered, "I didn't count them."

"Where's this briefcase now?," Richard asked.

"It's in the basement where I found it," Nina said, "It's hidden in a cubby hole near the washer and dryer."

"Do you still have the key?," Richard asked.

Nina nodded.

"Are the envelopes with the photographs still in the brief case?," Richard asked.

"I think so," Nina answered, "but I haven't looked inside the brief case since Anna left."

"But the envelope containing the photographs of the girl you thought might be Anna is gone," Richard said, "You gave that envelope to Anna when she left. Is that right?."

Nina again nodded yes.

"Why did you give her the envelope?," Richard asked.

"Because I thought it might help her find out who she is and were she came from," Nina said as tears began to fall from her cheeks, "I had no idea when all of this would end. I swear to God, if I'd known you would be coming this soon, I never would have given her the envelope or helped her escape. What have I done?"

Nina was now sobbing. Richard reached out a hand and touched Nina on the shoulder.

"You have to understand," Richard said sympathetically, "If you hadn't helped Anna escape, I wouldn't be here now. You did the right thing. I just want to find her. With your help, maybe we can discover who she really is."

"Do you really think I did the right thing?," Nina asked.

"No question about it," Richard responded, "Any information you give me now could be extremely helpful. I need you to think. Can you tell me anything more about the photographs of the little girl inside the envelope that you gave to Anna?"

"Like what?," Nina asked.

"Anything," Richard said, "Any detail you can remember might be the key to discovering who she really is."

"Let me think," Nina began, "I remember the photographs were taken from a distance. It was obvious that the little girl didn't know her photograph was being taken. A few of the photographs were of the little girl playing in front of a house. There were also photographs that seemed to be taken while the girl was standing at a corner waiting with other children. Like they were waiting for a school bus. I also remember some of the photographs were taken when the girl got off a school bus. I'm pretty sure there was a school bus in the photograph. Several of the photographs seemed to be taken while the girl was walking along a street. Like she was walking to or from her house. I remember there were also some photographs of the girl near a school. Some of them were in front of the school and some of them were in the school's play ground."

"How many photographs were in the envelope?," Richard asked.

"I'd say about thirty or forty," Nina answered.

"Did the photographs reveal any clue about where these photographs were taken?," Richard asked.

"No" Nina said as she shook her head.

"Do you remember what the house looked like?," Richard asked.

"Now that you ask me," Nina answered, "Yes. I remember the house very well."

"What do you remember?," Richard asked.

"The house was definitely in a small town," Nina began, "Definitely not in a city. I remember the house had orangish colored brick."

"One story or more than one story?," Richard asked.

"One story above ground, but I could tell it had a basement," Nina continued, "It had those metal things they put around basement windows. It also had an attached two-car garage on the left side of the house. I remember there was a basketball hoop on the left side of the driveway about half way between the street and the garage. I remember the house was on a very large corner lot. There was also a very large lot behind the house. The lot behind the house had something growing in it and it also had one of those great big steel farm buildings like farmers use to store their tractors and farm equipment. I remember seeing what looked like farm equipment along the farm building, like plows or something like that."

"Can you remember anything else?," Richard continued to press, "Anything at all?"

"Yes," Anna said, "I remember there were great big tall evergreen trees, like huge Christmas trees, that ran along the left side of the property along a road. There was also a hedge of what might be lilac or snowball bushes along the right side of the property. There were also two huge trees in the front yard."

"Do you know what kind of trees were in the front yard?," Richard asked.

"No," Nina answered, "But they were leafy trees, not evergreen trees."

"Do you remember anything else?," Richard asked, "Anything, no matter how small, could be extremely helpful."

"I remember a couple of other things," Nina said, "The front yard, the side yards and a back yard between the hayfield and the house were completely covered in grass. I also remember there was an irrigation ditch that ran along the street in front of the house. I can't remember for sure if there was an irrigation ditch along the road on the left side of the house."

"Can you give me a better description?," Richard asked.

"I'll try," Nina said, "On the left side of the house, there was a street, then the row of evergreen trees, then a grassy area, then the house and driveway. In front of the house, there was a street, then the irrigation ditch next to the street, then the front yard with two big trees, then the house. On the right side, there was a row of bushes that ran from about the front of the house to a fence behind the house. That's the best I can do"

"Were there any sidewalks?," Richard asked.

"No," Nina answered, "I don't remember any sidewalks.

"What about the photograph of the girl getting off the school bus," Richard asked, "Do you remember anything about that photograph?"

"Not really," Nina answered.

"Do you remember if the bus had the name of the school district on the side?," Richard asked.

Nina paused for a moment while she racked her brain.

"It probably did, but I don't remember the name," Nina finally answered, disappointed that she couldn't be more helpful.

"What about the photographs of the girl at school?," Richard moved on, "Do you remember anything about the school?"

Nina gave a detailed description of the school like

she had given of the house.

"You told me earlier that some of these photographs were taken in front of the school. Did you see the name of the school?"

"No," Nina said as she shook her head, "Not that I remember. I'm sorry I can't be more helpful."

"You have no need to apologize," Richard said, "You can't imagine how helpful you've been. With the information you just gave me, I feel extremely hopeful that I will be able to discover Anna's true identity if Anna is, in fact, the girl in those photographs."

"Do you really believe that?," Nina said, beginning to feel hopeful herself.

"Absolutely," Richard said emphatically.

"Do you think you could describe what you remember about the house and the school to a sketch artist?," Richard asked.

"I'm sure I could," Nina answered.

Richard asked Nina to take him to where the brief case was hidden. Nina led Richard down to the basement. She showed Richard where the brief case was and gave him the key. Richard took Nina back upstairs and told the first officer he ran into to take good care of her. Before Richard left, he again assured Nina that the information she had given was extremely helpful, beyond what she could imagine. He handed Nina his card and told her to call him if there was anything he could do for her. He gave Nina a hug.

"I'm so sorry about what you have gone through," Richard said, "I'm sure everything will get better for you from now on."

"What are you going to do about Jerry?," Nina asked.

"I'll do everything in my power to make sure he never bothers you again," Richard said, "I'm hoping that with the information you gave me, I'll find enough evidence to put him away for the rest of his life."

Richard found a pair of latex gloves, went back down to the basement and retrieved the briefcase. Richard returned to his office and opened the brief case. He found that it was full of cash just as Nina had described. Richard put the cash into an evidence bag, removed the large brown envelopes and put them on his desk. He put the empty brief case into an evidence bag and the key into a separate evidence bag.

Richard sat down at his desk and opened the first brown envelope. It contained twenty-eight photographs of a girl who appeared to be about three years old. The little girl had red hair and a complexion that was as white as snow. There were photographs of the girl being pushed in a shopping cart at a grocery store. There were also photographs of the girl being pushed in a stroller at the mall. Another photograph was of the girl being removed from a car in front of a house. Richard returned the photographs into the brown envelope and put the envelope into an evidence bag. Richard repeated this process fifteen more times and found similar photographs of various girls, each between what appeared to be about three and six years old. None of the photographs in the envelopes looked like girls that could have been a younger version of Anna. Unfortunately, Anna's envelope was now missing.

Richard sent the bags of evidence to the crime lab for processing and ordered several copies of the photographs that were in the envelopes. He also sent the photograph of Anna he had received from Ferraro to the crime lab and requested a computer generated image of what Anna would have looked like when she was about five years old. A few days later, Richard received several copies of the sketch artist's rendition of the house and school that were made from the description Nina gave from her memory. He also received several copies of the computer-generated image of Anna as a five year old and the photographs that were in the envelopes. Richard posted a copy of this information into the criminal investigation data base. This information would be available to all law enforcement agencies in the country. Richard placed a copy of everything he had compiled in his satchel and drove to the Salt Lake County Jail.

When Richard arrived at the Jail, he was escorted into a private cell where Hansen was waiting for him. Hansen was sitting on a metal bench that was secured to a concrete floor. Hansen's hands were handcuffed to the bench so that Hansen's movements were severely restricted. There was a metal table in front of Hansen that was also secured to the concrete floor. A man in a suit, who Richard recognized as a prominent defense attorney, was sitting on the bench next to Hansen.

"This Hansen fellow must have some stash of cash to be able to afford this guy," Richard thought to himself.

"What do you want, PIG?," Hansen yelled when Richard walked into the jail cell.

The attorney turned to Hansen and said,

"You need to remain calm like we talked about. Let me do the talking. You just sit there and listen."

The attorney turned to Richard.

"Hello Mr. Decker," the attorney said, "I'm representing Mr. Hansen. What can I do for you?"

"It's nice to see you again, Mr. Clarkson," Richard

said, "I have some questions that I want your client to answer."

"I'M NOT ANSWERING ANY OF YOUR F***ING QUESTIONS," Hansen screamed even louder as he tried to stand up. Hansen swore a string of curse words when he remembered that he was restrained to the bench.

Clarkson turned to Hansen.

"I told you to remain calm and quiet," Clarkson said with a firm voice, "My job is to do the talking. Your job is to sit there and be quiet. Understand?"

Hansen nodded his head. Clarkson then turned to Richard.

"As I was saying," Clarkson said, "how can I help you?"

Richard took out the papers from his satchel and spread them on the table in front of Clarkson and Hansen.

WHAT ARE YOU DOING WITH MY F***ING STUFF?," Hansen screamed even louder as he violently pulled on his handcuffs, "WHAT GIVES YOU THE . . ."

"YOU NEED TO KEEP YOUR MOUTH SHUT," Clarkson screamed at Hansen, "If you open your mouth one more time, I'm walking out of here and you can find another attorney. Do you understand me?"

When Hansen calmed down and remained subdued for a few seconds, Richard continued.

"I want to know about these photographs," Richard said pointing to the photographs on the table.

"What are these?," Clarkson asked with a laugh.

"These are photographs that were found in your client's briefcase," Richard said.

"So what?," Clarkson said, "First of all, I'm not agreeing that these photographs were taken from a brief case owned by my client. For all I know, the brief case could belong to anyone. Second, supposing it is my client's brief case, there's nothing illegal about taking photographs. Besides, those three, those aren't photographs. What are they?"

"Your client is a filthy child abductor and pervert," Richard said staring directly into Hansen's eyes.

Hansen made no attempt to look away.

"Your client is a slimy sexual predator," Richard continued, hoping to invoke another outburst from Hansen.

But other than the rage that flashed in Hansen's face, Hansen remained silent as he had been instructed.

"You can rant all you want," Clarkson said, "but I want to know about those three, what should I call them, . . . cartoons?"

"Your slime bag client," Richard said pointing to the computer-generated image of the five-year-old Anna, "abducted that little girl from her family."

Richard pointed to the illustration of the house and said,

"That's the house she lived in."

Richard then pointed to the illustration of the school and said,

"That's the school she went to."

Richard then pointed to the recent photograph of Anna that Ferraro had sent him.

"That's the little girl now," Richard said, "That photograph was taken within the last couple of weeks. I have your client right in my cross hairs and I am going to take him down."

Richard saw a moment of recognition in Hansen's face when Hansen looked at Anna's photo.

"I assume you have proof of that other than these photographs and cartoons," Clarkson said, "Let me talk to the girl and maybe we can make a deal."

Richard remained silent.

"Oh," Clarkson said, "you don't actually have the girl. I guess that's too bad for you. If all you have are these photographs and fancy cartoons, I expect you to release my client immediately. They obviously have nothing to do with your alleged victim. As for your cartoons, those are nothing but fairy tales as far as I'm concerned."

Hansen had a big grin on his face, obviously liking what his attorney was saying.

"Your client abducted a helpless little girl," Richard seethed, "and I'm going to wipe that smile of his face and put him away if it's the last thing I do."

"Good luck with that," Clarkson said, "but this conversation is now over. Call me when you have some real evidence."

Richard looked at Hansen.

"I'm going to put you away for life," Richard said, "Mark my words."

"I said this conversation is over," Clarkson stated firmly, "You don't have squat on my client and we both know it."

"The conversation may be over," Richard said, "But here's a warrant authorizing me to take your clients DNA."

"YOUR'RE NOT TAKING ANY DNA," Hansen screamed as Clarkson scanned the document.

"Your client can either do this voluntarily, or I can have some officers come in here and take his DNA involuntarily," Richard said, "I suggest you talk to your client."

"You don't have a choice," Clarkson said to Hansen

"DON'T YOU UNDERSTAND ENGLISH?," Hansen screamed, "I'M NOT GIVING ANY F***ING DNA."

"That suits me fine," Richard said.

Richard signaled for the officers to come into the cell. One burly officer held and restrained Hansen's head while another took a swab from inside Hansen's mouth. The officer holding Hansen's head inflicted as much pain on Hansen as he believed he could get away with.

"I'M GOING TO F****ING SUE YOU FOR THAT," Hansen screamed, "YOU CAN'T GET AWAY WITH THAT."

"By the way," Richard said to Clarkson, "I think your client has some anger management issues. Maybe you should get that taken care of before the trial."

When Richard returned to his office, he was still visibly angry from his visit to the jail. But his face immediately brightened when he read a note on his desk.

"We have a hit on the girl."

CHAPTER NINETEEN

REVELATION

As promised, Roger Hepner took Gabe to work with him when he reopened his jewelry store after the first of the year. Roger had a modest store on the corner of River Road and Main Street. Even though it was small, the store had good window frontage along both roads and there were several display cases along the glass so strollers by could window shop.

The jewelry store had very little business in January because people had spent themselves out of money during the Christmas season. This reality was causing Roger a lot of stress. He had grave doubts about whether the store could survive until Spring. But if by some miracle it did, wedding ring sales would pick up assuring that the store would survive for at least another year. Most of the store's business during this slow down after Christmas season was routine work such as resizing rings or repairing watches or jewelry. There were also a few people who traded up the jewelry they had been given as Christmas gifts. But this type of business didn't even bring in enough money to cover the rent and utilities on the store, let alone feed his family.

Roger discovered that Gabe had a photographic memory. Gabe seemed to learn things instantly and never forgot anything. Because of his remarkable memory, Gabe had already acquired a workable vocabulary and could communicate at least as well as Roger's five-year-old son, Carter. Gabe got along famously with his children and they already loved him. Even Mary seemed to be somewhat smitten by him in her cold, hard way. Gabe had become part of the family, albeit, one more mouth to feed. Being as large as he was, Gabe could eat a lot of food, which was a constant source of irritation to Mary.

When Gabe first came to the store with Roger, he would follow closely behind Roger wherever Roger went. This was extremely annoying to both Roger and his customers. Roger put a stool next to his work bench in the back room and told Gabe to sit on the stool and stay there. Roger thought how ironic it was that you spend the first few years of child's life teaching the child how to walk and talk, and then spend the next ten years telling the child to sit down and be quiet. After a couple of hours, Roger noticed that Gabe seemed to be in serious distress. Roger asked Gabe what was wrong.

"I have to go pee pee," Gabe answered.

Roger laughed as he thought about how exacting he had to be when giving instructions to a child.

"What I meant to say," Roger explained, "is that

you have to either stay in the workroom or you can go to the bathroom, but you can't go out into the sales floor. Understand?"

Gabe nodded and quickly skedaddled into the bath room.

When Roger wasn't helping a customer, he would sit at his work bench and do his work. Gabe sat on his stool closely watching everything Roger did. Gabe also asked questions about everything. What's gold? What's diamond? What's this? What's that? Where does that come from? How is that made? What does that do? Why are you doing that? Whenever Roger answered a question, Gabe would say,

"Oh,"

and immediately ask the next question. Gabe also studied everything he could find in the work room, including sketches of jewelry Roger had designed in the past. Gabe asked questions about that too. How do you make these? Why do you make these? What do you do with them? Even though Gabe's constant questions were extremely irritating to Roger in the beginning, he soon found that he enjoyed Gabe's company. His days seem to go by much faster and the conversations added new words to Gabe's vocabulary. In a short time, Gabe was talking almost fluent English. Near the end of the month, Roger returned to the work room after helping a customer. Roger found Gabe sitting at the work bench working on something.

"What are you doing?," Roger asked with alarm.

Gabe jumped with a start.

"I haven't left the work room," Gabe answered, "I'm still in the work room like you said."

"I know," Roger said a little bit calmer, "But what

are you doing?"

Gabe handed Roger a ring that had been left for repair. Roger inspected the ring and found to his amazement, that the repair had been made flawlessly. Roger began to wonder how extensive Gabe's skills actually were.

"Do you want to make a ring?," Roger asked.

"Yes," Gabe answered enthusiastically.

"Would you like to make a ring for yourself?," Roger asked.

"For me?," Gabe asked questioningly.

"Yes, for you," Roger said.

"Oh, no," Gabe said slowly, "I want to make a ring for Mrs. Mary."

Gabe had taken to calling Roger's wife Mrs. Mary. Upon hearing Mary's name, Roger thought how ironic it was that his wife's name was Mary since she was usually anything but merry. But a tear came to Roger's eye because he was so touched by Gabe's sincerity.

"OK," Roger said, "Why don't you make a ring for Mrs. Mary."

Roger watched as Gabe sketched out an amazing design that seemed to be several people interlocked together. He then watched as Gabe created the ring in wax, then made a mold. Gabe melted batch after batch of gold and silver, which he poured into the mold. When the gold was cooled, Gabe took the ring out of the mold. He then picked up tool after tool from the bench and worked on the ring. Finally, Gabe polished the ring.

With a big smile on his face, Gabe handed the finished ring to Roger. Roger was completely astonished as he examined the ring. It had various shades of gold and silver colors. It was the most exquisitely crafted ring

Roger had ever seen in his life. It seemed extremely delicate, but when Roger tried to squeeze the ring with his fingers, it was extremely rigid and sturdy. What's more, when Roger weighed the ring, Gabe had only used a quarter of an ounce of precious ore. Gabe had transformed gold and silver that were worth about a hundred dollars into something that was worth at least ten times that amount. It seemed miraculous and Roger was left speechless.

Roger closed the store early that day and he and Gabe went home. When they arrived home early from work, Mary went into a panic.

"What's wrong?," she asked, "Why are you home early."

"Nothing's wrong," Roger said with a big smile, "We have something we want to show you."

"What is it?," she asked, "Did you win the lottery?".

The grin left Roger's face.

"No," Roger said with a dejected voice, "Why do you have to be so cynical all the time. We came home early because Gabe made something special for you and we couldn't wait to show you."

Mary's first thought was that Gabe had made her something simple like a paper airplane. Roger told her to hold out her hand and close her eyes.

"OK, Gabe," Roger said, "Why don't you put it on her finger."

After Gabe put the ring on Mary's finger, she opened her eyes and stared at the ring in amazement.

"You want me to believe Gabe made this?," Mary laughed, "This ring's amazing. Come on. Tell me the truth. Where did you get it?"

"I'm telling you the truth," Roger said as his wife

took off the ring to inspect it, "Gabe made it."

Mary also found the ring to be extremely rigid and durable. This surprised her considering how delicate the ring looked. Mary continued to inspect the ring as Roger related the events of the day.

"It looks like there are people all mixed together as one," Mary said, "Does that mean something special, Gabe?"

"Yes," Gabe said, "That's all of us, you, your husband, your children and me, we are all together as one."

Mary looked at Gabe and smiled at him. As she did, Gabe seemed to shine as though he were an angel. In the time it took Mary to blink, Gabe returned to looking like an ordinary person. For the first time in her life, Mary seemed speechless. Mary turned and walked away.

"We still need money," Roger heard Mary say.

A couple of days later, an elderly man and woman walked into the store. Roger went out to the sales floor to greet them. They seemed to be especially affluent. They were immaculately dressed in tailored clothing. Roger couldn't help but notice that the woman was wearing jewelry worth tens of thousands of dollars. The man himself was wearing two very expensive looking rings and a top end Rolex watch.

"Hello," Roger greeted them cheerfully, "I'm Roger. Are you looking for anything in particular that I can help you with?"

"Yes," the man replied, "We'll be celebrating our fiftieth wedding anniversary in less than a week. I'm looking for a ring for my wife. By the way, I'm John O'Reilly and this is my wife, Susan."

"We have many rings to choose from here," Roger said, "Do you need some time to look around?"

"No," O'Reilly said, "I'm not looking for an ordinary ring. I want to have a ring made that is specially designed for the occasion."

"I also design and make custom jewelry here," Roger replied even more cheerfully hoping for a larger than normal profit.

"Yes," O'Reilly replied, "We were told that. That's why we came here."

"Let's start by having you describe the ring you want made," Roger said, "I'll go get my sketch book."

As Roger turned to go to the work room, O'Reilly said,

"Well that's the problem. It seems my wife has a very particular idea about what she wants, but nobody seems to be able to make sense of her description. I think we've been to every jewelry store in both St. George and Las Vegas and nobody has been able to get it right. Somebody told us about you and it seems that you're our last hope."

"Why don't you have her describe what she wants and I'll see if I can help," Roger said, "Let me get my sketch book. I'll be right back."

Roger returned with his sketch book and Susan O'Reilly began to describe the ring.

"I want a diamond for every year we have been married and I want some of the diamonds on top and some of the diamonds on the bottom and some in the middle," Mrs. O'Reilly said, "I want them to form a crescendo of magnificence that will radiate outward where they will be met in unison with emeralds and rubies to represent our children and grandchildren."

As Mrs. O'Reilly was talking, Roger's eyes began to glaze over and the only crescendo he envisioned was his hope for a hugely profitable sale spiraling downward into a crash. Mrs. O'Reilly continued on oblivious Roger's visible bewilderment until her eyes began to focus on something behind Roger. She slowly stopped talking and caught her breath.

"I think that man behind you wants to talk to you," she said pointing to something behind Roger.

Roger turned around and saw Gabe standing in the doorway of the work room. Gabe was motioning for Roger to come to him. Roger walked over to Gabe.

"What do you want?," Roger whispered impatiently, "Can't you see that I'm busy?"

Gabe handed Roger a piece of paper with a sketch on it. Roger looked at the sketch and nearly fell to his knees. He steadied himself against a nearby safe, then walked back to Mrs. O'Reilly. Roger held out the sketch. He could see that she was looking directly into Gabe's eyes and didn't even notice Roger at all. When Roger looked back at Gabe, it seemed like Gabe had been transformed into an angel, but when Roger blinked, it was just Gabe standing in the doorway.
Roger turned back to Mrs. O'Reilly.

"Is this what you had in mind?," Roger asked.

Mrs. O'Reilly looked at the sketch and squealed with delight.

"Johnny," Mrs. O'Reilly said enthusiastically, "This is exactly what I'm looking for. I'm so happy. It's like they could read my mind. I can't believe they understood me perfectly."

O'Reilly looked at the sketch.

"This is gorgeous," he said, "I had no idea you were

so talented. I always thought this was a second rate store. Can you really pull this off?"

"Of course we can," Roger said with more confidence than he really had.

"If you can," O'Reilly said, "I'll pay a premium given the short time frame. But if you disappoint my wife in any way, I'll make sure the entire town hears about it and do my best to put you out of business. How much would a ring like this cost?"

"Let me get a total for you," Roger said.

It seemed to Roger that his whole body was shaking out of control. Roger went into the work room and discussed the ring with Gabe. He calculated the amount of gold, platinum and jewels that would be needed and added it up. The total for the sale added up to more than one hundred and fifty thousand dollars. That was more than Roger's total sales from the entire previous year. His profit alone would be more than he had made the previous three years. Roger didn't know if he had the courage to tell the man, but Gabe gave him a reassuring nod and nudged him toward the show room. Roger took a deep breath and walked back into the show room. Roger handed the estimate to Mr. O'Reilly.

"I do an honest day's work for an honest day's pay," Roger said, "I take pride in not overcharging for my work, but this is the total I came up with."

O'Reilly looked at the estimate.

"Is that all?," he exclaimed, "I thought it would be a lot more than that. Don't worry, there's an extra ten thousand if you do the job right. Nothing is too good for my wonderful wife. But the ring has to be ready by no later than Monday. Are you sure you can do it by then?"

Since it was already Wednesday afternoon, Roger

looked at Gabe questioningly and said, "Can we do this by Monday?"

Gabe nodded and said yes.

"OK," Roger said, "It will be ready on Monday by four in the afternoon. Will that be soon enough?"

"That will be fine," O'Reilly said, "but don't disappoint us."

With that, John O'Reilly and his wife walked out of the store. Roger turned to Gabe.

"You can do this, Right?," Roger said just before he fainted.

When Roger came to, he and Gabe closed the store and went home early. When they arrived home, Mary took one look at Roger's deathly pale face and knew something terrible had happened.

"Are we finished?," she asked somberly.

Roger sat down and told her about the day's stunning event. Mary couldn't believe their good fortune. She was certain that it was too good to be true. For the next two days, Roger worked mostly in a daze. Roger met with customers and stayed out of Gabe's way while Gabe worked on the ring. When they left work on Friday, Roger asked Gabe if the ring was ready.

"Not yet," Gabe said, "but I promise it will be finished on time."

Roger spent the happiest weekend with his family that he had spent in a long, long, time. Roger was still nervous, but the whole family was energized by the luck they had experienced since Gabe arrived. For the entire weekend, Mary's mood matched her name. On Monday afternoon, Gabe announced he was finished. Roger ran to the work room where Gabe held out not a ring, but a broach.

"What's this?," Roger asked in horror.

"It's a funeral broach," Gabe said with a smile.

"A funeral broach," Roger yelled.

This was the first time Gabe had ever heard Roger raise his voice in anger.

"A funeral broach," Roger yelled again, "What have you done to me? You have destroyed me. Didn't you hear what the man said he would do if we disappointed him? What am I going to do now. It's too late to fix this."

"I'm done. I'm done," Roger kept repeating as he sat at his work bench and wept in despair.

About a half hour later, the door bell sounded and a woman walked in. Roger rose from his chair and tried to compose himself. He walked into the show room and before he could say a word, the woman said,

"My father, John O'Reilly, sent me here. He told me that he asked you to make a ring for my mother. But something tragic happened last night. My mother passed away unexpectedly."

"That's horrible," Roger said looking nearly as devastated as the woman, "I'm so sorry for your loss."

"Thank you," the woman said, obviously trying her best to remain composed, "It's a very difficult time for our family, but we felt blessed because the whole family was in town for the anniversary party. We were so blessed that we could all be together for her last hours on Earth. We had such a wonderful last weekend together."

"I'm happy to hear that," Roger said with empathy.

"My mother passed away quickly," the woman continued, "so she didn't suffer much. We are also grateful for that. I need to get going, but my father said he no longer needs the ring. He wants to know if you can make something appropriate for her funeral that would be just as beautiful as the ring. Something like a broach. It would need to be finished in two days in time for the funeral viewing. My father said he is so sorry to put you out like this, so he sent this check for twenty-five thousand dollars as appreciation for your efforts. In addition to the twenty-five thousand dollars, he will pay you the same amount he was going to pay you for the ring if you can make something for the funeral. Can you do that?"

"Yes," Roger said completely stunned, "We CAN do that."

"Thank you so much," the woman said thankfully and she quickly left the store.

Roger looked at Gabe in amazement.

"Exactly who is this man?," Roger thought.

SECRETS

D. K. DeGRAW

CHAPTER TWENTY

AWAKENING

"I'm sorry," Sergeant Jeffrey Johnson said, "No one has been reported missing who matches the description of - - what did you say his name is?"

"Gabe," answered Roger.

"That's right, Gabe," repeated Johnson, "May I come in?"

Roger invited Johnson to sit in his living room where they were soon joined by Mary.

"I would like to do some follow up work on Gabe," Johnson explained, "By the way, I never got his last name."

"He's never mentioned a last name," Roger responded.

"He's never told you what his last name is?," Johnson asked.

"No," Roger answered, "We only know him by Gabe."

"To start with," Johnson continued, "I would like to take his finger prints and run them through the NCIS database and see if anything pops up. Could I meet with Gabe?"

"What's the NCIS database?," Roger asked.

"NCIS stands for National Crime Investigation System," Johnson said, "It's a system that all law enforcement agencies in the county have access to."

"Why do you want to run his fingerprints through a criminal investigation system?," Roger asked. "I'm sure he's not a criminal."

"Gabe doesn't need to be a criminal for his fingerprints to be in the system," Johnson explained, "Gabe's fingerprints could be in the system for several reasons, such as he applied for a professional or child care license. I'm just trying to explore every option that's available to me. That's all."

"All right," Roger said "He's playing with the children out back. I'll go get him. Perhaps it would be easier to take his fingerprints in the kitchen."

Johnson agreed.

"Why don't you and Mary go to the kitchen and wait for us there," Roger said.

Mary and Johnson went into the kitchen. Johnson started setting up his finger printing equipment.

"So what's going to happen to Gabe?," Mary asked.

"I can take him with me if he's been too much trouble," Johnson said.

"Oh, no," Mary said quickly, "I didn't mean that. He's been no trouble at all. I meant what will happen to him if you never find out who he is?"

"I don't know," Johnson said, "He seems to be over eighteen years old. I guess that will be entirely up to him. I suppose he can go wherever he pleases."

"I would just hate to see anything bad happen to him," Mary said, "That's all I meant."

Roger walked into the kitchen with Gabe. Johnson explained to Gabe that he wanted to take his fingerprints and what that would entail. Gabe seemed totally confused by Johnson's explanation and looked at Roger for reassurance. Roger assured Gabe that it wouldn't hurt and that everything would be all right. Roger told Gabe to hold out his hand, which Gabe did. Johnson took hold of Gabe's wrist, then extended each finger one by one as he took Gabe's fingerprints. This was followed by a complete palm print. Johnson repeated this process with Gabe's other hand. Johnson also took a DNA sample from Gabe by swabbing Gabe's inner cheek. When Johnson was finished, Gabe washed his hands in the sink and went back outside.

Roger and Mary walked Johnson to the front door where Johnson assured them that he would let them know if anything turned up. Mary was secretly hoping that Johnson's search would find nothing, but didn't say anything. Johnson walked out the door and Roger closed the door behind him. Roger and Mary walked hand in hand to the living room couch and sat down close to each other.

"So who do you think Gabe is?," Mary asked.

"I have no idea," said Roger, "But whoever he is, I wish I could find ten more just like him. I still can't believe what happened with the O'Reillys."

"Neither can I," said Mary, "But it's more than that. I've had a couple of weird experiences with him."

"What do you mean by weird?," Roger asked.

"There's been a couple of times when it seemed like for just a split second, Gabe seemed to look like an angel," Mary said, "Do you think he's an angel?"

Roger didn't want to bring up his experience just yet, so he laughed.

"He's certainly our angel," Roger said, "I can't deny that. Things have certainly been going our way ever since he arrived."

"I'm serious, Roger," Mary said, "Do you believe in real angels?"

"I suppose so," Roger said, "but do you seriously think Gabe's an angel? What would make you think that?"

"The first time was on Christmas day," Mary said, "After I told Sergeant Johnson that Gabe could stay with us, I looked at him and he smiled at me. For just a fraction of a second, he seemed to shine like an angel. I mean he seemed to be as white as snow and radiant. But it was so brief I thought I just imagined it. Then it happened again just the other day."

"What?," Roger asked.

"The same thing," Mary said, "Gabe asked me why I was so sad. When I told him that I wasn't sad, he asked me why I always look sad. I told him that's just the way I am. I told him most of the time I'm happy. He said if I was happy most of the time, why was I always unhappy with you and the children. I told him I'm not always unhappy with you and the children, but he insisted that I was. I started to feel really angry towards him. Gabe told me that I was always critical of you and the children. That I always said that none of you could ever do anything right. Gabe said that I always pointed out the bad things about you and the children, but never praised anyone for the good things they did.

When I told him that's how I was raised, he asked me what I meant. I told Gabe that my mother always criticized everything I did and told me that I never did anything right. I told him I suppose I learned to be that way from my mother. When I said that, he smiled at me and for just a tiny second, he shone just like an angel again. The same as I saw before. Gabe said he understood. He said I wanted to teach that to my children since that was what my mother taught me. That really made me angry. I told him that I didn't want to teach that to my children.

Gabe told me that I was wrong. He said that just that very day, the children were giving me trouble and he asked them why they wanted to give their mother trouble like that. He asked them why they didn't obey without all the fuss. The children told him it didn't matter what they did because it wouldn't ever be good enough for me. He also said I keep trying to teach that lesson to you as well, but that you won't learn because your parents must have taught you something different. Do you think Gabe's right?"

"Do you seriously expect me to answer that question?," Roger said with surprise.

"Yes!," Mary said, "I want to know the truth. Do you really think that I'm just like my mother and that I'm passing that onto our children? I have never thought about it that way."

"Do you want me to be honest?," Roger asked.

"No," Mary said sarcastically, "I want you to lie to me."

"OK," Roger continued reluctantly, "But remember

you asked for the truth. I never thought anyone would have the guts to tell you the truth to your face. I know I didn't. Gabe's right about the children and about me. He's also right that my parents taught me something different."

"What were you taught?," Mary asked.

"My father struggled all of his life just like us," Roger explained, "But no matter how hard or bad things got, he never quit. He never gave up. That's what I was taught. My father used to say things like 'you haven't quit until you quit trying' and 'the tough get going when the going gets tough.' I remember he had this quote from Vince Lombardi"

"Who's Vince Lombardi?," Mary interrupted.

"I can't believe you don't know who Vince Lombardi is," Roger said, "He was a legendary coach of the Green Bay Packers"

"Is that a football team?," Mary asked.

"Yes," Roger laughed, "Lombardi said winners never quit and quitters never win. I remember my dad made me memorize this poem written by a guy named D. H. Groberg called 'The Race.' The poem went like this:

"Quit, give up, you're beaten"
They shout at you and plead
"There's just too much against you
This time you can't succeed".

And as I start to hang my head
In front of failures' face
My downward fall is broken by
The memory of a race

And hope refills my weakened will

SECRETS

As I recall that scene
Or just the thought of that short race
Rejuvenates my being

Children's race, young boys
Young men, how I remember well
Excitement sure, but also fear
It wasn't hard to tell

They all lined up so full of hope
Each thought to win that race
Or tie for first, or if not that
At least take second place

The fathers watched from off the side
Each cheering for his son
And each boy hoped to show his dad
That he could be the one

The whistle blew and off they went
Young hearts and hopes afire
To win and be the hero there
Was each young boys desire

And one boy in particular
Whose dad was in the crowd
Was running near the lead and thought
"My dad will be so proud"

But as they speeded down the field
Across a shallow dip
The little boy who thought to win
Lost his step and slipped

Trying hard to catch himself
With hands flew out to brace

And amid the laughter of the crowd
He fell flat on his face

But as he fell his dad stood up
And showed his anxious face
Which to the boy so clearly said
"Get up and win the race"

He quickly rose, no damage done
Behind a bit that's all
And ran with all his might and mind
To make up for the fall

So anxious to restore himself
To catch up and to win
His mind went faster than his legs
He slipped and fell again

He wished then that he had quit before
With only one disgrace
"I'm hopeless as a runner now
I shouldn't try to race"

But in the laughing crowd he searched
And found his fathers face
That steady look which said again
"Get up and win the race"

So up he jumped to try again
Ten yards behind the last
If I'm going to gain those yards he thought
I've got to move real fast

Exerting everything he had
He regained eight or ten
But trying hard to catch the lead

SECRETS

He slipped and fell again

Defeat, he lay there silently
A tear dropped from his eye
There's no sense running anymore
Three strikes, I'm out, why try?

The will to rise had disappeared
All hope had fled away
So far behind so error prone
A loser all the way

'"I've lost, so what", he thought
I'll live with my disgrace
But then he thought about his dad
Whom soon he'd have to face

"Get up" the echo sounded low
"Get up" and take your place
You were not meant for failure here
"Get up", and win the race

With borrowed will "Get up" it said
"You haven't lost at all"
For winning is no more than this
To rise each time you fall

So up he rose to run once more
And with a new commit
He resolved, that win or lose
At least he shouldn't quit

So far behind the others now
The most he'd ever been
Still he'd give it all he had
And run as though to win

Three times he'd fallen, stumbling
Three times he'd rose again
Too far behind to hope to win
He still ran to the end

They cheered the winning runner
As he crossed the line first place
Head high and proud and happy
No falling, no disgrace

But when the fallen youngster
Crossed the line, last place
The crowd gave him the greater cheer
For finishing the race

And even though he came in last
With head bent low, unproud
You would have thought he'd won the race
To listen to the crowd

And to his dad he sadly said
"I didn't do too well"
"To me you won", his father said
"You rose each time you fell"

He also had this quote from Theodore Roosevelt that he framed and hung on the wall. I'll never forget it. It went like this.

It is not the critic who counts: not the man
who points out how the strong man stumbles
or where the doer of deeds could have done
better. The credit belongs to the man who is
actually in the arena, whose face is marred
by dust and sweat and blood, who strives
valiantly, who errs and comes up short again

and again, because there is no effort without error or shortcoming, but who knows the great enthusiasms, the great devotions, who spends himself for a worthy cause; who, at the best, knows, in the end, the triumph of high achievement, and who, at the worst, if he fails, at least he fails while daring greatly, so that his place shall never be with those cold and timid souls who knew neither victory nor defeat.

"That's what I was taught," Roger concluded, "I swear I was brainwashed on stuff like that."

"You've never told me that before," Mary said.

"That's because you've never asked before," Roger said with a laugh.

"At least it was a good brainwashing, my poor little husband," Mary said as she laughed and jiggled Roger's cheeks with her fingers.

Roger laughed with her and said, "I don't know whether it was a good brainwashing or not, but I know it was a well-intentioned brain washing. Now that I think about it, I might have learned the wrong lesson. Maybe the lesson to be learned is that it's a good thing to never quit in life, never quit trying, but perhaps it's a good thing to quit doing something that isn't working and to try something else instead."

Mary looked directly into Roger's eyes.

"I must confess," she said, "it drives me nuts when you act way too optimistically and unrealistically for the situation. But now I think I understand where you're coming from. I also remember how much I admired this about you when we met. I wished I had even half of your optimism, enthusiasm and courage. I remember how much I wished that some of you would rub off on me. It's ironic that the same thing that I admired in you and attracted me to you in the beginning is the same thing that seemed to drive a wedge between us after we got married. But I never realized how critical I was being and how I was hurting both you and the children until I spoke with Gabe. It must be awful for all of you."

"To be honest with you," Roger said, "I remember how grounded you seemed to be when we first met and how much I admired that about you. I know I can be a space cadet from time to time and wished that I could be a little more grounded to mother Earth. I really love you and so do the children. Maybe we need to go about things a little bit differently from now on."

"Do you really think we can do that?," Mary asked, "My mother always said people never change. I think her exact words were 'a leopard never changes its spots'."

"Well," Roger said, "I think there are aspects about each of us that we can't change. I know I'm not going to get any younger and my eyes will always be brown. But now that we're beginning to see more clearly? Yes, I think we can change. What do you think?"

"I think we've changed a little even tonight," Mary said as she kissed him and gave him a hug, "I hope this is just the beginning."

It had been a long time since Mary had loved her husband as much as she did at that moment.

"At least," Mary added, "I know I've changed. I can feel it."

"By the way," Roger said, "I saw it too."

"Saw what?," Mary asked.

"The angel thing."

SECRETS

CHAPTER TWENTY-ONE

DEBUT

"Our next pretty lady is making her professional debut," the announcer said with a southern drawl, "Don't be stingy with your wallets, boys, because we don't want to scare her off on her first night."

The announcer chuckled and added, "So lets give a warm and generous welcome to Miss Amber Gould!"

Amber stood behind the curtain like a spectator until Kat gave her a shove from behind. Having been Amber Gould for such a short time, she forgot that the announcer was calling her name. When Kat learned that Amber was accidentally using the name Anna from time to time around the house, Kat angrily told Amber and the other girls that they needed to forget that name. She said that Anna didn't exist any more. The only person they knew went by the name Amber Gould. Kat told the girls to never, ever, forget that. Anna, or rather, Amber, automatically cringed when Kat walked over to her. But instead of a beating, Kat just looked at her sympathetically.

"That name can get you killed," Kat said, "Do you understand me?"

Amber nodded and said, "Yes."

That was the end of the incident and the first time Amber had been punished by words and looks alone. This, along with the fact that Amber had been treated very well at the house, made Amber want to please Kat all the more. Amber worked very hard to learn everything the girls taught her and practiced the various steps and moves from morning until evening. Before the second week was up, Kat could see that Amber was ready to perform.

But now it was time to actually perform in front of a real audience. Amber couldn't help feeling nervous as she heard the sounds of men whistling and hooting from the other side of the curtain. She was deep in thought as she reflected upon her past. Amber wasn't overly squeamish about what she was about to do because of what she had gone through with Gerald Hansen. It was more like a feeling of remorse. She hoped she would never have to do anything like this again. But so far, this was the easiest thing she had ever had to do and by far, was the best she had ever been treated. Amber took deep breaths.

"I can do this. I can do this," she repeated to herself over and over again.

The next thing Amber knew, she felt a shove from behind that propelled her through the curtain and onto the runway. Afer a momentary stumble and hesitation, an automatic pilot seemed to take over her body. She strode confidently down the runway in her stiletto heel shoes just as she had practiced. A huge cheer erupted from around her. The feeling of being alone in the spot light surrounded by a dark, anonymous sea of men seemed surreal. In an instant, the loud cheer was replaced by the sound of hands clapping to the beat of the music as she took each step. There was a momentary hush as she slowly took off her short, silky, golden robe. A thunderous storm of applause, cheers and whistles erupted when she threw her robe into the sea of men. With the robe now discarded, a golden outfit consisting of a G string and bra was now exposed.

As though in a trance, she continued through her routine. She grabbed onto a pole and swung wildly around it. Men had their hands stretched toward her. At first, this confused her, but then she saw they held money in their hands. Mostly dollar bills, but some had larger bills. She walked over to the men and leaned toward them. Amber unhooked the bra and it fell to the runway floor. She tried to gather as much money as she could. Amber gave extra attention to the men with the largest bills. She wagged her finger to say no to the men with mere dollar bills. The men reached for their wallets and produced larger denomination bills. Amber gave a broad smile as she slowly slid down the pole one last time and the music stopped.

The music was instantly replaced by another thunderous roar of applause, cheers and whistles. When Amber walked through the curtain, she started to count the money as the cheers and whistles continued. Kat approached Amber with her hand held out as if to say,

"Give me the money."

Instinctively, Amber gave Kat the bills she was holding in her hands and they both plucked at the bills that were in her G string. Amber didn't know exactly how much money there was, but she knew it was more money than she had ever seen in her life.

"Not bad for a beginner," Kat said approvingly.

Amber embraced Kat with a bear hug which took Kat by complete surprise.

"Thank you so much, Kat," Amber said almost in tears, "No one has ever treated me as good as you have. I can't believe how lucky I was to find you."

Amber continued to tightly embrace Kat until Kat, embarrassed by Amber's display of affection finally said,

"Now don't ztart getting all zentimental on me. It's only biznez."

Amber continued to hug and thank Kat.

"Vhy don't you go out and mingle vith za customers now, " Kat finally said.

Amber broke her embrace with Kat and bounded into the dressing room. Amber found that her discarded clothing was on her chair in the dressing room. She was beaming with delight.

"What are you so happy about?," one of the strippers asked.

She looked at the stripper and noticed that everyone was staring at her with a certain amount of contempt.

"I thought I did a very good tonight considering it was my first time," Amber said, "Even Kat thought so."

"Kat," the stripper laughed with a sneer, "is just using you. She's using all of us."

"Think what you want," Amber said, "I think Kat's wonderful."

The other strippers shook their heads in disgust and quickly dispersed. Amber put her clothes back on went into the show room. As soon as she emerged, men started calling out to her with wads of money in their hands.

"Hey baby," someone shouted, "I have something special for you."

"Don't listen to him," shouted another, "He's a schmuck. Come over here."

Suddenly, Amber had an idea.

"I want to be fair to everyone," Amber shouted back, "So let's have an auction."

Amber held an impromptu action. She gave her attention to the highest bidder. After she was finished with that customer, Amber held auction after auction until she was exhausted and needed a break. She went to the back of the show room and sat down at the bar. The bartender complimented Amber on her performance.

"What can I get for you?," the bartender asked, "It's on the house."

"What do you have?," Amber asked

"Look at the shelf," the bartender responded, "We have just about everything."

"No," Amber said, "I mean what kind of soda or juice do you have?"

"Soda or juice," the bartender laughed, "maybe something a little stronger will help you relax."

"Like what?," Amber asked.

"I don't know," the bartender said, "Maybe a shot of tequila or vodka."

"No thanks," Amber said, "I don't drink alcohol."

"Are you telling me you don't drink alcohol?," the bartender asked incredulously, "Not a drop?"

"That's right," Amber said, "My father was an alcoholic and he did terrible things when he got drunk. I swore I'd never touch a drop of alcohol as long as I live. So what kind of soda or juice do you have?"

The bartender paused for a moment.

"I guess we have Coke and Sprite," he said, "We also have tomato juice and orange juice. I think that's everything non alcoholic."

"In that case," Amber said teasingly, "I'll have an orange juice to celebrate my wonderful debut performance."

The bartender returned with a glass of orange juice and put it in front of Amber.

"Here's a virgin orange juice," he laughed.

"Thanks," Amber said.

Amber was taking her first sip of orange juice when she was approached by a man. He had followed her to the bar. She didn't recognize him, so he must not have won one of the auctions.

"I loved your performance," the stranger said with a drunken slur, "Are you sure that was your first time?"

"Very sure," Amber said.

Amber quickly turned away from the man. She found the man repelling because something about him reminded her of Gerald Hansen. Besides that, she wasn't interested in talking to a drunk. The man reached out, grabbed her shoulders and spun her around in her bar stool.

"Come on," the man said looking at Amber's breasts, "I have lots of money. If you're that good on your first try, maybe you can show me some of your other talents. I can pay for it."

Before Amber knew it, the man had one of Amber's

breast in one of his hands and her hair in the other. The man kissed Amber on the mouth, trying to pry her lips open with his tongue. The smell of his wretched alcohol breath filled her nostrils. Amber's body was frozen as if she were paralyzed. The thoughts of the many times she had been through this exact same experience were racing through her head. The man was groping her body. An automatic pilot took over and her mind was quickly in a distant place. As the hands groped her body, Amber could hear a voice in the distance. At first, it seemed like a dream. She tried to listen to what the voice was saying. As Amber concentrated on the voice, the voice became louder and clearer.

"Get your hands off the girl," the voice was yelling, "Security. Security."

It was the bartender's voice. Amber soon returned to reality and could feel hands groping her body and a tongue inside her mouth. Amber kicked and pushed with all her strength. It was enough to remove the tongue from her mouth.

"GET YOUR STINKING HANDS OFF ME," Amber screamed.

Amber could feel the man being pulled away from her. She saw two of Kat's security men dragging the man through a door next to the stage.

"Are you OK?," the bartender asked.

"I don't know," Amber said trying to regain her composure, "I guess so."

"That happens around here sometimes," the bartender said, "I'm sorry it happened to you on your first night, but don't worry, that man will be taken care of. He won't be bothering you again."

"What are they going to do to him?," Amber asked.

"You don't want to know," the bartender laughed, "but he'll be lucky if he can still walk when they get though with him. It'll be an experience he won't forget. By the way, my name is Dean."

"Thanks Dean," Amber smiled, "Thanks for calling for help."

"It's part of my job to look out for the girls," Dean said.

Amber sat in thought as she continued to compose herself. She took a few more sips of her orange juice. Finally, a smile came across her face. Amber realized that was the first time she had been allowed to say no, and for the first time in her life, she felt powerful.

SECRETS

CHAPTER TWENTY-TWO

HOSPITAL

Richard Decker, Detective Ferraro and Lieutenant Atkin remained in contact over the next two weeks. Ferraro told the others that, unfortunately, his trail had run cold. He told them that a man named Dwayne B. Goode had been seen with Anna at a diner during the early hours of Christmas morning. Ferraro also told them that he believed, without any doubt, that Goode had checked Anna into a nearby motel. Ferraro explained that Goode had used a fictitious name at the motel and that he could find no direct evidence positively linking Goode to the motel room. Ferraro told the others about the search warrant, but that the search turned up nothing. Ferraro told them that Goode had left town just hours before the search team arrived. He said there was nothing more he could do for now since he had no probable cause to issue an arrest warrant for Goode. Ferraro expressed his opinion that Goode had probably either hidden Anna or taken her with him when he disappeared. Ferraro also explained that it was possible that Goode, Anna or both of them, had left the country. Ferraro told them that the case had reached a dead end unless either Goode or some new leads turned up.

Richard told the others about his visit to Gerald Hansen's residence and his conversation with Hansen's girlfriend, Nina Larson. Richard reported that Anna had likely been kidnaped when she was a child. He said that Anna had been repeatedly raped by Hansen and was likely sold for sex. Richard explained that was how Anna became pregnant why she probably abandoned the baby. Richard further reported that Anna ran away with the help of Nina Larson and that Anna would probably take desperate actions to remain in hiding from Gerald Hansen.

Atkin, in turn, informed the others that the baby was alive in a temporary foster home. Atkin reported that blood samples were taken from the baby and that a DNA test confirmed that Gerald Hansen was the baby's father. The DNA tests also confirmed that the young woman on the bus, presumed to be Anna Hansen, was the baby's mother.

When all of this information was added together, it became clear that Anna was no longer the horrible creature that she seemed to be at first glance, but was a victim who deserved all the sympathy a young girl could get from the world. Knowing the truth, the three police officers made a pact to do everything in their power to find Anna and bring her tormentors to justice.

Richard told his wife everything he had learned

SECRETS

about Anna.

"Isn't it amazing how the truth can be so different from first impressions," Richard's wife said, "When I first heard about that baby, I wanted to crucify that girl. Now all I want to do is hug and comfort her."

Ferraro moved on to the next case. He opened a file and began to read that a badly beaten man showed up at Sunrise Hospital in a taxi. The man arrived completely unconscious and smelled of alcohol, throw-up and urine. Ferraro read that when the man regained consciousness, he claimed that he was beaten up by some bouncers at the Pussy Kat Club. The man's name was Larry Brown. He was hospitalized in room 342.

Ferraro took the elevator to the third floor of Sunrise Hospital. He found room 342 and looked inside. Ferraro saw a man laying in a bed being attended to by a nurse. The man's head seemed to be completely wrapped in bandages and the one arm that was laying outside the blanket was in a cast. Ferraro knocked on the door and the nurse turned her head in his direction.

"Is there something I can do for you?," the nurse asked.

"Yes," Ferraro answered, "My name is Detective Ferraro. I'm with the Las Vegas Metro Police. I'm looking for a man by the name of Larry Brown."

"Then you've come to the right place," the nurse said, "Why don't you sit down while I finish what I'm doing."

Ferraro sat in a chair that was inside the room next to the doorway.

"It looks like he got a pretty good beating," Ferraro said.

"I'd say it was pretty bad beating," the nurse

answered as the nurse continued about her duties, "His jaw was broken and his mouth is wired shut. He also has a severe concussion and was unconscious for almost two days. I could go on and on about a broken nose, broken ribs, a punctured lung, cracked vertebrae and other injuries, but you get the picture. This was a very severe beating."

"How long has he been here?," Ferraro asked.

"This is his fourth day," the nurse answered, "OK, I'm finished. He's all yours, but understand, the man has serious injuries, so be careful with him."

"If he's been here for four days," Ferraro continued, "he must have come in on Thursday."

"Yes," the nurse confirmed, "Late Thursday evening,"

"I'll be easy on him," Ferraro said as the nurse walked past him and out of the room.

Ferraro rose from his chair and walked over to the man laying in the bed. His head was completely wrapped in bandages so that only his lips and eyes could be seen. He was lying on his back and the rest of his body was now completely covered by a blanket. Ferraro looked into the man's eyes.

"My name is Detective Ferraro," he said, "I'm with the Las Vegas Metropolitan Police Department. Do you understand what I'm saying?"

Ferraro heard a soft, wheezy sound.

"Yes," the man said through his mouth that was wired shut.

"Is your name Larry Brown?," Ferraro asked.

"Yes," Brown said.

"Can you tell me what happened to you?," Ferraro asked as he put his ear closer to the man's mouth.

"I oz at the ussy cat ub," Brown said slowly. "There oz a neu girl. Airy ity."

"You mean a new dancer?," Ferraro asked.

"Yes," Brown said, "She oz ignoring ee. She oz at the rrr."

"The what?," Ferraro asked.

"The rrr," Brown repeated, "The ace where you get a drink."

"The bar?," Ferraro asked.

"Yes," Brown said, "She oz at the rrr. I alked o'er to her and asked eh she oz ignoring ee. She told ee to get lost. I told her I had honey and that she didn't need to act like an itch. The next thing I know there oz an ig ann holding ee i each arr and dragging ee outside. They started hitting ee and kicking ee. Hen I oak a, I oz here at the hosital."

"If I understand you correctly," Ferraro said, "You walked over to a dancer who was sitting at the bar. While you were talking to her, two big men grabbed your arms and took you outside. They beat you and kicked you. When you woke up, you were here at the hospital. Is that correct so far?"

"Yes," Brown said.

"Can you describe the girl?," Ferraro asked.

"Yes," Brown said, "She had owne hair and owne eyes. Her nay oz a'er Gold."

Ferraro wrote this information in his note book.

"What about the men who hurt you," Ferraro said, "Can you describe them."

"No," Brown said, "I only saw that they er airing ouncer uni'or's. They er airy ig. I don't know any thing else a'out these en."

"I want to make sure I've understood you," Ferraro

said, "The girl was new dancer at the club, had brown hair, brown eyes and her last name was Gold. Is that correct so far?"

"Yes, it oz her irst night at the clu," Brown said.

"It was her first night dancing at the club?" Ferraro asked.

"Yes," Brown confirmed.

"And the men who hurt you," Ferraro continued, "There were two of them, they were big and wore bouncer uniforms."

"Yes," Brown answered.

"Can you tell me anything else about these men?," Ferraro continued, "What about their ethnicity? Did they speak with an accent or have tattoos? Anything like that?"

"I don't remember," Brown said, "It oz airy ark. I don't know any thing else a'out the en."

"I want to make sure I have the story straight," Ferraro said, "The girl had brown hair, brown eyes and her name was Gold. It was her first night dancing at the club."

Is that correct so far?," Ferraro asked.

"Yes," Brown said.

"The men who took you out were wearing bouncer uniforms," Ferraro continued, "but you can't tell me anything else about them. Is that right?"

"Yes," Brown said.

"I need to take your blanket off so I can photograph your injuries, Ferraro said, "Is that OK?"

"Yes," Brown said.

Ferraro removed the blanket that was covering Brown's body. Brown was in a virtual full body cast that made Ferraro cringe. Ferraro took a digital camera out of his kit. He took several photographs of Brown from various angles. Ferraro put the camera back in his kit and placed the blanket back over Brown's body.

"Thank you." Ferraro said, "I need to get some information about you. I think the best way would be to get this information from your driver's license. Do you have a driver's license?"

"Yes," Brown said.

"Do you know where it is?," Ferraro asked.

"No," Brown said, "I don't know ere any ah i things are."

"I would also like to take your personal belongings with me." Ferraro said, "I want to examine your clothes for evidence. Maybe there will be blood or other evidence that will lead me to the men who did this to you. Do I have your permission look through your things and take what I think will be helpful to your case?"

"Yes," Brown said.

Ferraro pushed the attendant call button. He then leaned over Brown and looked into his eyes.

"I'm sorry about what happened to you," Ferraro said, "I will do my best to find out who did this to you. Do you understand me?"

"Yes," Brown said.

Ferraro saw tears fill Brown's eyes. Inwardly, Ferraro knew that the chances finding the exact men who did this were very slim given the fact that Brown could not describe either of the men to any useful detail. He also suspected that these men were experienced and smart enough not to leave any evidence. But Brown deserved his best effort. Ferraro took a few steps backward away from Brown and heard a voice behind him.

"What can I do for you?," the voice said.

Ferraro turned toward the door and saw the same nurse who had been in the room when he arrived.

"I need to look through Mr. Brown's personal belongings," Ferraro said, "Can you tell me where they're stored?"

"I need to get Mr. Brown's permission before I can do that," the nurse said kindly.

"I already got his permission," Ferraro said.

"Nevertheless," the nurse said politely, "I need to get his permission myself. It's hospital policy. I could lose my job if I gave you anything without his permission"

The nurse walked over to Brown.

"Do I have your permission to give Detective Ferraro access to your personal belongings?," the nurse asked.

Brown said "Yes."

"I also plan to take some of his things with me," Ferraro interjected, "So you might want to get his permission for that too."

"Does Detective Ferraro have your permission to remove your personal belongings from the hospital?," the nurse asked.

"Yes," Brown replied.

"I need to get a key," the nurse said, "Wait here and I'll be back."

Ferraro sat down in the chair next to the door and waited for the nurse to return. A few minutes later, the nurse returned with a key and opened a wall locker in the room.

"His things are in here," the nurse said.

Ferraro removed a pair of latex gloves and some

evidence bags from his kit. Ferraro put the gloves on his hands and began searching through Brown's belongings. He found a watch, a pair of shoes and a pair of socks. Ferraro immediately put each of these items into separate evidence bags. He found a button-down shirt and searched the front pocket. Finding nothing, he put the shirt into an evidence bag as well. He pulled a pair of jeans out of the locker and searched the front pockets. Ferraro found some small change and a key ring full of keys. He put these items back into the locker.

Ferraro could feel that there was a wallet in one of the back pockets of the jeans. Ferraro took the wallet out of the pocket and opened it. Everything seemed to be in place. The wallet was full of cash and credit cards. It seemed clear this was not a robbery. Ferraro found a driver's license and took it out of the wallet. It was a Nevada license, which meant that Brown was a local. He asked the nurse to make a photocopy. A few minutes later, the nurse returned with the photocopy. Ferraro put the driver's license back into the wallet and put the wallet into the locker. He put the jeans into an evidence bag and put all of the evidence bags into his kit. Ferraro snapped off the latex gloves and threw them into the trash can.

"Thanks for your help," Ferraro said to the nurse.

"If that's all," the nurse said, "I have other things I need to get to."

"One last thing," Ferraro said, "How much longer is Mr. Brown going to be here?"

"I would say at least another week. Maybe two," the nurse answered, "After that he will probably be transferred to a rehabilitation center. Why do you ask?"

"If I leave you my card," Ferraro said, "will you call

me when you find out which rehabilitation center Mr. Brown will be transferred to? I don't want to lose track of him."

"I'll do that," the nurse said, "I hope you can find out who did this to him."

"So do I," Ferraro said, "Again, thanks for all of your help."

"You're welcome," the nurse said.

Without further comment, the nurse spun around and walked out of the room. Ferraro watched as she hurried down the corridor.

SECRETS

D. K. DeGRAW

CHAPTER TWENTY-THREE

CLUB

When Ferraro returned to the precinct office, he sent Brown's belongings to the crime lab for analysis. He also ran Brown's information through the system. Other than two DUIs, Brown's record was clean. Ferraro also requested a print of Brown's photograph that was in the driver's license database. When the print arrived, Ferraro went to the Pussy Cat Club at around three o'clock in the afternoon. Ferraro parked his car in the south side parking lot close to the main entrance. The main entrance was on the left side of the building closest to the street. Ferraro got out of his car, walked to the entrance and pulled open the door.

When Ferraro stepped inside, he found himself in a show room that was dimly lit except for a stage and runway that were brightly lit. The stage itself was shielded by a red, velvet curtain that ran from the ceiling to the bottom of the stage. A runway, which was about eight feet wide and twenty-five feet long, protruded from the center of the stage. Three golden stripper poles were evenly spaced along the runway. Except for the red velvet curtain and golden stripper poles, the room was completely painted or decorated in black. On each side of the stage, there was a door where people could enter to or from the back portion of the building.

The show room was mostly empty, except for about a dozen men who were scattered about. One stripper was working the runway and two more were working the room. Every now and then, Ferraro heard the sound of men whistling or hooting. Ferraro spotted a bar to his right. A young woman was working behind the bar. Even from a distance, he could see she was a very attractive blond.

"That couldn't be Anna," Ferraro thought to himself.

Ferraro walked over to the bar, identified himself to the woman and saw that she had beautiful blue eyes.

"What's your name?," Ferraro asked.

"Tina," the woman replied.

"Tina what?," Ferraro asked.

"Tina Spencer," the woman answered.

Upon closer inspection, Ferraro knew this was not Anna Hansen.

"How long have you worked here?," Ferraro asked.

"A little over two years," Tina answered.

"I'm here," Ferraro continued, "because a man claimed he was beaten up by a couple of bouncers who work here. Would you know anything about that?," Ferraro asked.

"When did he say it happened?," Tina asked.

"Four days ago," Ferraro answered, "last Thursday

night."

"I wasn't working that night," Tina said looking away from Ferraro, "Maybe you should talk to the owner."

Ferraro held out Brown's driver's license photograph.

"Have you ever seen this man?," Ferraro asked.

Tina looked at the photograph and hesitated.

"I don't recognize him," Tina said

"Are you saying you've never seen this man before?," Ferraro continued.

"Not that I remember," Tina answered, "I think you should talk to the owner. Her name is Katia Marcova. Why don't you wait here and I'll go find her."

"Before you go," Ferraro interjected, "you still haven't answered my question. Have you heard anything about the man in the photograph getting beat up here last Thursday night?"

"I told you," Tina said with an annoyed voice, "I wasn't working that night."

"I didn't ask you if you were working that night," Ferraro continued, "I asked you if you heard anything about the beating."

Tina paused.

"No," she said with an even more annoyed tone of voice, "I haven't heard anything about the beating. Are you satisfied?"

"Not really," Ferraro said, "but I guess that's the best answer I'm going to get from you for now."

"I'll go find Kat," Tina said.

"Here's my card," Ferraro said he as held out a business card, "Please give this to Ms. Marcova. We go way back."

Tina took the card and quickly walked away. She disappeared through the door that was on the right-hand side of the stage.

Ferraro sat on a bar stool while he waited for Tina to return. A few minutes later, the beautiful, middle-aged Kat emerged into the show room. Kat was followed by a bouncer who was followed by Tina. The bouncer had some distinctive scars on his face. Kat gracefully walked toward Ferraro and held out her hand. Ferraro stood up.

"Deetectif Ferraro," Kat said seductively as they shook hands, "It's been zo long zinze I zaw you last. Vhere have you been zhis long time?"

"It's always a pleasure," Ferraro said, "Unfortunately for me, I don't get to visit here as often as I would like."

"I'll take zhat as a complement, Deetectif," Kat said as their hand lingered together, "Zo vhat brings you here now?"

Ferraro was feeling uncomfortable about how he was feeling about Kat flirting with him. Even so, it was with reluctance that broke the handshake.

"I'm here because a man claims he was beaten up by a couple of your bouncers last Thursday night," Ferraro said as he held out Brown's photograph, "This is what the man looks like. That was, I meant to say, before he was beaten up. Now he's wearing a body cast. Do you know anything about this beating?"

"I know nozhing about zhis," Kat said looking Ferraro directly in the eyes, "Zhis is za first time I've heard of zhis."

"Have you ever seen this man before?," Ferraro continued trying his best not to look at Kat's breasts.

"No," Kat answered, "but I don't come in to za

showroom very often. I ztay moztly in za back."

"Do you know who was working that night?," Ferraro asked.

"Of courze I do, Deetectif Ferraro," Kat answered, "I run zhis plaze completely. Vhy don't you come to my office and I can give you za names."

Ferraro followed Kat through the same door that she had entered into the showroom. He continued to follow her down a maze of hallways secretly enjoying the view of Kat from behind. Ferraro was followed by the bouncer. They walked through a door and into Kat's office. She motioned for Ferraro to sit down, which he did. Kat walked behind the desk and sat down herself. The bouncer stood next to the doorway.

"You need to know za names of everyone who vaz vorking zhat night?" Kat asked.

"Yes," Ferraro answered.

"Let me zee here," Kat said, "do you vant me to tells you za names, or do you vant me to vrite zhem down for you."

"Why don't you write them down," Ferraro said, "that will make it easier for me."

Ferraro waited as Kat wrote down the names on a note pad. She then tore off the page and handed it across the desk to Ferraro. Ferraro took the page and scanned the names.

"Are any of these people at the club now?" Ferraro asked.

"Yes," Kat answered, "three of zhem. Two of zhem are zecurity men. One iz a danzer."

"I would like to talk to the bouncers first?" Ferraro said.

"I prefer to call zhem zecurity men." Kat answered.

"Do you vant to talk to zhem right now?"

"Yes," Ferraro said, "if it wouldn't be too much trouble."

"I don't zink zhat vould be a problem," Kat answered.

Kat pointed to the bouncer standing in the doorway.

"You can ztart vith zhat man right zhere," Kat said.

Ferraro turned in the direction of the doorway.

"Were you working here last Thursday night?," Ferraro asked the bouncer.

The man nodded.

"Let's start with your name," Ferraro said.

"Serge," the man said, "Serge Korenovski."

"How do you spell that?," Ferraro asked.

"S-E-R-G-E   K-O-R-E-N-O-V-S-K-I," Serge answered.

"Your first name is pronounced Sergay?," Ferraro asked.

"Yes," Serge answered.

Ferraro looked at the paper and put a check next to Serge's name.

"What hours did you work that night?," Ferraro asked.

"From four o'clock in the afternoon until two o'clock in the morning," Serge answered.

Ferraro held out Brown's photograph.

"Have you seen this man before?," Ferraro asked.

Serge briefly looked at the photograph.

"No," he said.

"Are you sure?" Ferraro asked.

"Let me think about it," Serge said and paused, "As a matter of fact, the more I think about it, the more I'm sure that I've never seen this guy before."

"I guess I'm talking to a smart ass," Ferraro said as he pushed Brown's photograph into Serge's face, "Put your thinking cap on and tell me if you know anything about this man getting beat up here last Thursday night."

Serge's face flickered with anger and his fists clenched tightly as he took a step back. Kat shook her head slightly to say no. Serge instantly relaxed.

"I don't know anything about any beating," Serge said.

"Do you know if anyone got involuntarily escorted out of the club that night?," Ferraro asked.

"I might have heard something about that," Serge said.

"What did you hear?," Ferraro asked.

"I heard there was a man who got physical with one of our girls and was shown out the door," Serge replied.

"What was the man's name?," Ferraro asked.

"I don't know," Serge said, "I only heard about it."

"Who told you about it?," Ferraro asked.

"I don't remember," Serge replied, "I just over heard some people talking about it."

"Do you remember who you heard talking about it?," Ferraro asked.

"No," Serge said sharply.

"Do you know who escorted this man out?," Ferraro asked.

"No," Serge again said sharply.

"Was it you?," Ferraro asked.

"I told you," Serge said, "I only heard about it."

"Was it you?," Ferraro repeated matching Serge's sharp tone.

"No," Serge said a little less sharply.

"Do you have any theories about how this man came to this club and wound up at Sunrise Hospital beaten to a bloody pulp?," Ferraro asked.

"I might have a few," Serge said.

"What would your theories be?," Ferraro asked.

"Maybe," Serge said, "He stopped at a liquor store, got wasted, stepped into the street and got hit by a car. Or maybe he got bounced out of here and went to some other place and got beat up there. Or maybe he picked a fight in the parking lot. That's just a few of my theories. I have more if you have the time to hear them."

Ferraro knew he wasn't going to get any confessions out of any of Kat's bouncers, but he turned to Kat anyway.

"I'd like to talk to the other bouncer," Ferraro said.

Kat looked up at Serge and said "Pleaze get Pavel."

Serge left the room.

"You have your men well trained," Ferraro said to Kat.

"Yes," Kat said, "zhey are very professional."

"That's not what I meant," Ferraro said.

"Zhen vhat do you mean?," Kat asked.

"I mean they are well trained to give the right answers," Ferraro said.

"Zhey are trained to tell za truth," Kat responded.

"Right," Ferraro said as another man who was dressed just like Serge walked into the room.

"Zhis is Pavel," Kat said, "He vaz here zhat night alzo."

Ferraro interviewed Pavel and got the same answers that Serge had given him. He knew he would get those same answers from all of Kat's security men.

Ferraro thought he might have better luck with the dancers and bartenders.

"I'd like to talk to the dancer who was here that night," Ferraro said, "Can you bring her to me?"

"Of courze, Deetectif Ferraro," Kat said, "Anyzhing to cooperate. Pavel, pleaze get Candy."

"Candy, of all names" Ferraro thought, "Do all of these strippers go by the same name?"

A few minutes later, a red headed woman with oversized breasts walked in to the office.

"Zhis iz Candy,"Kat said, "She vaz vorking last Thursday night."

"Is her last name Cane," Ferraro asked with a laugh.

"How did you know?," Kat answered.

Ferraro took down Candy's information.

"Did you see a man get beat up here last Thursday night?" Ferraro asked.

"No," Candy answered.

"Did you see the incident at the bar with one of the dancers?" Ferraro asked. "I understand the dancer was new to the club."

"I heard about it," Candy said, "But I was busy doing my own thing. I didn't see anything myself."

"You didn't hear this dancer being assaulted?" Ferraro asked.

"No Candy said," the music's very loud in the club and I wouldn't have heard anything happening at the bar."

"Did you hear what happened to the man?" Ferraro asked.

"I was told he was escorted out," Candy said," I didn't hear anything else other than that."

"You didn't hear anything about the man getting beat up?," Ferraro asked.

"No," Candy answered, "I've never heard of anything like that happening around here."

Like the bouncers, Ferraro knew he wasn't going to get any useful information from the dancers either.

"What about the other people who were working that night," Ferraro said, "When are they scheduled to work?"

Kat scanned the schedule.

"All of zhem are zcheduled to vork on Thursday from four to closing," Kat answered.

"In that case," Ferraro said, "I'll be back on Thursday night to finish my interviews. I expect all of them to be here."

"Zhey vill be here," Kat said, "Zhat iz, if zhey vant to keep zheir jobs."

"One last thing," Ferraro said, "One of the names on your list is Amber Gould."

"Zhat iz right," Kat said.

"I see it is spelled G-O-U-L-D," Ferraro said.

"Zhat iz right," Kat responded.

"By any chance," Ferraro added, "was last Thursday night the first time this Amber Gould danced at your club."

"Az a matter of fact, it vaz," Kat said surprised that Ferraro knew this.

"Will she be working on Thursday night?," Ferraro asked.

Kat scanned the work schedule.

"Yez," Kat said, "She iz alzo zcheduled to begin vork at four. Vhy do you ask?"

"I especially expect here to be here when I come

back to finish my interviews."

D. K. DeGRAW

CHAPTER TWENTY-FOUR

CLARKSTON

Richard Decker picked up the telephone and dialed extension 3981.

"I got your message about the girl," Richard said.

"That's right," the voice on the other end of the telephone said, "We got a call from the Cache County Sheriff. He said that a girl matching the description you posted on the NCIS database was abducted from a town called Clarkston, Utah about ten years ago."

"I've never heard of Clarkston?," Richard asked, "Where is it?"

"It's about twenty-five miles northwest of Logan," the voice answered, "It's just south of the Idaho border."

Richard knew Logan well, a city in the far northern end of Utah near the Idaho and Wyoming borders. Logan is the largest city in a farming area known as Cache

Valley. A little under a hundred thousand people live in the valley, including almost twenty thousand students who attend Utah State University. About forty-five thousand of the valley's residents live in Logan itself. The remainder live in a multitude of surrounding towns that have a population of a couple of thousand or less. The primary occupation of most of these small-town residents is agriculture. Cache Valley is particularly renowned throughout Utah and Idaho for its dairy products, like Cache Valley Cheese and Casper's Ice Cream.

On the other side of the mountains that tower to the east of Logan is Bear Lake. Bear Lake is similar to Lake Tahoe, but far less crowded due to its isolated location. The northern half of Bear Lake is in sparsely populated Wyoming while the southern half of the lake is in an equally sparsely populated part of Utah. The only things of significance on the Utah side of Bear Lake are a few hundred homes, a small RV park and a condominium resort called Sweetwater. Sweetwater has a few hundred condos, a nine-hole golf course and a dock that rents various kinds of water craft. Richard and his family began spending a week there every summer ever since Richard purchased a timeshare interest in one of the condos twelve years ago.

During these summer visits to Sweetwater, Richard and his family traveled through Logan on their way back and forth from their home in Salt Lake. Richard had the routine down pat. The family would drive the hundred miles from their home in Salt Lake to Logan. Once in Logan, they would stop at the Smith's Grocery Store on Main Street and Highway 89. This was the last chance to use the restroom, make last-minute grocery purchases and fill up the gas tank. The family would then drive eastward up Highway 89 past the beautiful Logan Mormon Temple and the equally beautiful Utah State University campus. Once inside Logan Canyon, they would enjoy the beautiful scenery as the family drove past the three dams and their artificial lakes. The family continued northeasterly twenty-six miles until they came to the Beaver Mountain Ski Resort. Five miles later, they crested the mountain summit. The family could see the beautiful blue waters of the vast deep water lake as they descended into the beautiful Bear Lake Valley. Fifteen miles later, they would arrive at Sweetwater

"I have a contact number for you to call," the voice on the telephone said.

"What's the number?," Richard asked.

The voice on the telephone gave him a name and telephone number.

"Good luck," the voice said, "I hope this is the girl you're looking for."

"Thanks," Richard said not wanting to get his hopes up too high, "I hope it is too."

Richard called the telephone number and after a few rings, a voice answered.

"This is Sheriff Godfrey," a man said.

Richard introduced himself and explained why he was calling.

"Oh yes," Godfrey said enthusiastically, "We got a hit on the girl you posted on the NCIS database. A girl was abducted from our county about ten years ago. I think we have an exact match on the girl, the house and the school."

"What's the girl's name?," Richard asked.

"Becky Ann Clark," Godfrey answered.

"How certain are you that the girl I posted is this

Becky Ann Clark?," Richard asked.

"Not completely," Godfrey answered, "But the girl, the house and the school seem to match perfectly. Why don't you drive up here and we can drive by the school and the house. I don't want to bother the family if this turns out to be nothing. I can only imagine that the family has already suffered beyond anything imaginable. Beside that, if this turns out to be the girl you're looking for, I want to break the news to the family in person. What do you think about that?"

"I think that's a good idea," Richard said.

"When can you be up here?," Godfrey asked.

"I can be there in the morning," Richard answered, "I should be there around ten."

"I'll see you then," Godfrey said, "Let's keep our fingers crossed."

At eight o'clock the next morning, Richard got into his car and drove north on Interstate 215. Interstate 215 merged with Interstate 15 just north of downtown Salt Lake City. He continued driving north on Interstate 15 for forty-one more miles past a series of cities that were merged with Salt Lake City to the south and Ogden to the north. North Salt Lake, Bountiful, Kaysville, Layton, Clearfield, and Roy. The snow packed Wasatch mountains towered just a few miles to the east of the Interstate while the expansive Great Salt Lake stretched as far as the eye could see to the west and north. Just north of Ogden, the scenery quickly changed from city urban to country empty. Empty fields of snow surrounded the Interstate as Richard drove north another twenty-five miles.

Richard exited Interstate 15 at Brigham City and drove easterly into the snowy mountains. He continued up highway 89 until he reached the summit.

"This must be a mother of a drive when it's snowing," Richard thought to himself, "I'm glad it's nice and sunny today."

Richard continued driving northward on Highway 89 through the mountains. The road surface alternated from clear, to snowy, to slushy in no particular order. When Highway 89 veered eastward, Richard began a descent into Cache Valley. Cache Valley is nestled between towering mountains to the east and less towering mountains to the west. It is very similar to the Salt Lake Valley, but far less populated. The valley floor itself was covered in snow. Richard could make out where each farm began and ended by the fence lines that stuck out above the snow. To the northeast, Richard could see Logan in the far distance. Several small towns were dotted in between. The whole scene looked like it was from a Christmas card.

Thirty minutes after leaving Brigham City, Richard pulled into the Cache County Sheriff's Office. He arrived early. The Sheriff's Office was just a few miles due west of the Smith's Grocery Store where Richard and his family stopped on their way to Bear Lake. The Sheriff's office building was extremely small compared to the building that housed the Salt Lake City Police Department. In fact, it was smaller than Richard's house. Richard walked into a small foyer where a woman was sitting behind a glass booth.

"May I help you?," the woman said.

Richard walked to the booth and said,

"I have an appointment to see Sheriff Godfrey."

"What's your name?," the woman asked.

"I'm Richard Decker with the Salt Lake Police

Department," he said, "Sheriff Godfrey's expecting me."

"Yes," the woman said, "I'll let him know you're here."

The woman pushed a button on her telephone and Richard could hear Godfrey's voice.

"Yes," Godfrey said.

"Richard Decker from Salt Lake is here to see you," the woman said.

"Tell him I'll be right out," Godfrey said,

"Please sit down," the woman said, "Sheriff Godfrey will be right out. Is there anything I can get for you?"

"Do you have a restroom?," Richard asked.

He had not bothered to stop at the Smith's Grocery Store.

"Yes," the woman answered, "I'll show you where it is."

The woman opened a door and showed Richard the way to the restroom. When Richard walked out of the restroom, a police officer was waiting for him.

"Are you going to take me to see Sheriff Godfrey?," Richard asked.

"I'm sorry to disappoint you," the officer said, "But I'm Sheriff Godfrey."

"I'm terribly sorry," Richard said quickly, "You look way too young to be the Sheriff."

"I'll take that as a compliment," Godfrey said as he laughed, "I look way younger than I really am. It's something that's plagued me all my life. But the older I get, the less of a plague it is."

"I wish I had that problem," Richard laughed back.

Godfrey was a little over six feet tall and had a slender build. He had black hair that was perfectly combed and had a tanned complexion even in winter.

"You must like to ski," Richard said.

"Yes," Godfrey responded, "How could you tell?"

"How else can you get a tan like yours in the middle of winter," Richard answered, "You also have an outline of goggles around your eyes."

"I guess skiing has its hazzards," Godfrey shot back, "Did you bring the photographs and illustrations that you posted?"

"Yes," Richard said, "They're in my satchel."

"Let's go to my office and take a look at them," Godfrey said.

Richard followed Godfrey into an office that had a desk on one side and a small round conference table with four chairs on the other. They both sat down at the conference table.

"Let's take a look at what you have," Godfrey said.

Richard took out the recent photograph of Anna along with the illustrations of the house and school. Richard also showed Godfrey the computer-generated image of Anna as a little girl.

"These illustrations look exactly like the Clarks' residence and Richmond Elementary," Godfrey said quickly, "The image of the little girl looks almost exactly like Becky Ann Clark when she disappeared. There's no question in my mind that the illustrations and image are related to Becky Ann Clark. The question is whether or not your Anna Hansen is the same person as our Becky Ann Clark."

"If you're right," Richard said, "I think we should let the family know that their daughter might be alive. I would want to know that if I were them."

"But I'd hate to give them false hope," Godfrey said, "I can't imagine how devastated they'll be if this turns out to be a red herring."

"If I were them," Richard countered, "I'd rather have false hope than no hope."

"Let's start by going to the school," Godfrey said, "then we can go to the house. We can decide what to do after that."

Godfrey drove out of the parking lot and headed east. He turned left on Main Street and drove north. A few miles later, they were out of Logan and into the rural country side.

"Where are we going?" Richard asked.

"We're heading to Richmond," Godfrey answered, "That's where the elementary school is."

"How long have you been the Cache County Sheriff?," Richard asked.

"A couple of years," Godfrey answered, "Before that, I was a Cache County deputy for about five years. Before that, I was a Utah Highway Patrol trouper for about ten years."

"Are you Mormon?," Richard asked.

"Absolutely," Godfrey said, "My family's been in Cache Valley since they were sent here by Brigham Young in 1864."

"Did you go on a church mission?," Richard asked.

"Sure did," Godfrey answered, "San Antonio, Texas. That's probably why I became a police officer. It was the closest thing I could find to being a cowboy that paid money. And you? Are you Mormon?"

"Yes," Richard answered, "I went to Brazil on my mission. Did you go to college?"

"I graduated from Utah State," Godfrey answered.

"Based on what you've told me," Richard said, "you must be in your mid forties. I can't believe that because you don't look a day over thirty. I wish I had your genes."

"You have me pegged," Godfrey said, "But if you don't believe my age, I can show you my battle scars that prove it."

A few miles later, Godfrey pointed to a building about a mile to the west.

"That's the Casper's ice cream factory over there," Godfrey said.

"Is that the place that makes those Fat Boy Ice Cream Sandwiches and the Nut Sundaes on a Stick?" Richard asked.

"That's right," Godfrey answered, "My kids love to go there because they sell seconds dirt cheap. You can get a big box of those ice cream sandwiches and nut sundays for about ten bucks. They're all smashed up, but they taste the same."

"The elementary school's right there," Godfrey announced a few minutes later.

The elementary school looked exactly like the illustration that had been made by the sketch artist.

"This is definitely the school," Richard said.

"Wait until you see the house," Godfrey said.

"So where's Clarkston?," Richard asked.

"Straight west of here," Godfrey said pointing to the west, "It's on the lower bench of those mountains."

Godfrey put his four-wheel-drive SUV into gear and drove though Richmond. As soon as they were out of town, they were again driving through desolate countryside.

"Is Clarkson as small as Richmond?," Richard asked.

"What do you mean as SMALL as Richmond,"

Godfrey chuckled, "Richmond has almost two thousand people. This is a big town compared to Clarkston."

"Where's the high school?," Richard asked.

"That would be Sky View," Godfrey answered, "We passed by it just north of Logan."

"They go to high school way over there?," Richard said incredulously.

"Yep," Godfrey said, "That's also where I went to high school."

"So how big is Clarkston?," Richard asked.

"Do you mean how small?," Godfrey chuckled.

"I guess that's what I meant," Richard chuckled back.

"Maybe a little over five hundred people," Godfrey answered.

"Tell me about Clarkston," Richard said.

"Clarkston's main claim to fame is Martin Harris lived there until he died," Godfrey said, "He's buried in the Clarkston Cemetery. The town holds a pageant every year that celebrates his life at an amphitheater next to the cemetery. Actually, the pageant is more like a play they do."

"Martin Harris is buried in Clarkston?," Richard asked.

"That's right," Godfrey nodded, "There's a big monument next to his grave in the middle of the cemetery."

"I didn't know that," Richard said.

Richard, like all Mormons, knew that Martin Harris was one of three men who testified that an angel holding the gold plates from which Joseph Smith claimed to have translated the Book of Mormon appeared before them. They testified that they were able to hold the gold plates themselves and turn through the pages. Martin Harris' testimony of this event is printed at the beginning of every Book of Mormon in publication. Richard also knew that Martin Harris lived in Palmyra, New York at the time Joseph Smith translated and printed the first Books of Mormon. Martin Harris mortgaged his farm to give Joseph Smith the money he needed to print those first books. Richard and his family had visited Martin Harris' Palmyra cobble stone house, which is now on the national registry of historic places.

"There are still some old folks living in Clarkston who heard Martin Harris himself tell about when he saw the angel," Godfrey added.

"You mean there are people alive today who knew Martin Harris personally?," Richard asked.

"That's right," Godfrey said.

"That's amazing," Richard said, "I didn't know that. I guess you learn something new every day. How do people in Clarkston earn a living?"

"Mostly farming," Godfrey added, "There's also a huge pig farm and a few dairies."

"What do they grow on the farms?," Richard asked.

"Mostly alfalfa, wheat or barley," Godfrey answered, "A lot of the farmers around here also supplement their income by working at Thiokol."

"Is that the place where they make those space shuttle booster rockets?," Richard asked.

"Yep," Godfrey answered, "Thiokol is on the other side of the mountain over by the Great Salt Lake. How about you? What's your story?"

Richard told Godfrey his life story and finished just as a town appeared in the distance

"Did you say there was a pig farm?" Richard asked,

"Is that what I'm starting to smell?."

"Yep," Godfrey chuckled, "The smell can be quite strong if you're down wind."

They drove past a huge pig farm as they approached the tiny town.

"That's a lot of pigs," Richard said.

"It's the largest pig farm in the State of Utah," Godfrey said.

To his left, Richard saw the amphitheater and cemetery that Godfrey had described earlier.

"That must be the cemetery over there," Richard said.

"That's right," Godfrey confirmed.

Godfrey made a left hand turn where the tiny town of Clarkston began. At the second street, Godfrey made a right turn and began to drive up the lower bench of the mountain. Godfrey continued up two blocks past what had long ago been a gas station. The gas station was now abandoned, but it looked like somebody lived in the small building. Just before they came to the second cross street, Godfrey pulled to a stop in front of a house. The house looked exactly like the house in the illustration. The trees, the bushes, the irrigation ditch, the brick and even the basketball hoop were a perfect match.

"What do you think?," Godfrey asked.

"I think we should go in," Richard answered.

"I hope we're not making a mistake," Godfrey said.

"I think this is something we need to do," Richard said.

Godfrey pulled into the driveway and got out of the SUV. Richard got out of the SUV and followed Godfrey to the front door of the house. Godfrey pushed the doorbell button and they could hear a bell chime inside the house.

The door opened and a woman stood in the doorway. Her face turned as white as a sheet the instant she saw Godfrey.

"Have you found her body?," the woman said softly as she began to cry.

"We may have some good news, Deanna," Godfrey said, "May we come in?"

"Good news?," Deanna Clark said hopefully with tear filled eyes as the color began to return to her face, "I'm sorry, Sheriff, please come in."

Godfrey stepped into a formal living room. Richard followed him inside the house. The living room had a couch, several chairs, an upright piano and a small organ. There were family photographs and flowers scattered about the room. In a prominent place on the piano, there was what seemed to be a memorial to a little girl. The photograph of the girl on the piano looked just like the image in Richard's satchel.

"Is your husband home?," Godfrey asked.

"He's sleeping," Deanna Clark said, "He works the graveyard shift at Thiokol."

"I think you should wake him," Godfrey said.

"Why don't you sit down while I get him," Deanna Clark said.

She quickly disappeared down a hallway. Richard and Sheriff Godfrey sat on the couch and waited. A few minutes later, Godfrey and Richard stood up when Deanna Clark reappeared with her husband.

"How are you, Gene?," Godfrey said as he held out his hand and shook hands with Gene Clark, "This is officer Decker from Salt Lake."

"Deanna said you have some good news about Becky Ann," Gene stated.

"Why don't we all sit down," Godfrey said.

When they were all sitting, Godfrey said,

"We have reason to believe that your daughter might be alive."

SECRETS

CHAPTER TWENTY-FIVE

HOPE

"What do you mean, Becky Ann's still alive," Gene Clark exclaimed as his wife, Deanna, cried next to him, "Where is she?"

"This is going to be hard for you to hear," Godfrey said calmly, "But I said your daughter MIGHT be alive. We're not 100 percent certain at this point."

"You came here to tell us that?" Gene asked incredulously, "Is she alive or isn't she?"

"Look, Gene," Godfrey continued calmly, "We debated whether we should even tell you, but we thought you have a right to know. If your daughter's still alive, it's only a matter of time until we find her. But we're going to need your help."

"What do you want from us?," Gene asked.

"I'll let Officer Decker explain that to you," Godfrey

said.

Richard told the Clarks about his first encounter with Anna Hansen at the bus station. He explained that if Anna is their daughter, that's the name she's using now. He showed the Clarks the recent photograph of Anna he received from Ferraro.

"She's beautiful," Deanna said, "May I hold that photograph?"

"Yes," Richard said as he handed the photograph to Deanna, "She's very beautiful."

Richard told the Clarks about the baby who had been abandoned in St. George.

"We saw that on the news," Deanna exclaimed, "Are you saying this Anna Hansen abandoned that baby in St. George?"

"I believe so," Richard said.

"Is the baby alive?," Deanna asked.

"Yes," Richard answered.

"So if this girl in the photograph is our Becky Ann," Deanna said, "we have a grandchild?"

"That's right," Richard said.

Deanna began to sob audibly and tears began to fall from Gene's eyes as well. Richard paused to let them process this information.

"How did you find us?," Gene asked.

Richard explained that he'd traced Anna to a man named Gerald Hansen.

"Where's this man now?," Gene asked.

"He's in the Salt Lake County Jail," Richard answered.

Richard told the Clarks about his interview with Gerald Hansen's girl friend, Nina Larson. He also told them about the brown envelopes. He explained how Nina had helped Anna escape and that she had given Anna one of the brown envelopes. Richard went on to explain that Anna Hansen was last seen in Las Vegas. Richard further explained what happened at the Las Vegas bus terminal and that Anna had disappeared. Richard told them that Nina Larson had described some of the photographs that were in the missing envelope from her memory.

"I have some things to show you," Richard said.

Richard first showed them the computer-generated image of what Anna would have looked like as a five-year-old.

"That looks just like Becky Ann," Deanna gasped.

Deanna jumped up and quickly walked to the piano. She retrieved a photograph from the shrine and returned. Deanna held the two images side-by-side.

"They're almost identical," Deanna said showing the images to her husband, "What do you think?"

"I agree," Gene said

Deanna handed the two images to Richard and asked,

"What do you think?"

"I think that if they're not the same girl," Richard said, "they must be twins."

Richard handed the Clarks the illustration of the school.

"That looks just like Richmond Elementary," Gene exclaimed.

"Sheriff Godfrey and I drove past the school on our way here," Richard said, "I couldn't agree more."

Richard handed the Clarks the illustration of the house. Deanna audibly gasped.

"That's our house!," Gene exclaimed.

"I think that's a certainty," Richard confirmed.

"These illustrations were made based on photographs that were in the envelope?," Gene asked.

"That's right," Richard confirmed.

"So what does all of this mean?," Gene asked.

"That's the bad news," Richard said, "The only thing this proves for certain is that this Gerald Hansen took these photographs. We have already proven through DNA tests that Anna and Gerald Hansen are the parents of the abandoned baby. But these illustrations don't prove definitively that this Anna Hansen is the same person as your Becky Ann."

"But they must be," Deanna exclaimed, "The little girl you showed me looks just like Becky Ann. And that's her school and that's our house."

"I agree," Richard answered, "but the illustrations, by themselves, aren't enough proof to lock Hansen away. But I also have some good news."

"What's that?," Gene asked.

"There is a way to prove for certain whether Anna Hansen is Becky Ann," Richard said.

"How's that?," Deanna asked.

"We have the DNA samples from the baby and Anna Hansen," Richard answered, "If each of you will give us a DNA sample, we can determine if Anna Hansen is your daughter and whether the baby is your grandchild."

"We'll do whatever you need us to do," Gene said.

"Anything at all," Deanna added.

"I have some DNA kits with me," Richard said, "Can I take these samples now?"

"Absolutely," they both said in unison.

Richard took the DNA samples from the Clarks.

"This looks extremely promising right now," Richard said to the Clarks, "but I don't want to get your hopes up too much. If this turns out to be a dead end, I'll feel really bad if this only adds to your suffering."

Deanna looked into Richard's eyes.

"Don't you worry about that, Officer Decker," Deanna said earnestly, "This is the first time we've had even a small glimmer of hope in almost ten years. Even the smallest glimmer of hope is better than no hope at all."

"Those were my thought's exactly," Richard said looking at Godfrey, "By the way, do you have a photograph of Becky Ann that I can take with me."

"You can take this one," Deanna said, handing Richard the photograph that had been on the piano.

"I don't want to take that one," Richard protested.

"I want you to have it," Deanna insisted.

"OK," Richard said, "but I promise I'll return this photograph as soon as I can."

Richard told the Clarks that he would be in touch when the DNA test results came back. After saying a final goodbye, Godfrey and Richard left the Clarks' house, got in the SUV, and drove out of Clarkston. Godfrey took a more direct route back to Logan. Both of them remained silent as both were deep in thought. Godfrey broke the silence when he pointed to a large building on the left side of the road.

"That's the Cache County Cheese factory," he said.

Those were the only words that were spoken between the two on the return trip to Logan. Godfrey pulled into the Sheriff's office parking lot and the SUV came to a stop.

"What have you been thinking about?," Richard asked.

"I've been thinking about the suffering those poor

people must have gone through," Godfrey answered, "I can't imagine how they have held up. A lot of people like them end up divorced. But they seem to be pretty solid."

"I was thinking the same thing myself," Richard said, "I have two daughters and can't imagine what I would have done if one of them had been abducted. I hope for the Clarks' sakes, this turns out to be the real deal."

"Me too," Godfrey responded, "Let me know when the DNA results come back."

"I will," Richard said.

"How did you come into town?," Godfrey asked.

"I came in over the mountain from Brigham City," Richard answered.

"There's a safer way," Godfrey said.

Godfrey pointing to a road that headed straight west into the distance and over the mountains.

"That road will take you to Interstate 15," Godfrey said, "It's takes a little bit longer to drive, but it's a heck of a lot safer in the wintertime."

"Thanks for the tip," Richard said.

They said goodbye and Richard got into his car. He drove back to Salt Lake taking the road that Godfrey had suggested.

A few days later, the DNA results came back. The tests showed definitively that Anna Hansen was the Clarks' daughter and that the baby was the Clarks' grandchild. Richard was exultant and immediately called Atkin in St. George and Ferraro in Las Vegas. He told them the DNA test results proved that Anna Hansen had in fact, been abducted when she was five years old. Richard also told them about Anna Hansen's true identity and his visit with her parents. Ferraro and Atkin congratulated Richard on a job well done. Richard also called Godfrey and gave him the great news.

"Why don't you come up here and we can tell the Clarks together?," Godfrey said.

"I'd like that," Richard said, "How about tomorrow morning same time as before. I have a meeting with Gerald Hansen and his attorney this afternoon. That's one meeting I don't want to miss."

"I understand what you're saying," Godfrey said, "I'll see you in the morning."

Richard went to the Salt Lake County Jail with the DNA results and Becky Ann's photograph in hand. When Richard walked into the cell, Gerald Hansen was sitting on the same bench restrained like he was before. Clarkson was sitting next to Hansen.

"You told me to come back when I had proof," Richard said to Clarkson, "Here's the proof."

Richard threw the DNA results on the table in front of Clarkson.

"What's this?," Clarkson asked.

"These are DNA tests linking your scum bag client to the girl he abducted ten years ago."

"How so?," Clarkson asked.

"The DNA test results show that your client is the father of a baby who was abandoned in St. George, Utah," Richard said.

"So what?," Clarkson said calmly, "My client doesn't deny having sex with multiple women. So what if one of these women became pregnant and abandoned the baby. What does that have to do with my client?"

"Because we also know who the mother is," Richard said, "It's this girl right here."

Richard pushed Becky Ann's childhood photograph

toward Clarkson.

"Her name is Becky Ann Clark," Richard continued, "Your slime bag client abducted this little girl off the street ten years ago in Cache Valley."

"How can you prove that?," Clarkson asked.

"I tracked Becky Ann's parents down in northern Utah," Richard said, "I met with these people face to face. They have been crying over their missing girl for ten years."

"So what does that prove?," Clarkson huffed.

"The DNA test results prove that Becky Ann Clark, who your client named Anna Hansen, is the mother of the abandoned baby," Richard said, "The DNA test results prove that the abandoned baby is the Clarks' grandchild. This proves that your pervert client abducted this girl and had sex with her while she was a minor."

"My client may have had sex with her," Clarkson said, "but that doesn't prove he abducted her. This girl could be some prostitute for all I know."

"I have a witness who says otherwise," Richard said, "Your client's going down for a long, long time. I'm sure the district attorney will be in touch."

"This isn't over by a long shot," Clarkson said.

"Well, good luck with that," Richard said.

Richard turned around and walked out of the cell with a huge smile on his face. The next morning, he drove back to Logan and met Godfrey at the Cache County Sheriff's Office. They drove to the Clarks' residence and sat with them in their living room. Richard returned the photograph to Deanna.

"I have some terrific news," Richard said, "The DNA tests confirmed that you are the grandparents of the baby who was abandoned in St. George."

SECRETS

"So our daughter is alive," Gene Clark said.

"As far as I know," Richard said.

"And this baby is our grandchild?," Deanna asked.

"Yes," Richard answered.

"Where's the baby now?," Deanna asked.

"In a temporary foster home in St. George," Richard answered.

"If this is our grandchild," Deanna said, "We want the baby."

"I understand," Richard said, "I'm sure that will be arranged. But it will take a few weeks to go through the court system."

"So how long will it be before we get this baby?," Deanna asked.

"I'd guess within the next two weeks," Richard said, "But I can't make any guarantees."

"And that beautiful girl is really our daughter?," Deanna asked.

"No question about it," Richard said.

"What about that Gerald Hansen?," Gene asked, "What's going to happen to him."

"Based on the evidence I've collected," Richard said, "I'm sure he's going to spend a long time rotting in a prison cell."

"Now that we know Becky Ann's alive," Gene said, "how are we going to find her?"

"That's the next step," Richard said, "I need you to go on television."

CHAPTER TWENTY-SIX

ENCOUNTER

Ferraro returned to the Pussy Kat Club on Thursday evening as promised. One of Kat's bouncers met him at the door and escorted him to Kat's office. Kat greeted Ferraro and asked him to sit down.

"Is everyone here?," Ferraro asked.

"Yes," Kat answered, "Who do you vants to ztart vith?"

"I want to start with the bouncers," Ferraro said.

"Vhy do you insist on callings zhem bouncers," Kat asked.

"Old habit, I guess," Ferraro answered.

The bouncers came into Kat's office one by one. As expected, each one gave the same answers as Serge and Pavel. Ferraro interviewed each of the strippers one by one. Each of them gave the same answers that Candy

Cane had given him.

"I want to talk to the bartenders," Ferraro said.

"I'll have zhem brought in," Kat said.

A few minutes later, a man who looked to be in his late thirties walked in.

"Zhis is Dean," Kat said.

"I understand you were working the bar last Thursday night," Ferraro said.

"That's right," Dean said.

"Why don't you start by giving me your full name," Ferraro began.

"Dean Crawford," answered the man.

"What's your current address and telephone number?," Ferraro asked.

"Why do you need my address and telephone number?," Dean asked.

"In case I need to get in touch with you in the future," Ferraro answered.

"You can reach me here at the Club," Dean said.

"Yeah," Ferraro said, "but just in case, I need your address and telephone number."

Kat gave a slight nod and Dean gave the requested information.

"How long have you lived at that address?," Ferraro asked.

"Four years," Dean answered.

"How long have you worked here at the Club?," Ferraro asked.

"Five and a half years," Dean answered.

Ferraro handed Larry Brown's driver's license photograph to Dean.

"Did you see this man in the Club last Thursday?," Ferraro asked.

"I think he looks familiar," Dean answered after he studied the photograph for a while, "But I'm not sure."

"Sure about what?," Ferraro asked.

"A guy assaulted one of our dancers last Thursday," Dean said, "This might be the guy, but I'm not sure."

"Why don't you tell me what you remember about that incident?," Ferraro said.

"There was this new dancer at the club," Dean said, "She was really popular."

"Does this dancer have a name?," Ferraro asked.

"Amber Gould," Dean answered.

"Go on," Ferraro said.

"After she made her rounds through the club," Dean continued, "she came over to the bar to get a drink. While we were talking, some guy came up and started harassing her."

"What do you mean by harassing her?," Ferraro asked.

"If I remember right," Dean said, "something like he had a lot of money and he was trying to purchase some sexual favors. When Amber rejected his advances, he became irrate and started yelling at her. He said that Amber thought she was too good for him and things like that. When Amber continued to ignore him, he started groping her and shoving his tongue down her throat."

"What did you do?," Ferraro asked.

"I called for security," Dean answered, "What else could I do. I was on the other side of the bar."

"What happened next?," Ferraro asked.

"A couple of security men came over and pulled the guy off her," Dean answered.

"Which security men?," Ferraro asked.

"I don't know," Dean answered, "Everything

happened so fast. My attention was focused on Amber. Everything else was like a blur."

"Did you see where these security men took the guy?," Ferraro continued.

"No," Dean answered, "I didn't pay attention to that. I was only worried about Amber. I could tell she was really shaken up by what happened. Especially since it was her first night at the Club."

"Did you hear anything about what happened to the guy?," Ferraro asked.

"No," Dean answered, "I assume he was thrown out of the Club and told to never come back. That's the standard practice around here."

"Sure it is," Ferraro thought to himself.

Ferraro handed Dean a photograph of Brown that he had taken at the hospital.

"This is what he looks like now," Ferraro said, "Are you sure nobody here had anything to do with this?"

When Dean looked at the photograph, a hint of horror flashed across his face.

"Not that I know of," Dean answered somberly.

"You didn't see anyone beat this guy up?," Ferraro asked.

"Absolutely not," Dean answered.

"You didn't hear the sounds of anyone getting beat up?," Ferraro asked.

"No," Dean said, "It's very loud in the showroom, so I wouldn't have heard anything anyway."

"What did you and Amber talk about at the bar?" Ferraro asked.

"Not much," Dean answered, "We didn't have much time to talk before that guy attacked her."

"What did you talk about during your short

conversation?," Ferraro pressed.

"I remember she ordered an orange juice," Dean said, "I teased her because she didn't order an alcoholic drink. She told me that she didn't drink alcohol because her father was a drunk. That was about it."

Ferraro ended the interview with Dean and interviewed the other bar tender who had been working that Thursday evening. The other bar tender had nothing more to say other than what Dean had already told him.

"I want to talk to Amber Gould," Ferraro said to Kat.

"Go get Amber," Kat said to Serge.

A few minutes later, a stunningly beautiful woman dressed in a golden silk robe and stiletto heels walked in the room. The woman had amber colored hair like her name and brown eyes. Amber was wearing brown contact lenses to disguise her natural blue eyes. Amber sat in a chair across the room from Ferraro. She crossed her legs exposing her upper thigh. There was something about this woman that seemed familiar to Ferraro, but he couldn't put his finger on it.

"I understand you want to talk to me about something that happened at the bar last Thursday evening," Amber said.

The woman's beauty initially left Ferraro temporarily speechless.

"That's right," Ferraro stammered, "I understand you were attacked by a man at the bar that evening."

"Attacked," Amber said, "would be overstated. I would say the man was a little too drunk and a little too ambitious for his own good. Nothing that doesn't happen around a place like this from time to time."

A slight smile came across Kat's face. She had

prepared Amber for this interview for the past two days. Amber was handling the interview perfectly. She even remembered to sit as far away from Ferraro as possible just like Kat had instructed her to do. It was apparent to Kat that Amber was as intelligent as she was beautiful.

"I want to start with some preliminary questions," Ferraro said, "I understand your name is Amber Gould, spelled G-O-U-L-D. Is that correct?"

"That's right," Amber said.

"How old are you?," Ferraro asked.

"Didn't your mother teach you it's not proper to ask a woman her age?," Amber responded seductively.

"I guess I'm just stupid," Ferraro replied, "But I still need to know your age."

"Twenty-one," Amber answered with a seductive pout.

"Where are you from?," Ferraro asked.

"All over," Amber said just as Kat had rehearsed with her, "My father was in the Air Force and we moved all over the country. We also lived in Germany."

"Exactly where have you lived?," Ferraro asked.

"When I was little," Amber continued, "I remember my dad was stationed at Hill Air force base in Ogden Utah. Then we went to Ellsworth Air force base in South Dakota. After that, we went to Ramstein Air Force Base in Frankfurt, Germany. Then my dad was stationed here at Nellis. That's when I was in Junior High. Then we went back to Ramstein. My dad retired after that and we moved to Idaho where he was from."

"What's your dad's name?," Ferraro asked.

"Tony," Amber answered.

"And your mom's name?" Ferraro continued.

"Peggy," Amber answered.

"Did you go back to Idaho with them?," Ferraro asked.

"Yes," Amber answered.

"So what brought you back to Las Vegas?," Ferraro asked.

"When my mom and dad moved to a tiny little town in Idaho," Amber answered, "it was great for them since they had a retirement income. But it wasn't so great for me. There were no jobs and nothing to do. My father also had a drinking problem. When he got drunk, he also got violent. My mom put up with it, but I didn't want to any more."

"So that's why you don't drink alcohol?," Ferraro asked.

"How do you know that?," Amber asked surprised.

"Dean told me," Ferraro said.

"That's right," Amber said, "I remember telling him that at the bar."

"When was the last time you saw your parents?," Ferraro asked.

"My parents died in a car accident a little over a year ago," Amber answered.

"I'm sorry for your loss," Ferraro said, "When did you leave this town in Idaho? What was it called?"

"St. Anthony," Amber said, "I left there about six months after we moved there. I went to Pocatello to go to school."

"What school was that?," Ferraro asked.

"Idaho State," Amber answered.

"Did you graduate?," Ferraro asked.

"No," Amber said, "I only went there for two years before I dropped out."

"Why'd you drop out?," Ferraro asked.

"Because I could make a lot more money as a dancer," Amber said.

"You became a stripper in Idaho?," Ferraro asked, "I didn't know they had strippers in Idaho."

"Dancers," Amber said, "You must be naive, Detective Ferraro. You can find anything, anywhere, if your looking for it. You don't think men in Idaho are interested in sex? Men are men wherever you go. Trust me on that."

"When did you become a stripper?," Ferraro asked.

"I started dancing after my Freshman year," Amber said, "I became friends with a girl from one of my classes. I told her that I was going to drop out of school because I didn't have the money to continue. She confided in me that she worked as a dancer to pay her way through college. At first, I was appalled, but when she told me how much money she made, I started to think about it. She made as much on a weekend as my father made in a month while he was in the Air Force. She told me to stop by the club where she worked and check it out. So I went to the club and the rest is history as they say."

"How old were you?," Ferraro asked.

"Nineteen," Amber answered.

"How could you work at a strip club when you were under twenty-one?," Ferraro asked.

"I plead the fifth amendment on that question, Detective Ferraro," Amber said in her seductive voice, "Let's just agree that it's not hard to get around that requirement."

"That reminds me," Detective Ferraro said, "I need to see your I.D."

"I knew you were going to ask me for that," Amber

said, "so I came prepared."

Amber took out a driver's license from a small purse she was holding and handed it to Serge. Serge walked across the room and handed the license to Ferraro. Ferraro examined the Idaho driver's license and wrote the birth date in his note book. He also compared the photograph on the license to the woman sitting across the room from him. He saw they matched. Ferraro handed the license back to Serge who returned it to Amber.

Ferraro asked Amber for her social security number, which Amber gave to him by memory.

"When did you leave Idaho?," Ferraro asked.

"A few weeks ago when I came here," Amber asked.

"Why did you come to Las Vegas?," Ferraro asked.

"Are you kidding?," Amber said laughing, "Everyone in this business knows you can make twice as much money in Las Vegas than anywhere else. I liked Vegas when I lived here before, so I said to myself 'Why not go to Vegas?' I know I have what it takes to be successful here."

Ferraro had to admit that Amber was right about that. She was going to be very successful in Las Vegas.

"Tell me about what happened last Thursday evening at the bar," Ferraro said.

"What do you want to know?," Amber asked.

"Tell me about the man who assaulted you," Ferraro said.

Amber told him a story that matched Dean's version of the event.

Ferraro showed Amber Brown's driver's license photograph.

"Is this the guy who assaulted you?," Ferraro asked.

"It could be," Amber said, "but I was really frightened at the time. I can't be sure."

"Do you know which bouncers dragged the guy away from you?," Ferraro asked.

"No," Amber said, "I was really frightened. I didn't even see the security men. I only felt them pull the man off me."

"Do you know anything about Mr. Brown getting beat up afterward?," Ferraro asked.

"Beat up?," Amber said, "Nothing like that."

"Something else?," Ferraro asked.

"I don't know," Amber said, "I'm new here. I have no idea what happened to the guy after they pulled him off me. I'm just glad they did. I'm not even sure this Mr. Brown is the man who assaulted me."

"So you don't know anything at all about what happened to the man who assaulted you?," Ferraro said.

"Nothing," Amber answered, "I was told he wouldn't be allowed back in the Club. That's all."

"Who told you that?," Ferraro asked.

"Dean, the bartender," Amber answered, "He said it was standard practice at our Club when a man assaults a dancer."

After a pause, Ferraro said,

"I think I'm finished here."

"Good," Kat said, "I'll have my man show you out, Deetectif. Don't hezitate to call me if you have any more questions."

After Ferraro was escorted out of the building, Kat stood up and walked over to Amber. She gave Amber a big hug.

"You vere perfect," Kat said, "You did everyzing I told you to do."

"You think so?," Amber said, "I was so nervous. I thought I was going to break down any moment."

"I azzure you," Kat said, "You did vonderful. I'm zo proud of you."

"What about all the lies I told?," Amber said, "What if he checks out what I told him."

"You don't have to vorry about zhat," Kat said, "Everyzing vill check out fine."

"What if he finds the real Amber Gould?" Amber asked, "Then what?"

"Za real Amber Gould iz a drug-addicted vagabond who vent back to Germany after she dropped out of za college," Kat said, "She died zhere a nameless perzon. Everyzhing vill be fine. Trust me on zhat. Zhat's vhy vee paid za big dollars for your new I.D."

Ferraro drove away from the Pussy Kat Club. His instincts were gnawing at his brain. He knew he was missing something, but he didn't know exactly what it was.

CHAPTER TWENTY-SEVEN

SNATCHED

Atkin received a telephone call about a missing girl in Dixie Downs. He immediately sent Sergeant Jeffrey Johnson to take a report. St. George is divided into several separate sections because of the natural terrain. The original town of St. George is completely surrounded by red rock hills and mesas leaving only a limited amount of contiguous space for expansion. The white Mormon temple towers over this part of the city. It wouldn't be accurate to call this section "the old part of town," because a majority of the houses and buildings in this section are relatively new. But when the city's growth exploded from seven-thousand residents in 1970 to nearly fifty-thousand residents thirty years later, the city's growth spread to areas on the opposite side of the surrounding hills and mesas. One of these growth areas is Dixie Downs. It is on the other side of a mesa west of the original town.

Johnson arrived at the missing girl's home to find a grief-stricken mother and father. It took him nearly fifteen minutes to calm the parents down enough so that he could interview them.

"Why don't you start by giving me your names," Johnson began.

"My name is Roberto Martinez," the father said, "but I go by Rob. This is my wife, Cathy."

"What's the name of your missing daughter?," Johnson asked.

"Bethany," Rob said.

"How old is Bethany?," Johnson asked.

"She just turned sixteen," Cathy responded.

"I'm assuming she goes to Snow Canyon High School," Johnson said.

"No," Rob answered, "She goes to Tuacahn."

Tuacahn High School for the Performing Arts is a charter school a few miles northeast of Dixie Downs. In addition to the high school, Tuacahn also has a nearly two-thousand seat outdoor amphitheater. The high school and amphitheater are situated in a stunningly beautiful location near the mouth of Snow Canyon. Johnson knew the place well because he attended several of the events that Tuacahn hosted throughout the years.

"How long has she attended Tuacahn?," Johnson asked.

"She started when she was a freshman," Cathy said, "She's now a sophomore. She decided to go to Tuacahn instead of Snow Canyon because we thought it would be a better fit for her. She loves playing the piano and dancing. She was also learning to act. She even had a couple of small parts in the plays last summer. We thought moving her to Tuacahn was a good idea because she is naturally very shy. The opportunity to perform and act was bringing her out of her shell. Besides that, she never really fit in at the Junior High. We thought it would be a chance for her to get a fresh start."

"How does she get to school?," Johnson asked.

"Normally," Cathy said, "she rides the school bus. She usually rides her bike if she has to go to school early. She can't drive yet because she doesn't have a driver's license. Sometimes a friend picks her up."

"Is her bike here now?," Johnson asked.

"Yes," Rob answered, "That was one of the first things I checked."

"When was the last time you saw her?," Johnson asked. "When she went to bed last night," Cathy answered.

"What time was that?," Johnson asked.

"I'd say around ten o'clock," Rob answered.

"Did either of you see her this morning?," Johnson asked.

"No," Roberto answered.

"What about you, Mrs. Martinez?," Johnson asked, "Did you see her this morning?"

"No," Cathy answered.

"Was that unusual?," Johnson asked.

"No," Cathy answered, "There's always early morning rehearsals for the activities she's involved in. She wakes up and goes to school early several times a month. We weren't concerned at all until she didn't come home for dinner. We started calling her friends and they told us she wasn't at school. That's when we became alarmed."

"Where do you work, Mr. Martinez?," Johnson inquired.

"I own a landscaping business," Rob answered, "My office is on Sunset Boulevard."

"What time did you wake up this morning?," Johnson asked.

"I woke up at Five-thirty and left the house at six," Rob answered.

"Did you see Bethany before you left for work?," Johnson asked.

"No," Rob answered, "I assumed she was still asleep."

"You didn't check her room before you left?," Johnson asked.

"No," Rob answered.

"So it's possible that she was already gone when you left for work," Johnson said, "Is that correct?"

"'I suppose so," Rob answered, "but that wouldn't be like something she would do."

"When she leaves for school early," Johnson said, "does she always leave the house after you've left for work?"

"As far as I know," Rob answered.

"Does she have her own bedroom?," Johnson asked.

"Yes," Rob answered.

"So no one would have seen her leave the house then," Johnson said.

"I guess not," Rob replied.

"What time did you return home from work?," Johnson asked.

"At about five-thirty," Rob answered.

"You put in some long days, Mr. Martinez," Johnson

said, "I assume Bethany wasn't here when you arrived home."

"That's correct on both accounts," Rob answered.

"What about you, Mrs. Martinez?" Johnson asked, "Do you work?"

"What are you trying to say," Cathy said, "That because I work I must be a bad parent?"

"I'm not trying to say that at all," Johnson said sympathetically, "I'm just trying to gather information that might help us find your daughter. I know this is a very difficult time for you. But understand, I'm only here to help. Sometimes people blame themselves when something like this happens. Maybe you're blaming yourself because you weren't here for her today. But that isn't going to help find your daughter. This could have happened whether you were home or not. This happens more than you would ever think and happens to all kinds of people regardless of their situation in life."

"I'm sorry," Cathy said, "I didn't mean to take this out on you, but you're right, I wish I would have been here."

"Don't worry about that," Johnson said, "I understand completely. Now, can you tell me where you work?"

"I work at a veterinarian's office on St. George Boulevard," Cathy answered.

"What time did you wake up this morning?"

"I woke up at seven," Cathy answered, "That's when I wake up to get the kids off to school."

"You have more than one child?," Johnson asked.

"Yes," Cathy answered, "We also have a son."

"What's his name?," Johnson asked

"Joshua," Cathy answered, "But we call him Josh."

"How old is he?," Johnson asked.

"Eleven," Cathy answered.

"What did you do when you woke up?," Johnson asked.

"I woke up Josh," Cathy answered, "After that, I went to Bethany's room to wake her up, but she was gone."

"So Bethany was already gone from the house by seven," Johnson said to clarify.

"Yes," Cathy answered, "After that, I took a shower and made breakfast. After breakfast, I drove Josh to school and went to work."

"What time did you get home from work?," Johnson asked.

"About a quarter past five," Cathy answered.

"I assume Bethany wasn't home when you arrived," Johnson said.

"That's right," Cathy said.

"What did you do after you arrived home?," Johnson asked.

"I made dinner," Cathy said, "We always have dinner together as a family at six o'clock. When Bethany didn't come home, we started to worry. By seven, we were in a panic."

"What have you done to look for Bethany so far?," Johnson asked.

"The first thing we did was call her friends," Rob said, "They're the ones who told us that Bethany wasn't at school today. After that, Cathy drove around the surrounding neighborhoods and I went to the school and to the mall."

"Why did you go to the mall?," Johnson asked.

"Because Bethany likes to go there after school

sometimes," Cathy said, "We thought maybe she was there and lost track of time."

"When we couldn't find her," Rob said, "we called the police."

"Do you have any reason to believe she might have run away?," Johnson asked.

"No," Rob answered, "We've had our arguments like any parents have with a teenager, but nothing that would cause her to run away."

"Has she ever threatened to run away?," Johnson asked.

"No," both parents responded.

"Do you know if she has a boyfriend?," Johnson asked.

"Not that we know of," Cathy answered.

"Is it possible that she's with a friend you've never met?," Johnson asked.

"I suppose it's possible," Rob answered, "But that wouldn't be something she would do without calling us."

"Does she have a cell phone?," Johnson asked.

"No," Rob answered, "We're not crazy about kids having cell phones."

"Do you mind if I talk to Josh?," Johnson asked.

"Not at all," Rob said, "I'll go get him."

Rob returned with his son a few minutes later.

"I understand you go by Josh," Johnson said, "May I call you that?"

Josh nodded.

"My name is Sergeant Johnson," he began, "I work for the St. George police department. I'm here to help find your sister. I want you to understand that you're not in trouble. There's nothing for you to be afraid of. Do you understand?"

Josh nodded again.

"I want to ask you some questions," Johnson said, "Is that all right?"

Josh nodded a third time.

"When was the last time you saw your sister?" Johnson asked

When Josh said nothing, Rob reassured his son that it was all right to answer Johnson's questions. Rob told his son that he needed him to answer the questions truthfully so that Johnson could help find Bethany.

"The last time I saw her was last night," Josh answered.

"Do you remember what time that was?," Johnson asked.

"My mom and dad made me go to bed at nine-thirty," Josh said, "I wanted to stay up longer, but they said no. Bethany was still watching TV. That was the last time I saw her."

"Did you see her this morning?," Johnson asked.

Josh shook his head.

"What time did you get home from school?," Johnson asked.

"Three-thirty," Josh answered.

"How did you get home?," Johnson asked.

"I took the bus," Josh answered.

"Did you see Bethany after you came home from school?," Johnson asked.

Josh shook his head no.

"What did you do after you came home from school?," Johnson asked.

"I did my homework and watched TV," Josh said, "I also went outside and played with my friends for a while."

"But you never saw Bethany after you came home

from school," Johnson said, "Is that right?"

"That's right," Josh answered.

"Do you have any idea where Bethany might be?," Johnson asked.

When Josh remained silent, Cathy hugged him and said,

"If you know anything, Josh, you have to tell the policeman."

"But I don't want to get into trouble," Josh said.

"Why would you get into trouble?," Cathy asked.

"Because I promised Bethany I wouldn't tell," Josh said,

"Tell what?," Rob asked.

"I think she's with her boyfriend," Josh said.

"What boy friend?," Cathy asked, "Why do you think she has a boyfriend?"

"Because she's been acting all weird lately," Josh said, "so I started teasing her. Every time I saw her, I would say 'Bethany has a boyfriend, Bethany has a boyfriend.' She would get really mad at me and tell me to stop. I told her I wouldn't stop until she told me her boyfriend's name. She told me it was some boy she met at the mall, but she wouldn't tell me who he is. She told me not to tell you because you would freak out."

Josh started crying.

"I'm sorry I didn't tell you, but she told me not to," Josh whimpered.

"That's OK," Cathy said, "You did the right thing by telling us now."

"She told you she met this boy at the mall and not at school," Johnson said, "Is that correct?"

"Yes," Josh said.

"Do you have a recent photograph of Bethany?,"

Johnson asked.

"Yes," Cathy answered, "It's her school picture. I'll go get one for you."

Johnson completed his report and assured the Martinezes that the police department would do everything they could to find their daughter.

Atkin read Johnson's report the next morning when he arrived at work. He thought for a while, then picked up the telephone. He dialed Ferraro's telephone number.

Ferraro answered the telephone.

"This is Lieutenant Atkin in St. George."

"How you been?," Ferraro asked.

"I'm doing well," Atkin answered, "but I have a family in St. George that's not. I want to talk to you about it."

"I'm listening," Ferraro said.

"A girl was abducted in St. George yesterday," Atkin said, "I have a strange suspicion that your missing Dwayne B. Goode might have something to do with the girl's disappearance."

"Why do you say that?," Ferraro asked.

"Can you tell me more about the way Goode operates?," Atkin asked.

"He's never been convicted of anything," Ferraro said, "But the way I understand it, his people go looking for attractive young women."

Ferraro described how Goode and his men were suspected of looking for girls at places like a mall. One of them would befriend the girl and start meeting the girl in secret. They would always avoid meeting the parents. When the girl was comfortable in the relationship, they would have the girl sneak out at night and abduct her.

"That's exactly what I think happened to this girl in St. George," Atkin said, "Has Goode returned to Las Vegas?"

"No," Ferraro said, "He's still missing. Do you think he's hiding in St. George?"

"This would be as good a place as any," Atkin said, "By any chance, do you have a photograph of Goode?"

"Yes I do," Ferraro answered.

"Will you send me a copy?," Atkin asked.

"It will be in the express mail today."

CHAPTER TWENTY-EIGHT

MANHUNT

Gene and Deanna Clark stood in front of the television camera flanked by Sheriff Godfrey and Richard Decker.

"I'm standing here today," Sheriff Godfrey began, "with Gene and Deanna Clark. Ten years ago, a man named Gerald Hansen kidnaped their five-year-old daughter, Becky Ann Clark. This is a photograph of Becky Ann at the age when she was abducted. The photograph of Becky Ann filled the television screen. Through the efforts of Officer Decker, who is standing to the left of the Clarks, and others, we have discovered that Becky Ann may still be alive. This is a photograph of Becky Ann taken just weeks ago in Las Vegas, Nevada. This photograph now filled the television screen. That was the last place she was seen alive. She's fifteen years old, has golden blond hair and blue eyes. She's about five-feet, six-inches tall and weighs about one hundred and ten pounds. We believe she's going by the name of Anna Hansen. The television screen now showed Godfrey standing in front of the microphones. We are asking for your help in locating Becky Ann and reuniting her with her family. If you've seen this girl, please call the toll-free number on the screen. Becky Ann's parents would now like to make a statement."

Gene Clark stepped forward in front of the microphones.

"Becky Ann," Gene Clark said, "We know you're out there somewhere. Please come back to us. Wherever you are, whatever you've done, just come back to us. We're here waiting for you. Please come home."

Deanna Clark then stepped forward with tear filled eyes.

"If anyone has seen our girl or if anyone knows where she is," Deanna said, "please, please, please, call the number. Becky Ann, if you're watching, please call the number or go to the nearest police station. We have been waiting so long for you to return to us."

When Deanna Clark withdrew from the microphones, Sheriff Godfrey again stepped forward.

"Again," he said, "we're asking for your help. If anyone has seen Becky Ann Clark or a person by the name of Anna Hansen, please call the toll-free number on the screen immediately."

When Sheriff Godfrey finished making his statement, the reporters covering the press conference were invited to ask questions.

"How did you learn this girl may be alive?," a reporter asked.

"I'll let Officer Decker answer that question," Godfrey said.

Richard stepped forward to the microphones.

"This girl first came to my attention on Christmas Eve at the Salt Lake City bus station," Richard said, "I was suspicious of the reasons why such a young girl would be traveling alone on Christmas eve, so I approached her. She told me she was a student at the University of Utah and was traveling home to Los Angeles for the holiday. When I later learned that she purchased a ticket to Las Vegas instead of Los Angeles, I suspected that she was a run away. For her protection, I requested that the Las Vegas Police Department intercept her at the Las Vegas bus terminal; however, she was able to elude the bus station security man when she arrived in Las Vegas. It was only in the past couple of days that we were able to positively identify this girl as Becky Ann Clark."

"How did you identify her?," another reporter asked.

"As you know," Richard answered, "a baby was found abandoned in St. George a few weeks ago. We were able to positively determine that Becky Ann Clark is both the baby's mother and the Clark's missing daughter through DNA samples taken from the baby and the Clarks, together with trace DNA that Becky Ann Clark left on a bus."

"Is Becky Ann Clark the woman who abandoned the baby in St. George?," another reporter asked.

"Yes," Richard answered, "We now know that the baby was conceived as a result of her rape, which we believe is the reason why she abandoned the baby."

"Do you know who the father is?," a reporter

shouted.

"Yes," Richard answered, "We were able to determine that Gerald Hansen, the man who abducted Becky Ann Clark, is the father of the baby through DNA testing. He is now incarcerated in the Salt Lake County Jail."

"How do you know he abducted Becky Ann Clark?," the same reporter asked.

"I have a witness who can establish that," Richard answered.

"Who is the witness?," the first reporter asked.

"I'm not at liberty to give you that information," Richard answered.

"Where do you think Becky Ann is now?," another reporter asked.

Godfrey stepped forward to the microphone.

"We know she was last seen in Las Vegas," he said, "If we knew where she is now, we wouldn't be having this public press conference. It was only through the excellent work of Officer Decker and others that we've arrived at this point. I cannot thank Officer Decker enough for the outstanding job he did in following up on leads and putting this case together. I, as well as the Clarks, owe Officer Decker a huge debt of gratitude. The Clarks have their hope restored and we need your help to bring this case to a close. That's all for now"

When Richard returned to his office, the county attorney was waiting for him.

"You do know," the county attorney said, "because of that press conference, it's going to be almost impossible to get an impartial jury to try Gerald Hansen in Salt Lake?"

"I figured as much," Richard said, "but right now,

the only thing I care about is finding Becky Ann Clark. I'm prepared to do whatever I need to do to make that happen."

"Luckily for you," the county attorney said, "he entered into a plea agreement this morning. I came by to congratulate you on a job well done."

"What are the terms?," Richard asked.

"He'll plead guilty to one count of aggravated kidnaping and one count of the rape of a child," the county attorney answered.

"What's the sentence?," Richard asked.

"Ninety-nine years," the county attorney answered.

"That means he'll be eligible for parole in thirty-three years," Richard said, "That's a lot better than what he deserves."

"He'll be a convicted child rapist," the county attorney said, "We both know what happens to child molesters in prison."

"Then I guess I'll have to hope he doesn't live to serve out his sentence," Richard said.

———————

Dwayne B. Goode entered a bowling alley and scanned the bar. He spotted a woman sitting by herself. She looked to be around forty years old. She had a worn look about her but was still reasonably attractive. At one time, she was probably extremely attractive. This woman was too old and too used to be the type of woman Goode would recruit for his business. But he was bored, so he thought he would give her a try. She was good enough for at least a one night stand. The past few weeks of hiding in St. George had not suited Goode very well. He was looking for some company, even if the company was a little substandard. Goode walked over to the bar and sat in the bar stool next to the woman.

"I'll have whatever she's drinking," Goode said to the bartender.

"That would be a Daiquiri," the bartender said.

"I'll have one of those then," Goode said, "and bring another one for the lady."

The bartender returned with two Daiquiris and put one on the bar in front of each of them.

"Do you like to bowl?," Goode asked the woman.

"What?," the woman asked.

"This is a bowling alley," Goode said, "I'm wondering if you like to bowl."

"I don't come here to bowl," the woman said, "I come here to drink. This is one of the few places in St. George that has a bar."

"That's what I was told," Goode said, "I'm more of a drinker than a bowler myself. Hi, my name's Duane."

"I'm Teresa," the woman said, "You must be new in town. I've never seen you here before."

"Yes and no," Goode answered, "I've owned a place here for several years. But I only come here once every couple of years. So I guess that makes me new in town."

"Why did you buy a place here if you only come once every couple of years?," Teresa asked, "Why don't you stay at a hotel?"

"It's a retirement home," Goode answered, "but I'm not retired yet."

"Where're you from?," Teresa asked, "I detect an accent."

"East Texas," Goode answered.

"How about you?," Goode asked.

"I was born here," Teresa answered.

"Are you one of those Mormons?," Goode asked.

"My great-great-grand-parents were," Teresa answered, "but not me."

"Why them and not you?," Goode asked.

"My great-great-grandparents were sent here to grow cotton by Brigham Young in the early 1860's," Teresa answered, "My parents were baptized into the Mormon religion when they were eight years old, but stopped going to church by the time I was born. I was never baptized and never went to church. Because of that, I've always felt like an outsider and never really fit in here."

"So why don't ya leave?," Goode asked.

"I did leave," Teresa answered, "I got married to a guy I met in Vegas who was in the Air Force. We had two children and then we got shipped off to Guam. But the marriage didn't work. After the divorce, I came back to St. George to live with my parents. It was the only place I could go at the time."

"Why didn't the marriage work out?," Goode asked.

"Because my ex is an ass hole and I cheated," Teresa answered.

"What about the kids?," Goode asked.

"They're with their father in New Jersey," Teresa answered.

"What are they doing in New Jersey?," Goode asked.

"He's an air traffic controller at an Air force base there," Teresa answered.

"I didn't know there was an Air force base in New Jersey," Goode said.

"Yeah, there is," Teresa said, "It's Patterson Air force base. It's in the middle of the State, next to Fort

Dix."

"Did you ever live in Jersey?," Goode asked.

"No," Teresa answered, "We got divorced in Guam. He got transferred to New Jersey after the divorce."

"At least New Jersey is closer to here than Guam," Goode said, "It probably makes it easier for you to see your kids."

"The ass hole doesn't let me see my kids," Teresa said, "and I don't have the money to take him to court over it."

"That must be hard not to see your kids," Goode said sympathetically.

"It is," Teresa said, "That's why I'm here. At the bar I mean."

"If you need some company," Goode said, "I have a listening ear."

Goode had been glancing at the television while he was talking to Teresa. He noticed that a man, a woman and two cops were holding a press conference. Suddenly, there was a photograph of the girl who had caused him all this trouble.

"You're not even listening to me," Teresa said with agitation.

"What?," Goode said.

"You told me you had a listening ear," Teresa said angrily, "and now you're not even listening to a word I'm saying."

"I'm sorry," Goode said, "I wanted to hear what they're saying on the television."

"Again," Goode heard Sheriff Godfrey say, "we're asking for your help. If anyone has seen Becky Ann Clark, please call the toll-free number on the screen."

Goode listened as the reporters questioned Officer

Decker. He smiled with a sense of relief. They had no idea where the girl was. This was a big break for Goode. He returned his attention to Teresa.

"I'm sorry," Goode said, "I'm all yours now."

— — — — — —

Amber Gould walked into Kat's office.

"I called you in here becauz I zaw a prezz conferenze on za TV," Kat said.

"What does that have to do with me?," Amber asked.

"Becauz I zhink za press conferenze vaz about you," Kat answered.

Amber went as white as a sheet and began to sweat profusely.

"Why do you think it was about me?," Amber asked after she sat down to regain her composure.

"It zaid zhat a little girl named Becky Ann Clark vaz abducted vhen she vaz five yearz old," Kat said, "It zaid zhat za name of za abductor vaz Gerald Hansen and zhat zhis girl may now be called Anna Hansen. It also zaid zhat zhis girl abandoned a baby in St. George, Utah. Zhey asked zhis girl to turn herself in to za police or for people to call a number if zhey zee her. Her parents vere zhere as vell."

By now, the energy was completely drained from Anna's listless body.

"What am I going to do?," Amber said to no one in particular.

"I zhink you should turn yourself in," Kat said, "Zhis should be good news for you."

"I can't do that," Amber answered.

"Vhy not?," Kat asked.

"The baby," Amber answered, "I left that baby to die. I can't turn myself into the police."

"Za baby iz dead?," Kat asked.

"Yes," Amber said.

"Zhey didn't zay anyzhing about zhat in za news conferenze," Kat said, "Zhey only zaid zhat zhey took a DNA sample from za baby. I didn't know za baby iz dead. Zo zhis is za trouble you are in?"

"Yes," Amber said somberly, "So what should I do? If I turn myself in, I'll go to prison,"

"If you vant to hide," Kat said, "I zhink za best way iz to hide is in plain zight."

"What do you mean?" Amber asked.

"It means," Kat answered, "Zhat you should do nothing to hide yourself ozher zhan vhats vee have already done. People are looking for a fifteen-year-old girl, not an adult voman. You need to appear confident. Like you have nozhing to hide."

"But I do," Amber said, "How can I pretend like that?"

"Very zimple," Kat answered, "becauz you must. If zomone zeems to recognize you, you muzt zay zhat people tell you all za time zhat you look like zhat girl, but zhat it's not you. Zhey are looking for a teen age girl who iz running and hiding. Not a confident voman. Zhey vill never know it iz you. Besides, zhis is vhy I gave you zhat new ID. It vill be nearly impozzible for za police to track you down. You can do zhis. I know it."

"I don't know," Amber said, "I don't want to spend the rest of my life running. Maybe I should just kill myself."

"Don't even talk like zhat," Kat said, "In a few years, no one vill be looking for you anymore. You can do zhis.   I know you can. Take za night off. Trust me. Everyzhing vill zeem better in za morning."

"I'll think about it," Amber said.

"No," Kat said, "you must not zink about it, you muzt do it."

CHAPTER TWENTY-NINE

HIDEOUT

Dwayne B. Goode returned home from the Bowling Alley feeling like he had dodged a big bullet. As long as the girl remained missing, he had nothing to worry about.

"Maybe this is going to turn out just fine," Duane proudly thought to himself.

Goode was in a particularly good mood because Teresa came home with him. Goode had kept a low profile since from the day he arrived in St. George. Instead of wearing his typical cowboy get up, he had adopted a style more compatible with the conservative values of the local population. Tennis shoes, polo shirts and khakis or jeans. His goal was to blend in and not draw attention to himself. Goode religiously monitored any news that might affect his potential return to Las Vegas. This included watching every Las Vegas television news broadcast that aired in St. George. He also subscribed to and read every page of the Las Vegas Review Journal. To be on the safe side, Goode also subscribed to and read the local newspaper, the St. George Spectrum. On the day he arrived in St. George, Goode saw the television report about the search of his Las Vegas house and property. He also read about it the next day in the Review Journal. Detective Ferraro, the same guy who had been snooping around the Starlight Motel, led the search. Detective Ferraro refused to comment about what the police found, but Goode knew that Ferraro found nothing that could incriminate him.

There was one positive development since the time Goode arrived in St. George. He discovered that St. George was a potential treasure trove for new recruits. St. George seemed to be filled with children. When Goode drove through the residential streets of the city, there were literally dozens of kids playing in the street. That was something he never saw in Las Vegas. On top of that, St. George had a far more relaxed atmosphere than the people had in Las Vegas. Attractive teen-aged girls were everywhere.   Even though Goode initially believed that the population of St. George was mostly retirees, it turned out that almost thirty percent of the city's population was under the age of eighteen. The city also had a junior college that drew thousands of students from around the region. The city was full of girls between seventeen and nineteen years old and to his surprise, Goode had landed on a gold mine.

Goode continued to direct his Las Vegas operation by telephone and even brought some of his subordinates to St. George. It wasn't long until they found their first recruit. One of his subordinates met a girl at the food court in the local mall. She was sitting by herself reading a book. After talking to her, the subordinate learned that she was mostly a loner and was viewed as an intellectual geek by her peers. Her name was Bethany. The subordinate used his charm and set up a clandestine rendevous with Bethany for the next day. He continued meeting Bethany after school, making sure that he was never seen with Bethany in public. He also made sure that Bethany was home by the time her parents came home from work. He would drive Bethany to remote locations near the city, which were plentiful. There was Snow Canyon and Pine Valley to the north. There were isolated dirt roads that led to the Grand Canyon to the southeast of the city. There was practically nothing west of St. George for hundreds of miles except for desolate terrain. He would take Bethany on hikes or drive her to the middle of no where and they would just talk. Once he gained Bethany's trust, they made love. The next night, Bethany was kidnaped and she vanished into thin air. There was an article about her disappearance in the local Spectrum two days later. As far as Goode could tell, the matter was being treated as a runaway.

Teresa spent the first night with Goode and never went back to her parents' house. Since Teresa was good in bed, Goode decided he would continue to use her for sex until he left town. Goode bought her a new wardrobe and threw a few bucks her way now and then. For her part, Teresa really didn't care how long the relationship lasted because it was a nice break from living with her parents. As long as Goode didn't hit her, the trade was worth it. Teresa had lost all of her self esteem and believed that a guy like Goode was the best she could ever do anyway.

The erosion of Teresa's self esteem began when she was still a child. Her parents were quick to criticize her and slow to praise. If her grades didn't measure up, which they never did, she was told she was stupid and that she would never amount to anything. This only caused Teresa to put less and less effort into her school work. She learned that nothing she did would ever be good enough for her parents. Because of that, Teresa fell prey to every boy who whispered something sweet in her ear. Teresa became sexually promiscuous by the time she was twelve and became known as the school slut. This only further eroded her self esteem. She had three abortions by the time she graduated from high school. Teresa was convinced that no decent man would ever accept her. She also didn't know the difference between sex and love. To her, they were the same thing.

When Teresa met her ex husband in Las Vegas, he was, she thought, the first decent guy who ever accepted her for who she was. He had a stable job and showered her with gifts, praise and attention. She was quickly swept off her feet. When Teresa told her parents that she was getting married, her father asked what was wrong with the guy. Teresa said there was nothing wrong with him. Her parents later learned that he was divorced and already had two children.

"I told you so," her father said, "I knew there had to be something wrong with him."

Just weeks after the wedding, her ex husband began to change. He was no longer the attentive, caring man she had dated. He became increasingly verbally abusive and spent more and more evenings with his friends away from home. Teresa stayed in the marriage for two simple reasons. She had no better options and

SECRETS

she hoped her husband would eventually change. At least he never physically abused her she rationalized. Over time, Teresa suspected he had other women on the side, but she had no solid proof. She thought this might be her own insecurities talking. She purposely became pregnant because she secretly hoped having a child would motivate her husband to change.

But having a child didn't change anything. If anything, it made things worse. The child only annoyed her husband and he spent more and more time away from home. The child also made Teresa feel more and more trapped in the marriage. One child soon became two, and they were all shipped off to Guam by the Air force. Once they were in Guam, the physical violence began between them. Because Teresa usually started the altercations, including the physical violence, she believed that she deserved what she got when he beat her up.

About a year after their arrival in Guam, Teresa began having an affair with another man. This man, who was also serving in the Air force, showered Teresa with the gifts, compliments, praise and physical intimacy that her husband no longer gave her. Her new lover promised that he would marry her if and when she got a divorce. Because her lover was scheduled to be transferred within a few months, they started making plans for their new life together away from Guam. Teresa's lover made her feel like a princess. Nothing could go wrong. Teresa filed for divorce the day after her lover received his transfer papers. Because Teresa had to stay behind in Guam until her divorce was finalized, her lover moved ahead without her. At first, everything seemed fine. But over time, her lover started calling less and less. Within two months, her lover stopped calling or even answering her telephone calls all together. Shortly after that, she received a letter telling her that he had a new girl friend and that she should move on with her life. Teresa felt completely betrayed and this affair only further depleted her self esteem.

Her husband hired a private investigator to follow her and knew everything about the affair. He used the affair against her to get sole custody of the children and avoid alimony. Being completely ashamed, Teresa simply signed the divorce papers that were put in front of her rather than have this affair exposed in open court. Teresa's whole life had gone down the toilet. Begging her parents to let her come live with them in St. George was the final humiliation. Teresa now turned to the bottle for her only source of comfort. Her favorite place to drink and avoid her parents' house was the bowling alley. That's how she came to meet Dwayne B. Goode.

Goode planned to hide out in St. George for a few more weeks. This would give him time to monitor whether Becky Ann Clark ever turned up. But before that time was up, something happened that forced his hand. One morning, Goode opened the local Spectrum and saw a photograph of himself right on the front page. The headline read,

"HAVE YOU SEEN THIS MAN?"

Goode read the article that accompanied his photograph. It said that he was a person of interest in the disappearance of Bethany Martinez. The article asked anyone who saw the Goode to call the police immediately. Since to the best of Goode's knowledge, Becky Ann Clark had not been found, and because he knew there was no way the police could possibly link him to the Martinez disappearance, Goode decided to be proactive and turn himself in. Goode called his attorney who drove up to St. George that same day. They both went to the police station and walked in. When the officer at the front desk asked them why they were there, Goode's attorney held out his card.

"My name is Michael Allen," he said, "I'm here with my client Mr. Goode. I believe his photograph is on the front page of the local newspaper. I understand you're looking for him."

The officer at the front desk looked at Goode and immediately recognized him as the person on the front page of the newspaper. The officer took the card and led them to a conference room. The officer left and about fifteen minutes later, he returned with his superior.

"I'm Lieutenant Atkin," the man said looking at Goode, "I understand that you're Dwayne B. Goode."

"That's right," Goode said, "Let me introduce you to my attorney, Mr. Allen."

Goode had the routine down pat. Those were the last words he would speak himself.

"I understand you consider my client to be a person of interest in a disappearance," Allen said.

"Actually, two disappearances," Atkin said, "One in St. George and one in Las Vegas."

"Let's start with the one in St. George," Allen said, "Why is my client a person of interest in that disappearance."

"A girl," Atkin said, "Bethany Martinez, disappeared sometime after ten o'clock p.m. on the evening of February second."

"So what?," Allen said, "What evidence do you have that suggests that my client had anything to do with that?"

"I just want to ask Mr. Goode a few questions," Atkin said.

"My client's not answering any questions," Allen said "unless you show me evidence, any evidence at all, that suggests my client had anything to do with her disappearance."

"Where was your client between ten o'clock on February second and the same time on the third of February?," Atkin asked.

"Without any evidence against my client," Allen said, "that's none of your business. But I can assure you, if my client needs to answer that question, he has rock solid alibis that will prove he was no where near that girl during that time period. Mr. Goode voluntarily walked in here today precisely because he has nothing to hide. Is my client under arrest?"

"No," said Atkin.

"In that case," Allen said, "we'll be leaving."

"I would like to ask him some questions about a disappearance in Las Vegas," Atkin said.

"What disappearance in Las Vegas?," Allen said.

"The disappearance of a girl named Becky Ann Clark," Atkin said, "She may have been going by the name of Anna Hansen."

"She was the girl the news conference was about," Allen said, "Why do you want to ask my client questions about her?"

"Because we have witnesses who place your client with Becky Ann Clark just before she disappeared," Atkin said.

"What questions?," Allen asked.

"I would prefer to ask those questions when a detective from Las Vegas is present," Atkin said, "He's more familiar with that case."

"When will that be?," Allen asked.

"I think I can arrange it for tomorrow," Atkin said.

"I would like to have a private conversation with my client," Allen said.

"I'll give you some time alone," Atkin said.

"I'll come get you when we're ready to talk again," Allen said.

Atkin left the room and closed the door behind him. Allen had a quiet discussion with Goode. Goode told Allen that he had met the girl, but assured Allen that he had nothing to do with her disappearance. Based on that, they both agreed it would be best to submit to the questions in order to nip this accusation in the bud. Allen opened the door and waived Atkin back into the room.

"My client has agreed to answer your questions about this Becky Ann Clark," Allen said, "He has assured me that he has nothing to hide."

"I'll set up a meeting for tomorrow," Atkin said, "I'll call you with the time. I assume I can reach you at the number on your card."

"That's right," Allen said, "but I prefer that you set the meeting for as early in the morning as possible. I need to get back to Las Vegas."

Atkin went to his office and called Ferraro.

"You're not going to believe who just walked into the police station," Atkin said.

"Who?," Ferraro asked.

"Dwayne B. Goode," Atkin answered.

Atkin explained that he had put Goode's photograph in the local newspaper as a person of interest in the disappearance of Bethany Martinez. Atkin relayed that Goode walked into the police station with his attorney that same day. Atkin also told Ferraro that he set up a meeting with Goode and his attorney for the next day.

"I think it would be a good idea if you came," Atkin said.

"I agree," Ferraro said, "I can't wait to ask that scum bag a few questions."

"They would like to do it as early in the morning as possible," Atkin said, "How soon can you be here?"

"I'd say nine o'clock," Ferraro answered.

"Are you remembering that there's a one hour time difference between St. George and Las Vegas?," Atkin asked.

"I forgot about that," Ferraro said, "Since you're one hour ahead, let's make it for ten o'clock."

The next morning, Atkin and Ferraro met with Goode and his attorney.

"Hey," Goode said when he saw Ferraro, "I understand you're the douche bag who tore my place apart in Las Vegas."

"That's right," Ferraro said with a smile, "I enjoyed every minute of it."

"I hope you enjoy paying the bill that I'm going to send you for the damage you did," Goode said as he smiled back, "By the way, did you find anything?"

Ferraro ignored the question and placed the recent photograph of Becky Ann Clark on the table.

"Do you recognize this girl?," Ferraro asked.

Goode picked up the photograph and studied it.

"Maybe," Goode said, "She looks familiar."

"Where have you seen this girl?," Ferraro asked.

"If it's the girl I'm remembering," Goode said, "she's a girl I met on Christmas Eve near Fremont Street and Maryland Parkway."

"What was the girl's name?," Ferraro asked.

"She told me her name was Cindy," Goode answered, "But I think she might've been lying."

"Why do you think she was lying?," Ferraro asked.

"Because she acted like she was on the run," Goode said, "It seemed like she had something to hide."

"Tell me what you remember about this girl," Ferraro said.

Goode told about how he had found the girl sleeping on the sidewalk by a diner. He told them that he felt sorry for her and invited the girl into a diner and bought her something to eat.

"Hey," Goode said, "I was only trying to help the girl out. Is that a crime?"

"Was that all that happened between the two of you?," Ferraro asked.

Good thought for a moment. He calculated that in this case, the risk of lying was greater than the risk of being honest.

"After we finished eating," Goode said, "I checked her into a nearby motel."

"The Starlight Motel?," Ferraro asked.

"That's right," Goode answered, "It was obvious that she needed somewhere to stay. I was just trying to help the girl out. Like I said, when does that become a crime?"

"If you had good intentions," Ferraro said, "Why did you use a false name when you checked her in?"

"Because," Goode said, "These sorts of things have a way of being misconstrued. Just like what's happening right now. I didn't want some person with bad intentions to find out I was helping this girl and drag my name though the sewer."

"How do you explain the fact that the girl has not been seen since that night?," Ferraro asked.

"It's not his job to explain every possible scenario that would explain why this girl is allegedly missing," Allen interrupted, "I'll let you ask questions that Mr. Goode has personal and direct knowledge about, but I won't allow him to speculate."

"Then let me ask you a direct question," Ferraro said, "did you abduct that girl or did you have anything to do with her disappearance."

"No," Goode answered, "The last time I saw her, she was alive. I haven't seen her since I left her at the Starlight Motel. I will even take a lie detector test if that's what I need to do to prove my innocence."

"I'm advising you not to do that," Allen interrupted.

"I hear what your saying, Michael," Goode said, "but I have nothing to hide. I have no problem taking that test."

Goode took the lie detector test after his attorney carefully reviewed each of the questions. When the results came back, to Ferraro's great surprise, Goode's response to each and every question was truthful.

SECRETS

D. K. DeGRAW

CHAPTER THIRTY

KNOWLEDGE

Over the next several months, Gabe read every book he could get his hands on. In no time, he could speak not only fluent English, but fluent Spanish as well. Gabe seemed to need very little sleep and he spent all of his free time reading and watching educational channels on the television. Gabe was already the smartest man Roger knew. Gabe also enjoyed helping the children with their homework every day after work. This pleased Mary a lot since it was one less thing she needed to worry about. One day, while Roger and Gabe were at work, Gabe blurted out,

"I can't believe the nonsense the schools are teaching your children."

"What do you mean?," Roger asked.

"Things like the earth is four or five billion years

old," Gabe answered, "I also have problems with the way they're taught things like evolution and the big bang theory."

"You think it's nonsense that the earth is four or five billion years old," Roger asked surprised.

"No," Gabe answered, "but that information is absolutely useless."

"I don't understand what you're saying," Roger said perplexed, What do you mean?"

"Let me try to explain," Gabe said, "I read an article in a magazine about a man named Warren Buffet. He's one of the wealthiest men in the world. He said there's a proverb that a bird in the hand is worth two in the bush."

"I've heard that proverb," Roger said, "but what does that have to do with how old the earth is?"

"Let me continue," Gabe said, "Warren Buffett said that the proverb is useless unless you know when you're going to get the two birds in the bush. Is it in a second? A minute, A month? Ten years? Buffett says that unless you know when you're going to get the two birds in the bush, you can't know the value of the bird in the hand compared to the two in the bush. He said he's made a fortune on that idea."

"OK," Roger said, "I get that. But I still don't understand what that has to do with how old the earth is?"

"Because," Gabe answered with an expression like he had just pulled a rabbit out of a hat, "to say the earth is four or five billion years old is useless information unless you know what time clock you're talking about."

"What do you mean time clock?," Roger asked "Time is time. I have no idea what you're talking about."

"Didn't they teach you anything about Einstein's theory of relativity when you were in school?," Gabe asked.

"Sort of," Roger answered, "but I never understood it."

"That's exactly what I'm talking about," Gabe said, "Unless you understand Einstein's theory of relativity, you can't possibly understand how useless it is to teach children that the Earth is four or five billion years old."

"What does Einstein's theory of relativity have to do with how old the earth is," Roger said completely confused, "I still don't get it."

"I'll explain it to you," Gabe said, "Until Einstein introduced his theory of relativity in 1905, every physicist on earth believed that there was one universal time clock throughout the universe. Einstein came along and said that wasn't true. He said that objects moving through the universe at different speeds use different time clocks. For example, an object moving faster through the universe compared with another object is using a slower time clock. He said time is not constant throughout the universe, but it's variable based on how fast the object is moving compared to another object. It's simple. You can't just say the earth is four billion years old. You also have to specify the time clock that's being used."

"Maybe it's simple to you," Roger shot back, "but not to me. I still don't get it."

"Can't you see," Gabe said, "If the earth was moving at a slower speed through the universe at some time in its past, it could be trillions of years old in present Earth time. Or if the earth was moving at a faster speed at some time in its past, it could be twenty thousand years old in present Earth time. Because no one can possibly know how fast the Earth has been moving throughout it's history, there's no way anyone can possibly know how old the Earth is in present Earth time. It would be complete speculation."

"I guess if you say so," Roger said, "The only thing I remember about Einstein is that he said a man traveling at the speed of light ages slower than a man on Earth, I had no idea that had anything to do with how old the earth is."

"I came across something astounding on that subject the other day," Gabe said.

"What's that?," Roger asked.

"I found a book called the Pearl of Great Price on your bookshelf," Gabe said.

"That's one of the Mormon scriptures," Roger said, "I've read it several times. But I don't remember anything in that book that has anything to do with how old the earth is?"

"It doesn't," Gabe said, "I'm talking about Einstein's Theory of Relativity."

"I don't remember anything in that book about Einstein's Theory of Relativity either," Roger said.

"There is," Gabe said, "The book says that one day on a planet called Kolob is equal to one thousand years on Earth."

"So what?," Roger said, "Every Mormon knows that."

"Don't you understand the significance of that statement?," Gabe asked incredulously.

"No," Roger answered, "One year on Kolob equals a thousand years on Earth. So what?"

"You really don't get it," Gabe said.

"I guess not," Roger said.

"Joseph Smith wrote that in 1842," Gabe said, "If Joseph Smith had gone to the best universities in the world and been taught by the most preeminent physicists living at the time, he would have been taught that time was constant throughout the Universe. That there was only one universal time clock. If he had raised his hand in class and said that he knew about a planet called Kolob where one day equals a thousand years on Earth, he would have been laughed out of the building."

"Yeah," Roger said, "All non-Mormons poke fun at the name of the planet Kolob."

"He wouldn't have been laughed out of the building because of the funny sounding name of the planet," Gabe said, "He would have been laughed out of the building because of the concept of variable time, one year here being equal to one thousand years there, would have been preposterous to the physicists of his day. It wasn't until more than sixty years later that Einstein proposed his Theory of Special Relativity. The Theory of Special Relativity, which has now been proven as scientific fact, confirms that it is completely possible that a day on one planet can be equal to one thousand years on another, just as Joseph Smith wrote in the book. In fact, any ordinary physicist today can calculate how fast this Kolob must be moving relative to the Earth so that one day on this Kolob equals one thousand years on Earth. It's now simple science."

"I have been a Mormon all of my life," Roger said, "and I have never been told what you just explained to me."

"I don't think even Joseph Smith was educated enough to understand the significance of what he wrote," Gabe said, "If he had, maybe he would be known as the scientific genius instead of Einstein."

"That's amazing," Roger said, "You're saying that evolution and the big bang theory are nonsense as well?"

"I'm not saying they're nonsense as ideas," Gabe said, "But its nonsense that these theories are being taught to your children as though they are scientific truth, instead of theories that have huge scientific holes."

"What holes?," Roger asked.

"Let's start with evolution," Gabe said, "Evolution is based on the law of natural selection. Natural selection is a scientific truth that says that all creatures are created based on the combination of parental genes. It's proven science that the characteristics of every living thing is determined by genes that are passed down from its progenitors. But evolution takes this a step further. The theory of evolution says that all life on earth began as some simple cell that involved into more and more complex creatures. But there is a big reason why this is called the theory of evolution and not the law of evolution."

"Why's that?," Roger asked.

"Because there are still some huge scientific holes in this theory that have not been explained," Gabe said.

"Like what?," Roger asked.

"For example," Gabe said, "there is no archeological evidence that shows that life evolved on the earth from simple cells to complex creatures. In fact, the archeological evidence shows that one day there was rock, and the next day there were complex plants and animals. No one can explain this. There are also several other unexplained holes that have yet to be answered. That's why it's still a theory and not a law."

"I didn't know that," Roger said, "It has always

been taught to me that evolution is a fact. I'm starting to wonder if anything I have been taught as science is true."

"I came across a book called the Discourses of Brigham Young that had another concept of a creation that intrigued me," Gabe said.

"I'm afraid to ask," Roger said, 'but I'll give it a shot.

"According to Brigham Young," Gabe said, "there are many worlds just like ours that exist in the universe. He said that when this Earth was created, God didn't create everything from scratch. He said that God took seeds from existing planets and planted them on earth. He also said that God took animals from existing planets and put them here. I'm not saying this is correct, but this idea's intriguing to me because it seems to be consistent with the archeological evidence that one day there was rock on earth, and the next day there were complex plants and animals."

"How would that explain the fact that scientists have proven that creatures here on Earth show millions of years of genetic evolution?," Roger asked "I remember being taught that in one of my science classes."

"That's not even a hard question," Gabe said, "First of all, the term millions of years has no meaning whatsoever unless the time clock is specified. We already talked about that. Second, if Brigham Young is correct and worlds are created by a God taking plants and animals from an existing planet to another, the creatures on earth would reflect genetic changes that have been occurring over eons of time. In simple terms, the creatures on Earth would not only reflect genetic changes that have occurred while they have been on this planet, but also genetic changes that occurred while they and their progenitors lived on prior planets."

"I give up," Roger said, "I'm not sure I understand everything you just said. But I know one thing for certain. There's no point arguing with a walking encyclopedia. My brain is already about to explode. Let's talk about the big bang theory another day."

"That one has even bigger holes," Gabe said.

"I know, I know," Roger said, "That's why it's called the Big Bang Theory and not the Big Bang Law."

"Exactly," Gabe said.

"Even if you're right," Roger said, "What difference does it make if my children are taught nonsense. I don't think it hurt me that much."

"My point," Gabe said "is that we're doing the children of the world a great disservice by teaching them theories as though they are facts."

"Why do you say that?" Roger said.

"Because as far as I can tell," Gabe said, "All great scientists became great, not because they could repeat what was taught to them, but because they found answers to unanswered questions."

"Like who?" Roger asked.

"Let's start with Copernicus," Gabe said.

"Of course," Roger said, "Let's start with him."

"In his day," Gabe began, "Everyone believed that the Earth was in the center of the universe. It made sense to them. When they looked up into the sky, the sun, the moon and the stars rose in the East and continued across the sky until they set in the West. There was only one problem."

"What was that?" Roger asked.

"There were these things in the sky called planets,"

Gabe said, "That means wanderers in Greek. Instead of rising in the East and continuing across the sky to the West, they would travel west, then do an about turn and travel east, then they would do another about turn and travel west again. For centuries, scientists tried unsuccessfully to develop a model of the universe that could explain these wanderers if Earth was in the center. Then Copernicus came along and put the sun in the center of the solar system and the problem was solved. The funny thing is, the powers that be at the time didn't thank Mr. Copernicus for solving this mystery that had plagued them for centuries. Instead, they treated him like he was a heretic. But centuries later, Copernicus is known for his genius while those who persecuted him are forgotten. But he's not famous for what he knew. He's famous because he solved a great mystery of science."

"I can see that," Roger said.

"Einstein was exactly the same," Gabe said, "For centuries, physicists thought the law of gravity was the end all and be all of physics. But there was one problem."

"I'm afraid to ask,' Roger said, "but what was that."

"The planet Mercury," Gabe said, "All of the planets orbited the sun according to the equations developed by Newton under his law of gravity except for Mercury. Einstein was determined to explain this anomaly and as a result, he developed his Theory of General Relativity which has now been proven. The scientific mystery was now solved. In fact, the law of gravity is no longer even the truth, it is only a simplified version of the truth. The law of gravity continues to be taught only because the General Theory of Relativity is too difficult for most adults, let alone children, to comprehend. But Einstein did not become famous for what he was able to learn or what he knew. He is regarded as a genius because he found an answer to an unsolved scientific mystery."

"OK," Roger said, "and the point is?"

"Children should be taught everything as it really is," Gabe said, "Both what is known and what is not known. They should not be taught theories as though they are fact, but should be taught the theory and the unanswered holes that keep these theories from becoming laws. Hopefully, one of these children will be inspired to find answers to these unanswered questions and become the next Copernicus or Einstein."

"I can agree with that," Roger said.

When Roger and Gabe returned home from work that day, both Sergeant Johnson and Lieutenant Atkin were sitting in the Hepners' living room.

"Thanks for dropping by," Roger said, "Have you learned anything new about Gabe?"

"Yes," Johnson said.

"What have you learned?," Roger asked excitedly.

"I'll let Lieutenant Atkin explain that to you."

"Right now," Atkin said, "I'm sorry to say we have more questions than answers."

"I'm sorry," Roger said, "but I've just spent the entire afternoon listening to Gabe expound upon the mysteries of the Universe. My head's already about to explode. Can you please get to the point?"

"We ran a DNA test on Gabe," Atkin said.

"Did you find a match with someone?," Roger asked.

"No," Atkin said as he glanced oddly at Johnson, "You may not believe this, but Gabe doesn't have any DNA."

SECRETS

CHAPTER THIRTY-ONE

SUSPICION

"What do you mean Gabe has no DNA?," Roger asked.

"According to the lab," Atkin said, "they found no trace of DNA when they ran Gabe's DNA test."

"What does that mean?," Roger asked.

"I don't know," Atkin answered, "Have you noticed anything unusual about Gabe?"

"Other than the fact that the guy has a photographic memory, has gone from knowing virtually nothing to being a genius in just a few months, that he never seems to get sick and he can read people's minds," Roger answered, "I'd say he seems perfectly normal."

Atkin and Johnson glanced at each other.

"What do you mean when you say he has a photographic memory?," Atkin asked.

"Exactly what I said," Roger said, "He remembers everything he hears, sees and reads. It's unbelievable. Didn't you hear me what I just said? He spent the whole afternoon lecturing on the Universe. If I show him how to do something, he can immediately do what I show him perfectly. I never have to tell him or show him how to do anything twice."

"Have you noticed whether Gabe's involved in any unusual activities?," Atkin asked.

"Yes," Roger said, "He reads every book he can get his hands on."

"That's not what I meant," Atkin said, "What I mean is, does Gabe ever leave the house at unusual times or are there any unexplained absences."

"No," Roger answered, "The only time he leaves home is when he's with our family or goes with me to work. I don't think he's some kind of spy, if that's what you're getting at."

"Has he ever left the house at unusual times during the night?," Atkin asked.

"No," Roger said with irritation in his voice, "Now what are you trying to say? That he's some kind of night prowler stalking the neighborhood?"

"I'm not saying that either," Atkin said, "I'm just trying to get an idea about who Gabe is, that's all. I'd like to ask him some questions. Do you mind getting him for me?"

"Not at all," Roger said.

Roger left the living room for a few minutes and returned with Gabe.

"Hello," Johnson said to Gabe, "Do you remember me?"

"Yes," Gabe said, "How are you, Sergeant

Johnson?"

"I'm fine," Johnson said, "This is Lieutenant Atkin. He would like to ask you a few questions. Would that be all right?"

"You can ask me anything," Gabe said.

"We're trying to gather information that might help us discover who you are," Atkin began, "Let's start with the night Mr. Hepner found you. Do you remember anything about that night?"

"Yes," Gabe said.

"What do you remember about that night?," Atkin asked.

"I remember it was very dark and cold that night," Gabe said.

"I understand," Atkin said, "that Mr. Hepner found you on Highway 59 between Kanab and Colorado City. Is that correct?"

"I don't know where he found me," Gabe answered, "I only know it as on a road."

"You don't know where Mr. Hepner found you?," Atkin asked.

"No," Gabe answered, "I only remember it was dark and cold. I remember seeing a light."

"A light?," Atkin asked.

"Yes," Gabe said, "It came toward me, then went past me, then the light was shining on me. After that, I saw Roger."

"Do you remember being naked in a road when Mr. Hepner found you?," Atkin asked.

"Yes," Gabe answered, "I remember that."

"What happened to your clothes?," Atkin asked.

"I didn't have any clothes," Gabe answered.

"I know," Atkin said, "What happened to your

clothes before you were naked?"

"I didn't have any clothes," Gabe repeated.

"Do you remember how you got there?," Atkin asked, feeling like Gabe was trying to avoid answering his questions.

"Where?," Gabe asked.

"In the road," Atkin said with a frustrated voice.

"Yes," Gabe said.

"Tell me how you got in the road," Atkin said.

"I woke up there," Gabe said.

"Where did you fall asleep?," Atkin asked.

"I don't know," Gabe said.

"What do you remember before you fell asleep?," Atkin asked.

"Nothing," Gabe answered.

"You don't remember anything before you fell asleep?," Atkin asked.

"No," Gabe answered, "I only remember waking up."

"Do you know if someone put you in the road?" Atkin asked.

"No," Gabe answered.

"Do you remember if it was a man or a woman?," Atkin asked.

"No," Gabe answered.

"Was there more than one person who put you there?," Atkin asked.

"I don't know how I got there, Lieutenant Atkin," Gabe answered, "I only remember waking up."

"What happened when you woke up?," Atkin asked.

"I saw a light coming toward me," Gabe answered, "and then I saw Roger."

Feeling frustrated that he was getting no where,

Atkin decided to follow a different line of questions.

"Can you tell me about your parents?," Atkin asked.

"My parents?," Gabe asked.

"Yes, your parents," Atkin said, "Do you remember anything about your mother or your father?"

"I don't remember having a mother or a father," Gabe answered.

"You don't remember anything about your mother or your father?," Atkin continued.

"No," Gabe answered, "I don't remember having a father or a mother."

"I see," Atkin said quizzically, "Do you remember anything about where you were born?"

"Where I was Born?," Gabe asked.

"Where did you grow up?," Atkin said, "From a baby to an adult."

"I don't remember growing up," Gabe answered.

"You don't remember being a child?," Atkin answered.

"No," Gabe answered.

"Do you remember anything about your life before Mr. Hepner found you?," Atkin asked.

"No," Gabe answered, "Only the light."

"Nothing else at all?" Atkin asked.

"No," Gabe answered.

"Mr. Hepner tells me that you like to read," Atkin continued, "Is that correct?"

"Yes," Gabe answered.

"Why do you like to read?," Atkin asked.

"I like to learn," Gabe answered.

"Is there anything in particular you're trying to learn about?," Atkin asked.

"I don't understand your question," Gabe answered.

"Is there anything specific that you're trying to get more information about?," Atkin asked.

"No," Gabe answered, "I like to learn about everything."

"Why are you so curious?," Atkin asked.

"I don't know," Gabe said, "It's just the way I am. Aren't you that way, Lieutenant Atkin?"

"Not so much that I spend all my time reading books," Atkin answered, "Mr. Hepner tells me that you never get sick. Is that correct?"

"My body has not experienced sickness," Gabe answered."

"Do you know why you don't get sick?," Atkin asked.

"I've never thought about it," Gabe said, "I guess it's just the way I am. Maybe I'll get sick sometime in the future."

"I would like to take you to the hospital for some tests," Atkin said.

"What kind of tests?," Roger interjected.

"Just some routine tests to follow up on the DNA tests," Atkin said.

"I don't like the sound of that," Roger said, "I don't want him to wind up locked away like some extraterrestrial being like ET."

"I can assure you," Atkin said, "that he won't be locked away like that."

"How can you be sure about that?," Roger asked, "You already said he has no DNA. I also know he has remarkable abilities. What if these test show he's some kind of super human? How do I know someone in the government won't start running experiments on him? I don't like the sound of this at all."

Atkin turned to Gabe.

"Will you come to the hospital with me?," Atkin asked.

"I read a book about the United States Constitution," Gabe said, "The book explained that you have no right to make me go to the hospital for these tests without a warrant. Do you have a warrant?"

"No," Atkin said, "but I'm asking for your cooperation on this matter."

"Do you have any reason to believe that I'm involved in any criminal activities?," Gabe asked.

"No," Atkin answered.

"Then I don't wish to have these tests," Gabe said.

"Don't you want to help us find out who you are?" Atkin asked.

"I don't think these tests are intended to help you find out who I am," Gabe said.

"Mr. Hepner says you can read people's minds," Atkin said, "Is that true?"

"No," Gabe answered, "I can't read peoples minds. But I can sense what people are thinking."

"Can you sense what I'm thinking about you?," Atkin asked.

"Yes," Gabe answered, "You're thinking that I'm a dangerous man."

"Are you?," Atkin asked.

"Not at all, Lieutenant Atkin," Gabe said.

"I can assure you," Roger interjected, "that this man has been nothing but a Godsend to us ever since the day he arrived. If you think he's a dangerous man, you can think again."

"I suppose we've asked enough questions for now," Atkin said, "I think it's time for us to go. But just to be safe, we'll be keeping an eye on Gabe for now. I want you to know that."

"You can watch him all you want," Roger huffed, "A dangerous man. You've got to be joking. He's practically an angel."

"I can assure you," Atkin answered, "that I haven't told a joke while I was on duty in almost twenty years. I hope you're right, Mr. Hepner."

When Atkin and Johnson left the house, Atkin told Johnson that he believed Gabe was evading his questions. It was just too unbelievable that Gabe just appeared out of nowhere. The man had to have a reason to keep everything so secretive. Atkin ordered that Gabe be kept under twenty-four-seven surveillance until Atkin ordered otherwise.

"We need to keep a close eye on this fellow until we know exactly who he is," Atkin said.

"Understood," Johnson said.

When Roger and Gabe left for work the next morning, there was an unmarked police cruiser in front of the house. The car followed them to work and parked in a stall in front of the jewelry store. It remained there until it was relieved by another unmarked car at noon. The unmarked car followed them home at the end of the day. A similar car continued to follow Gabe everywhere he went. After a few days, Roger confronted the man in the car.

"Who are you and why are you following us?" Roger demanded to know.

The man in the car showed Roger his police badge and told Roger that he was following orders.

"How long are you going to follow us?" Roger asked.

"Until I'm told otherwise," the officer said.

"All you're doing is wasting taxpayer money," Roger said, "I can't believe you don't have anything better to do."

"I understand what you're saying," the officer said, "but I'm obligated to follow my orders."

At the end of each shift, the officers conducting the surveillance sent a report to Atkin. They observed no suspicious activities or behavior from either Gabe or the Hepners. However, the night shift officer reported suspicious behavior unrelated to the objects of the surveillance. She reported that every night, numerous people came to visit a house down the street from the Hepners. The visits would last less than ten minutes, then the visitors would leave and drive away. That report caused Atkin to conduct an investigation of the house that led to a major drug bust. It turned out the house was rented by members of a notorious Los Angeles gang who were growing marijuana and manufacturing methamphetamine in the house. They were also selling cocaine and other drugs that they got from their suppliers in Los Angeles. The neighbors were completely shocked when the drug bust went down. They couldn't believe these drug activities were happening in their quiet neighborhood right under their noses. But Gabe and the Hepners, remained squeaky clean.

EPILOGUE

EIGHT YEARS LATER

Richard Decker retired from the Salt Lake City police department and moved to St. George, Utah with his wife just like they had planned. Solving the case of the missing Becky Ann Clark was by far, the highlight of his career. But it was also the source of his deepest disappointment. Becky Ann Clark was never found. His only solace was that Becky Ann's abductor, Gerald Hansen, killed himself in prison six years into his sentence. Richard worried that he wouldn't be alive when Hansen came up for parole. Richard made it his personal business to make sure that Hansen would never be set free. From what Richard was told, Hansen was a target of the other inmates from the time he was put in prison. Eventually, Hansen couldn't take it anymore and hung himself in his prison cell.

Richard kept in touch with Hansen's girlfriend, Nina Larson. She has lived a quiet and peaceful life from the day she first met Richard. She stopped drinking and hanging out at bars. One thing for certain is that she never again invited a stranger to live with her. Nina was relieved when she heard about Hansen's death in prison. She would never have to see or deal with that dirt bag ever again. Richard also kept in touch with Detective Ferraro and Lieutenant Atkin.

Ferraro continues to work as a Detective for the Las Vegas Metro police Department. Ferraro has never forgotten about Becky Ann Clark and a day doesn't go by that he doesn't think about her. Every now and then, he spots a woman in Las Vegas who he thinks might be Becky Ann Clark, but it's always a mistaken identity. A feeling keeps gnawing at his brain like there was something that he missed, but he still can't figure out what it was.

Lieutenant Atkin is now the Sheriff of Washington City, a city north and adjacent to St. George. He and Richard developed a close relationship when Richard moved to St. George. They go to lunch together almost every week, but they avoid talking about Becky Ann Clark. Their emotions still remain too raw to talk about that subject. They are sometimes joined by Johnson who continues to work for the St. George Police Department. He took Atkin's place as a lieutenant when Atkin took the Sheriff's position in Washington City.

Dwayne B. Goode returned to Las Vegas a few weeks after he took the lie detector test. His house had been completely trashed by the police search. But his staff managed to put the house back in order by the time he returned. He could sense that he was being closely watched by the police, so he decided it was time to get out of the prostitution business. But because he belonged to a ruthless gang, this wasn't going to be easy. Because once he was in, he was in and there was no way out except through death. However, Goode was one of the lucky few who had saved enough money to buy his way out. Therefore, he reached a buyout agreement with the prostitution ring that required him to pay twenty million dollars. Despite the hefty sum, Goode still has enough money left over to live comfortably for the rest of his life. He was also able to keep his houses and properties. Most important, he kept his status in the Las Vegas community. Goode continues to be involved in charity work and lives a typical life for a man of his wealth and status. Goode is considered to be among the elite members the Las Vegas society. Teresa met another man at the bowling alley bar after Goode returned to Las Vegas. She continues to live with him.

Becky Ann Clark's abandoned baby was united with Gene and Deanna Clark less than a week after their press conference. Because of the publicity surrounding the baby and Becky Ann, the matter was put on a fast track. The Clarks gave the baby the name of Helene, the name of Deanna Clark's grandmother who was originally from Denmark. Helene has golden blond hair and blue eyes just like her mother. She is also, like her mother, turning into a beauty. The old Richmond Elementary school was torn down before Helene began attending school and was replaced by a new one. This helped Gene and Deanna Clark somewhat, since they didn't have to send Helene to the same school that was filled with such bad memories for them.

But Deanna, in particular, tends to over protect

Helene. Deanna continually hovers over Helene and goes into a panic every time she unexpectedly loses sight of the little girl. Gene worries about his wife and whether his wife's overprotective behavior will have an adverse effect on Helene's development. In some ways, having Helene in their house has created more strain on their marriage than having a missing daughter. At least they are united in their feelings about their missing daughter. But they have been unable to resolve their sharp disagreements over how Helene should be raised.

Gabe continues to live with Roger Hepner and his family. The police never found any clues about who Gabe is or where he came from.   The police ended their surveillance on Gabe three months after it began. The surveillance netted nothing. As promised, John O'Reilly kept his word and told all of his wealthy friends and family, both in and out of St. George, about Roger's jewelry store. That word of mouth spread exponentially and within a year, Roger prospered to the point that he needed to hire two additional sales people and three additional jewelers. Within that same year, he was able to purchase a much larger, two-story house across the street from where he was living. Roger also moved his store into a much larger location because his business is booming. He has picked up a large clientele from both Utah and Nevada, including corporate clients like the casinos.   His store is currently the highest grossing jewelry store in the intermountain area that includes the States from Nevada to Montana.

Five years later, Roger and his family built an even larger house on the exclusive Foremaster Ridge. This house is situated on a three hundred-foot high mesa on the east side of the original town of St. George. From their house, they have a wonderful panoramic view of the city that surrounds them as well as the surrounding red rock canyons and hills. The house could properly be called a mansion. Roger and Mary have no idea why Gabe wants to live with them instead of living on his own. Gabe has made enough money to retire and could go any where or do anything he wanted. But Gabe insists on living with the Hepners and going to work every day with Roger. Gabe will always be welcome to stay with the Hepners for as long as he wants. The Hepners know there is no possible way for them to ever repay Gabe for the blessings he brought to their family, both financially and emotionally.

With Gabe's straightforward comments and suggestions, the Hepners are as happy as any people alive. It's not because they don't have problems, but they have learned how to deal with their problems much more effectively. Roger encouraged Gabe to attend classes at the local community college, but it quickly became apparent that Gabe knew far more than his professors. Because of that, Gabe is officially a college dropout. Gabe doesn't encourage anyone else to follow his example, but college wasn't for him.

Amber Gould fulfilled her three-year contract with Kat and promptly left the Pussy Kat Club. She took a sizable wad of cash with her. Kat was sorry to see Amber leave because Amber made more money than any dancer who had ever worked at the club. Amber remains a loyal friend to Kat and considers Kat to be the best thing that ever happened to her.

Knowing her true identity, Amber went to Cache Valley and visited Clarkston, Utah. She only went there once because it was too painful for her to ever do it again. She first drove to Richmond and pulled the photographs out of the brown envelope. She compared the photograph in her hand to the school in Richmond. Tears were streaming from her eyes. She then drove to Clarkston and quickly drove past the Clarks residence. She did this at night because she didn't want to draw any attention to herself. The house was the same house that was in the photograph from the brown envelope. She could see lights on in the house behind closed drapery. She only stayed for a couple of minutes, the quietly drove out of town. When the town was out of sight behind her, Amber turned onto a dirt road and stopped the car. She started crying uncontrollably.

"THAT SHOULD HAVE BEEN MY HOUSE. THOSE PEOPLE SHOULD HAVE BEEN MY FAMILY," she screamed over and over again.

It took Amber nearly an hour for her to compose herself. She knew she would never be able to forgive Gerald Hansen for what he did to her. She could feel the bitterness and hatred rage in her heart. This never went away even after she heard about Gerald Hansen's suicide in prison. If she knew where to find it, she would spit on his grave.

Amber continuously took formal dance classes and developed her dancing skills throughout the time that she worked at the Pussy Kat Club. Just before her contract with Kat expired, she auditioned to become a show girl at one of the strip casinos. She got the job and is working as a show girl on the Las Vegas strip. She's now taking acting lessons. She still dreams about becoming an actress one day.

To be continued . . .

SECRETS

www.ingramcontent.com/pod-product-compliance
Lightning Source LLC
Chambersburg PA
CBHW032225010726
47494CB00002B/350